WHITEWATER

RACHEL HATCH BOOK SIX

L.T. RYAN

BRIAN SHEA

Copyright © 2021 by L.T. Ryan, Liquid Mind Media, LLC, & Brian Christopher Shea. All rights reserved. No part of this publication may be copied, reproduced in any format, by any means, electronic or otherwise, without prior consent from the copyright owner and publisher of this book. This is a work of fiction. All characters, names, places and events are the product of the author's imagination or used fictitiously. For information contact:

contact@ltryan.com

http://LTRyan.com

https://www.facebook.com/JackNobleBooks

THE RACHEL HATCH SERIES

Drift

Downburst

Fever Burn

Smoke Signal

Firewalk

Whitewater

Aftershock

Whirlwind

Tsunami

Fastrope (Coming Soon)

RACHEL HATCH SHORT STORIES

Fractured

Proving Ground

The Gauntlet

ONE

"You know I honor family above all else? For me, there is nothing greater than that. Our family is stronger than any other. The only reason for this is simple. We built our family's name brick by brick through our blood, sweat, and tears. The toils my father endured secured our place at the throne. That kind of thing only happens when each member of the family is strong. As with any building's foundation, we're only as strong as the sum of its parts."

Raphael Fuentes stood in the corner of the room and listened on as his father, Hector, delivered his ceremonious speech. This wasn't the first time Raphael had heard it, or at least a variation of it. The man had raised Raphael. And over his twenty-three years of life, he'd listened to his father espouse the meaning of family, and its worth. He'd grown up loving the man, not just for the power he wielded, but for the love he had shown Raphael and his two younger brothers, Gabriel and Jesus. And just three months ago, Raphael became big brother once again to Guadalupe.

He could see that his father hadn't been as pleased when his sister was born. Hector wanted only boys. As a child Raphael knew his father's love was true and genuine but doubted his sister would ever come to know it. His father didn't give his love freely, it came at a hefty price, its tolls increasing with each passing year. As the oldest male heir to his father's fortune and power, Raphael learned at an early age what it meant to rule and lead as his father had. At seven years old, Raphael watched his father use a dull machete to separate a man who had wronged him.

Even witnessing the beheading and the many to follow in its wake, Raphael went to bed every night praying for the strength of his father, to walk in the man's gigantic footsteps. And every morning when he woke, was saddened to see he was still the same old Raphael. He did his best to prove himself worthy. By the age of thirteen, Raphael knew deep down the differences between his father and himself spread as wide and long as the Rio Grande River cutting its path outside his hometown of Juarez. As he matured, his father took him to places, showed him things, and taught him what the family business was all about.

Raphael had felt the disconnect before learning the true source of his father's power and influence, then after he felt like he never had known the man at all. He saw it in his father's eyes too, the darkening. Over time, Raphael's disagreement became more obvious, and his father had begun to question whether Raphael was fit to lead. This was why his father put on such a big show. It was another lesson, another opportunity to test Raphael to see if he had proved his worth.

"But even the smallest fracture in the foundation of any building can lead to bigger cracks, until it all crumbles down." Hector Fuentes lectured the room's attendees, to include Raphael who remained silent while his father addressed the group. No one ever interrupted Hector Fuentes without consequence. Depending on your status within the family, some of those consequences had life-altering repercussions.

"What we do here matters. What we say to others matters. The money, the power, it means nothing if we don't have family. If I cannot trust every member in this room to carry forward the ideals and the secrets that our family holds, then it is all for naught. That's why today saddens me as much as it angers me."

Seated in the center of the room was a woman bound to a chair. Thick plastic zip ties held her and her ankles in place. A rope wrapped around her midline just under her ample breasts sealing her to the back of the chair.

    Hector reached down and grabbed the top of the hood shrouding the woman's face and head and ripped it off. Raphael's eyes moistened at the sight of his mother's tear-soaked face. Raphael did not make eye contact with her. Raphael couldn't afford to let his father see the pain in his eyes, nor the hate that would surely follow. Instead, he looked just to the side of her at the hulking shoulders of a mountainous man. His father's right-hand security man, Juan Carlos Moreno.

    Moreno had done a stint in the military before returning home to serve as Hector's most trusted soldier. He stood by with his deadpan golden eyes and scanned the crowd. Even in the close circle of friends, family, and upper echelon of the Fuentes Cartel, his father was smart enough to know that threats could come from anywhere. The woman bound to the chair was testament to that.

    Hector worked the room, moving around and making eye contact with each member present as if he were a politician at a speaking engagement. "Isabella my love, to see you sitting here tears at my soul." The words sounded genuine, and maybe at some point they would've been. Even now they might still hold some truth of the love they used to share. To Hector Fuentes, though, loyalty trumped all else. Even love.

    But to Raphael, his father's words sounded rehearsed. He figured they were. Everything his father did was done to perfection. That's why when things did not go according to his meticulous plans, there were repercussions. This was one of those moments.

    "But you betrayed me." Hector turned and bent down, bringing his face inches from his wife's.

    "Please," she uttered, barely above a whisper. Her voice quivered. She choked it down like an overcooked piece of steak. Then came a flash of defiance in her deep-set eyes. This resistance only seemed to energize Hector's fervor.

    He stepped back and panned out to the audience. "I loved her. I still love her. She is the mother of my children and just gave birth not three months ago to my daughter, Guadalupe. Your sons stand by and watch." His voice darkened. "Because of what you did, they have to suffer. Because of what you did, our family must suffer. There is no worse crime than turning on your family." Raphael heard his father's words and recognized the hypocritical connotation.

"Please," Isabella Fuentes sobbed. "I did it for—"

"Save your breath," he barked. A froth of spit came out of his father's mouth in contrast to his normally reserved demeanor. He was enraged and nearly launched at her. "Not only did you go behind my back, you also went to the police. The POLICE! There's no reason you could give that would ever justify what you did. But just like a crack in any foundation, if it's addressed early enough, it can be patched up. It can be repaired. And that is what I'm going to do here. The police officers you spoke with have already been dealt with. There's just one more small crack that needs filling."

"No," she whimpered. Isabella brought her head around, twisting it, craning her neck to look at her first-born son.

Raphael could no longer avoid the eye contact. He met his mother's tearful eyes, and the sight of it nearly broke him. He bit the inside of his lip so hard that he could taste the blood. She pleaded with him without uttering a sound. Her silent cry for help tore at his soul.

"You have been called here today to bear witness to this...so that no other crack, no other fracture in our foundation, will ever happen again. Remember this moment."

Hector moved quickly. Slipping in behind Isabella's seated position, he grabbed her forehead and jerked it back against his chest, breaking her eye contact with Raphael. He looked on as his father ran the sharpened edge of a long-bladed knife across his mother's throat.

Raphael Fuentes remained motionless as the blood spurted. He listened to the choking and gurgles of his mother's dying breaths. He willed himself not to look away as his mother's life slipped from her body.

TWO

It was dark, but the sandy ground she laid on still carried the warmth of the day, even though the air around her had cooled dramatically in the shift from day to night. A wind began kicking up sand. It still carried a note of the remnants of the nearly contained wildfire seven miles away. The massive efforts to contain the wildfire had been successful, and they worked now to extinguish the remaining embers, but the air continued to reek of the fire's damage. It had burned in a twenty-mile crescent extending from Nogales. Hatch still felt the memory of its sting.

Ash and soot drifted like dirty snow, laying a thin coat over Hatch during the seven hours of waiting. She accepted the gift of gray camouflage now covering her body. She'd returned to the area in which the traffickers had taken Angela Rothman. She had travelled the same road where the first gunfight with Colton Gibbons and his fellow traffickers had taken place. When she passed by the spot, she was surprised to see no evidence of the violence that had taken place less than a day before. She stopped and looked for any shell casings. She found none. Even the blood was gone. None of the media sources she'd searched had covered the event. Her trail was clear, as well as the traffickers. She was dealing with a highly organized group of individuals.

It would only be a matter of time until she found what she was looking for. So she hunkered down and waited. Patience born by necessity. She skirted the border until coming to an empty swath of open space. There was no way she could enter Mexico legally without a passport or identification. Since she was legally dead, neither one of those things were available. To have it done through an alternative channel would've taken time she didn't have. So, she waited.

Hatch lay on the ground seven miles west of the Nogales border crossing. She selected her current location by asking herself one simple question, where would I try to cross the border? It had taken nearly eight hours before she'd proven her decision right.

She heard it before she could see it. There were no buildings nearby, no streetlights, no lamps, or sources of man-made light anywhere in sight. The only light provided came through the cloudy ash covering the sky. To Hatch's benefit, she was bathed in the darkness, giving her more flexibility in her choice of concealment.

There was a crunch up ahead followed by the coo of a baby and the mother trying to quiet it. Somebody snapped, yelling in Spanish a phrase Hatch didn't understand, but the tone of which was easily discerned. Anger. The cooing stopped and the procession continued. They weren't quiet by any stretch, although Hatch could tell they were trying to be.

As they came into view twenty feet from her position, she counted seven heads: an old man, a pregnant woman, a young mother carrying a baby, and two men. One of the men was heavyset and older and used a walking stick to navigate the uneven terrain in the dark. He stumbled once, and the younger man at the back of the pack kicked him hard, hard enough for Hatch to hear. The older man grunted softly, and then got back to his feet, offering no form of resistance to the violence he'd endured. Hatch knew why. The man who had kicked them was their coyote, a paid shepherd of human beings. Most of the people in that group undoubtedly gave their life savings for this journey, or would be indebted upon arrival, possibly for the remainder of their lives. Crossing the border from Mexico to the United States, with the hope of a better life, was no easy task. Often, the American Dream was more a nightmare than anything else.

Human trafficking was a modern form of indentured slavery. These people each had a predetermined destination, where they would serve out whatever sentence until their debts were paid. Hatch watched as the group came to a stop, now only fifteen feet from where she lay.

Hatch remained tucked tightly to a rock, making herself as small as her 5'10" frame would allow. The large rock aided in masking her from the headlights of the approaching van. The small boulder casting Hatch in the shadow cut the beams, keeping her invisible to the man driving. The coyote shoved the other six border crossers into the back of the van. A very brief exchange between the coyote and the driver followed and within a minute, they were gone.

Hatch remained still. She waited until the van was out of sight. The brake lights disappeared as the van crested the small rise in the dune nearby. Twenty seconds later Hatch's night vision returned. The details of her surroundings came back in full view as she watched the man who had just offloaded the six people into the van.

He took a moment to smoke a cigarette. The embers burned, casting him in an orange glow, and blinding him to her movement as she broke cover and stood up. He wasn't looking in her direction. And he didn't turn.

She crept along the dirt and rock beneath her feet, rolling heel to toe on the outside edge of her boot. She moved forward, keeping her knees bent just above a half squat. Like a tiger, she was ready to pounce. She wanted to get close to the man before addressing him. Within five feet, he still had not noticed Hatch. She could see now that he was armed. She hadn't expected otherwise. He carried a revolver, a strange weapon for a man in his line of work. With six shots and six people, he could've easily been overwhelmed. The power of a coyote didn't come from the ammunition in their gun, but from the influence they had over people's lives. The families left behind could easily be gotten to. Death, or worse, was just a phone call away for those who did not comply. There was power in the control mechanisms at play that went well beyond that of a one-hundred-eighty grain Hollow Point, like the ones in Hatch's gun. She didn't draw it or plan to. Hatch had other plans for the man in front of her.

He blew out a long puff of smoke, and Hatch spoke. "Hola. Cómo estás?" She knew little Spanish but figured it might put him more at ease if she started in his native tongue.

The man spun and reached for his gun.

Hatch threw her hands up. "Wait, wait, wait!"

He paused and looked back toward the massive fence dividing the two countries. He was frantic and looked as though he were about to run. "No policía," she said.

He looked around, expecting a hoard of border patrol agents rushing in his direction. But there were none. There were no cars. Hatch had parked her vehicle nearly three miles away. After clearing her DNA from the car, she lit it ablaze, and walked the rest of the way here.

He was curious now. His hand went off the gun, and he squinted his eyes at her as he took another drag of the cigarette. "What the hell do you want, lady?" he asked in broken English, but easy enough for her to understand.

"I don't want any trouble. I just need to get across the border."

"You need to get across the border?" He looked confused. "Why don't you...?"

She knew what he was going to say. "Why would any American citizen need to illegally cross the border into Mexico?" Her answer couldn't be given, but this was a man of secrets, this was a criminal, and her reasons didn't matter. Only one thing mattered to a man like this.

"I've got a thousand dollars. Take me across and get me into Mexico. Half now, half when you get me across." Hatch pulled out an envelope with five hundred dollars cash inside. She showed it to him, but didn't give it to him, not until he agreed, which he did with a shrug, before she allowed him to snatch the money from her hand. He stood there and counted it for himself. He flicked the cigarette off into the dry dirt beside him and didn't bother to squash it out. "Get you across the border and there's five hundred more?"

"That's it." She knew he had other plans in mind when they got across, but she'd deal with that when it arose.

"Nobody smuggles themself into Mexico. You must be either crazy or desperate."

Hatch knew better.

She was both.

THREE

Hatch followed the coyote through the desolate landscape, among the dark shadows. The sure-footedness with which the smuggler navigated the uneven terrain, with limited to no light to guide him, spoke volumes to the countless times he'd taken this path before. Hatch thought of the innumerable human lives he'd shuttled across this same path. She thought of how this man, and men like him, had subjected his own people to suffering over the course of his career. Up close and personal, modern day slavery didn't look all that different when compared to smugglers of old, in a world with a long and ugly history of this unforgivable abuse.

She despised the man ahead of her. The smell of his stale cigarettes mixed with the funk of his body odor made the already repugnant man even more so. She hated needing to use his services. Hatch would've favored putting a bullet in the back of his head, but small fish needed to be thrown back. Killing the sour smelling man would do little to help the girl she'd come to save. Missing an opportunity to rescue the feisty redheaded teen, Angela Rothman, from a group of human traffickers in Arizona had led her here. Hatch couldn't allow her disdain for the coyote to affect her decision to follow. She'd had to illegally cross borders during her time in the military, in particular the years she was assigned to Task Force Banshee, with varying results. Working with indigenous people was the only way to effectively move about in a foreign land. It was one of the Green Berets' specialties and Hatch, being qualified on that front, understood it better than most. Still, she wouldn't hesitate should the smuggler turn on her. But that hadn't happened yet, and therefore he continued to breathe.

Two miles into their trek, light penetrated through the high, rust-covered steel of the twenty-foot fencing which separated the United States from Mexico. They were close, just shy of a hundred feet from the border when the coyote stopped in his tracks. Hatch stopped, too. A gap of five feet separated Hatch from her guide. He turned to face her. Hatch's left hand was already behind her back. The web between her thumb and index finger pressed firmly into the tang of the Glock she'd taken off the dead traffickers in Arizona. The coolness of the steel slide against which her index finger rested calmed her.

No way he would have been able to unholster his six shooter before Hatch dropped the hammer. In the split-second action versus reaction equation it would take to end this standoff, Hatch was confident in her probability of victory. Knowing this still didn't remove the tension she now felt. Maybe it was the calmness in his dark eyes that gnawed at her nerves. He had a smug look, like he knew something she didn't. Was it a trap? She scanned her peripheral and saw no other indication of a threat.

He didn't seem to notice her hand or the intensity in her eyes. Or if he did, he didn't seem to care. "The hard part comes next. If you're ready?"

"Lead on." Hatch's grip on the Glock loosened, but she maintained her position.

The coyote slowly scanned the wall in both directions before squatting by a small rock and shrub. Hatch's eyes tracked his movements. Atop the rock was a coiled rattler. She didn't hear the familiar tat-tat-tat of its tail warning of an impending strike. It didn't react to the coyote's proximity. In that moment, she thought of Dalton Savage, the sheriff of

Hawk's Landing who'd given Hatch a new lease on life, and the snake that had nearly ended his.

The smuggler must've seen her reaction to the nearby snake, subtle as it was. His thin-lipped smile exposed the yellow stains of the few teeth left in his rotten mouth. "El senuelo."

"No entiendo." Hatch shrugged.

"Decoy." He grabbed the snake and set it on the ground next to him.

Hatch squinted and realized the rattler was a fake, albeit a very realistic one. The coyote then pushed aside the rock. Using his hand, he began clearing away the dirt and sand, exposing a circular wooden door roughly three feet in diameter. He pulled a long knife from the sheath on his belt and began digging the tip into the seam. A few seconds later, the coyote pried it open.

Hatch stepped forward. The hole was pitch black and the coyote offered no light. She then looked out toward the wall. In that moment, Hatch realized the next hundred feet would make the two miles they'd just traversed seem like a walk in the park.

"You first." The coyote gestured his hand toward the hole.

"Not going to happen." Hatch was poised to strike. Unlike the fake rattler on the ground nearby, her venom came in the form of the match grade ammunition loaded into the semi-automatic pistol tucked in the small of her back.

The crooked smile fell away from the dark-skinned smuggler's face. He was silent for the few tense seconds following Hatch's comment. He shifted on his heels and grunted. He pulled out a cell phone and mashed his weathered fingers onto the buttons of the flip phone before dropping his feet into the hole. He looked like a kid wading into a pool. "Five hundred?"

Hatch slapped the thigh pocket of her tan cargo pants. "It's right here. Just get me across and it's yours."

"Pull it closed."

"What about the rock?"

He tapped the closed cellphone in his hand before returning it to the front pocket of his jeans. "They fix."

The text message she'd just watched him send made sense. A tunnel like this would require a team not only to build, but also to maintain its secrecy.

"After you." Hatched stepped closer. There was a new smell, a worse smell, and it emanated from the hole, making the coyote's stink seem like a bouquet of roses in comparison.

No further discourse followed. The tenuous deal had been brokered. The coyote disappeared, swallowed by darkness as he dropped into the hole.

Hatch waited half a minute to avoid piling on top of the smuggler before sliding in feet first as she'd seen him do. With her body halfway in, she grabbed at the wood door and inched it closer so that the outer lip protruded past the hole's edge. Hatch shimmied herself underground. Using her fingertips, she slid the door closed.

The limited ambient light above was now only visible through the imperfect gaps in the wood door's slats as Hatch began working herself deeper into the restrictive space of the tunnel.

Hatch inched downward. The tunnel dropped in at an angle like a crude playground slide. Instead of a smooth ride down, the surface she scraped along was lined with jagged bits of rock poking out from the packed earth. The butt of her Glock banged noisily as she moved deeper. She thought of the pregnant woman and the woman who'd been carrying her baby and the challenges they'd faced when navigating their way.

She could hear the coyote ahead but couldn't see him. The soles of her boots hit bottom at twenty feet down. From there, the tunnel leveled out and was slightly wider than the confines of the angled descent she'd just endured. The additional foot of space in the excavated tunnel enabled Hatch to assume a crawl. She edged forward in the dark, her knees banged painfully into the hardpack while the coyote led the way.

Her right hand pressed into something moist. She didn't need to see to know what it was. The repulsive stinging in her nostrils immediately answered that question. Whether the fecal matter was of animal or human origin was the only thing up for debate. She wiped off the remnants against the dirt wall as best she could before she continued.

Hatch kept track of the distance she had travelled by placing her hands tip to palm. Every time her right hand struck the dirt floor, she counted one foot. It was a rough system of estimation, but it helped ease the strain of forging ahead into the unknown. By her assessment of her underground trek, Hatch figured she had just passed the halfway mark.

She banged her head hard on an unseen object. Hatch ran her hand along the edge of what felt like the rim of a wood support beam. It was splintered at the center. She could still hear the coyote scraping his way along ahead of her. The weight of the ground above had collapsed at some point. Hatch blindly felt her way around the opening.

She pressed her body flat against the dirt and snaked forward in a low crawl. The tunnel walls gripped at her shoulders like a boa constrictor. Each breath filled her mouth with the dust and dirt kicked up from her exertions.

She shifted her torso and hips as she snaked her way for the next ten feet before the tunnel opened back up to its original size. Taking up a crawl, Hatch made up for lost time and quickly caught up with the coyote.

They continued unimpeded until they came upon a slight incline. The coyote stopped and Hatch ran her dirty fingertips into the worn treads of his cowboy boots, nearly jamming her knuckles.

"Just up there." It was the first time she could see his face again as light above penetrated a seam in another door, this one made of metal instead of wood.

He crawled up the rest of the way to the door and banged twice on its metal exterior. After the long silence, the noise was deafening. A few seconds later, a metal latch release signified the message had been received.

A hinge barked its request for oil as the hatch opened. The coyote's body shielded Hatch from the light pouring into the tunnel, bathing the once darkened surrounds in its pale glow. It took only a few moments for Hatch's eyes to adjust to the brightness.

A long-haired, leather-faced man stared down into the hole at Hatch. He then assaulted the coyote in a barrage of rapid Spanish. Hatch was worried the lid was going to come crashing down on her and the man who'd brought her here. Instinctively, her hand drifted back to the weapon tucked against the small of her back.

The coyote returned a volley of Spanish. The argument ended when the coyote tossed the cash-filled envelope out. The gatekeeper's long greasy hair flopped over his tanned face when he ducked to catch it. If Hatch were looking to kill these men, now would've been the perfect time to strike. But she didn't. She chose to wait.

The coyote went first. Hatch half expected them to close, or try to close, the lid on her, but apparently the money in her pocket meant more than her life. She saw the glint in the long-haired smuggler's eyes held a different intent, a lustful one, that may have contributed to his concession. Neither reason mattered. The only thing that mattered was that Hatch was now out of the tunnel and standing on Mexican soil.

The room was empty of people, minus the two smugglers. The space looked to have once been a cheaply designed bar, long since out of use. A table nearby was covered in empty and some not so empty beer bottles. A half-eaten plate of beans and rice indicated their arrival had interrupted the greasy one's dinner.

The two smugglers were shoulder to shoulder, blocking Hatch from the only door she saw. She towered five inches over both men. The coyote's right hand drifted toward the revolver on his hip.

"Don't go for yours and I won't go for mine," Hatch said.

It seemed to take the men a second to realize that a) she had a gun of her own, and b) the gun she had was already in her hand behind her back.

The coyote threw his hands up. The broken smile, worse in the light, reappeared. "Easy, pretty lady. This is just business."

Hatch slid her filth-covered right hand along the seam of her pants to the cargo pocket containing the remainder of the promised money. Hatch had another, more sizable, pouch of cash strapped along her ankle which she had no intention of sharing. The two men didn't move as Hatch retrieved the envelope. The brown stains from her encounter in the tunnel marked the white surface of the paper. She handed it over and the long-haired smuggler greedily snatched it up.

"Anything else you need?" The coyote asked.

"Did you two move a girl through here within the last day?"

The two men laughed, but it was the greasy haired man who spoke. "We run girls through here all the time."

"You'd remember this one. Red hair, pale skin. Young girl, seventeen." Hatch stared at them with her hand firmly rooted against the gun. "Ring any bells?"

"No."

"There's money in it if you cooperate." Hatch wouldn't pay that fee though. If she got a sniff these two were involved in the abduction and transport of Angela Rothman, Hatch would extract the information in a more brutal way.

"As much as I'd like to take your money, still no. And if she was anything like you, I'd remember."

Hatch read both men. Despicable as they were, neither gave any indication in their body language that they'd had contact with the teen.

Hatch stepped forward and the two men parted. Her shoulder forced the greasy haired smuggler back, almost causing him to drop the cash he was counting as she made her way to the door.

Hatch stepped into the warm night air. It smelled like a sewer line had broken nearby, but better than the hundred feet of tunnel she'd crossed to get here. She hoped to find some help, but first she needed to find a change of clothes, and a place to wash the filth from her.

FOUR

Splinter wood clawed Hatch's thighs as she sat on the wooden milk crate she'd used as a makeshift stool for the past couple hours. She'd allowed herself a brief reprieve from her crossing, resting but not sleeping in the alley between a bakery and a clothing shop aimed at tourists. The bakery had opened an hour ago. Hatch's filth covered clothes caught some looks from women behind the counter when she ordered.

Hatch consumed the last bite of her torta de tamal. She wiped the crumby remnants of the soft bolillo roll from her lips before washing the chicken filled tamale down with the black coffee. The nutty scent wafted into her nostrils and battled the overwhelming odor of human waste. Only one more hour until the clothing store opened. As strange as it was, at that moment, Hatch longed for her morning run. She felt off. New environments always made more sense to her after a run.

Exhaust from a passing bus swirled its noxious fumes as sunlight crept its way out from behind a building across the street. Daybreak spread across Nogales. Within seconds, Hatch felt the temperature rise, and with it, the smell of her own filth solidified her reason for remaining in her current location a little longer. A change of clothes was warranted before she presented herself at the Police Department.

Vacant eyes of the homeless wandering the alley passed over Hatch with little interest. An older man staggered along rattling a tin cup along the broken stucco of the graffiti covered alley wall. The sad tune of the thin metal against the wall's rough edges stopped abruptly. The old man's ambled gait quickened. Hatch followed the beggar with her eyes, watching him as he hurried toward the street. A rush of movement filled her view as others appeared out of nowhere. They were all drawn to a light blue ambulance pulling to a stop near the alley's opening.

As the ambulance driver exited, Hatch was surprised to see he was not wearing a paramedic's uniform. Instead, he was in a powder blue button-up, rolled to the elbow, and tight-fitting jeans. His potbelly protruded just slightly over the belt line, but his frame was thin, making him look like a half-used tube of toothpaste. She guessed him to be in his early to mid-sixties. Standing nearly six feet high, he towered over the crowd. Sun bounced off the top of his bald head giving his walnut skin an orange hue. He rubbed his neatly groomed beard, yawned, and then stretched his arms high into the air before closing the door and making his way toward the rear of his vehicle.

As the crowd clustered around him, he worked like a politician on the campaign trail, hugging and shaking hands with nearly every one of them. Hatch remained seated on her prickly perch and watched from a distance while she continued to wait for the store's opening.

About a half hour later, most of the crowd had gone, and those who lingered behind clustered in small groups. But the ambulance idled in the same spot. She had watched the man who'd driven there dispense basic necessities, toiletries, water, diapers, and clothes. A young mother walked away with a package of diapers and a box of formula balanced in one arm while her infant child clung to the other. He closed the rear doors to the ambulance, passing a worried glance in Hatch's direction as he did.

She dipped her head and rolled her shoulders forward. Hatch wanted to obscure her face and height from the approaching ambulance man, hoping to dismiss any good-natured attempt to help her. The people she was hunting were likely to have eyes everywhere. Coupled with a recent critical misread of character in Arizona that nearly left her dead, Hatch had no intention of letting her guard down again any time soon.

Her subterfuge did nothing to stop his approach. If anything, it worked to broaden the smile cresting his face as he stopped in front of her. The toes of his worn sneakers nearly touched her boots.

"Estas bien, querida?"

She understood enough Spanish to know he was asking if she was okay. Hatch could've likely inferred it from his body language. Although she was fluent in three languages, Spanish was not one of them. She did, however, have a passable knowledge for conversational Spanish, but was by no means fluent.

"Please leave me alone," she said back in his native tongue, but poorly delivered and without the proper inflection. Hatch saw the expression on his face and knew immediately her ruse failed.

His knees cracked as he squatted, putting his face in front of hers. She peered out from beneath the dirty tendrils of greasy hair splayed across her face. She met his brown eyes and registered their surprise.

"You're an American?" His English was good. Hatch picked up on a slight drawl. Texas or maybe Arizona.

"I'm fine."

"You look miserable. Can I call somebody for you? Maybe I can take you back to your hotel?"

"I don't have a hotel." He looked even more confused now. Looking down at Hatch as she no longer tried to hide her face. She pulled back her hair and sat up. The kind-eyed man stepped back, taking her in.

She looked at the man and then over at his ambulance. "You a medic?"

"No." A permanent smile was stamped into his beaming face. "I am a certified EMT—well—at least I was when I lived in Chihuahua. Retired now."

"The ambulance?"

"Bought it, fixed it up, and put it to good use." He waved a hand in the direction of the ambulance where the crowd had been. "I help the homeless whose numbers grow daily. Many are desperate for asylum and find themselves lost and cast away."

"You do what, exactly?"

"I provide basic needs. Food, water, hygiene, and medicines like Tylenol and cough syrup."

"Are you government funded?"

He laughed. "No. I started this on my own and been doing it that way ever since. I like it that way."

"That's a big load to shoulder."

"Depends. I try to keep things in perspective." The perma-smile dimmed but did not recede altogether. "I was born in an alley much like the one you're sitting in."

"Must've been rough."

"Especially when you're brought into this world at the hand of a murderer's blade. I was cut from my mother's belly a month premature."

"Why? Who would kill a pregnant woman?"

"The who and why doesn't matter. What matters is the perspective such events bring to one's life." Hatch thought of the long list of tragedies and the direct impact it had on her view of the world as he continued, "So, yes, to some, this work that I do would come at great cost. But not to me. Each day I wake and get to help my fellow humans is a good day to me."

"Listen to me ramble on. I didn't even introduce myself. I'm Javier," he outstretched his hand as he stood. "But everybody calls me Azul. Because of the color I painted my ambulance."

"You probably don't want to do that." She looked down at the filth covering her body and Azul's eyes followed. "That's not just dirt."

"Sounds like you've got a bit of perspective too, eh?

"Listen, I don't want to press. You don't have to tell me what happened to you. I probably wouldn't want to know. I just want to make sure you're okay?"

"I am."

"At least let me give you some things to help you get cleaned up." His eyes pled his case.

The idea of getting cleaned up trumped any other options as she counted down the seconds until the clothing shop opened. Hatch stood. Being only two inches shorter than the six-foot man shocked him.

"I didn't realize you were so tall."

"Just the way I was made." Hatch gave a shrug.

"I didn't mean it that way. I have a change of clothes in the back that just might fit."

She looked down at the dark smears on her pants and shirt, knowing full well that not all of it was dirt. The smell of her own stink had stopped registering with her a while ago but seeing the expression on Javier's face told her it was bad. "I think I might take you up on that offer."

"They were my son's."

"How old?"

"Dead."

"I'm sorry," Hatch said. He gave a smile, but not as genuine. He struggled to mask his pain. Hatch recognized the look, having seen it in herself too many times to count.

Azul sighed as he led Hatch out of the alleyway to the back of the ambulance. "It's not a safe place by any reasonable measure. Lot of bad people out here doing bad things. But there's lots of good being done by good people."

"Your vision of retirement may not be what other people envision, but I'm sure the people you serve are grateful. I sure am."

Azul opened the doors and climbed inside. He slithered his way down the neatly packed rows of shelves containing Tylenol and other over-the-counter drugs. Boxes of diapers filled a corner along with bottles of water and other odds and ends. He stooped at the dividing wall separating the cab from the back. Azul grabbed a yellow plastic grocery bag tucked beside a stack of baby formula. He returned a moment later, bag in hand which he handed to Hatch.

The bag contained a pair of jeans, worn thin at the knees but otherwise in good condition. Underneath was a long-sleeved collarless white cotton t-shirt.

"Sorry. I know it's getting warm. Maybe you can tear the sleeves off if you need to."

"This is more than generous. It's perfect." She looked at the white fabric and her dirty hand holding the bag it was in. "Mind if I use one of those water bottles to rinse off a bit?"

"I've got something better." The smile never left his face as he turned his back to her and fished around in a brown cardboard box. He spun around holding a package of sanitizing moist wipes. "Use as many as you need."

Hatch went to work getting the grime off her hands, using every inch of the damp toilettes to dig into every crack and crevice. She made a neat stack of the soiled cloths on the back fender. With her hands clean, she set about cleaning her face. A few minutes later, Hatch was cleaned up as good as she was going to get.

"Gotta do something about those clothes." He investigated the van. "It's tight but you can use it to change if you want."

Hatch thought on the offer for a second. And in that second, Azul must've seen the hint of concern at voluntarily getting into a stranger's van. Some things are just universal.

"I'll stand outside and keep watch."

Hatch decided this was the best of all options right now. Plus, it gave her the opportunity to transfer her personal items, cash, and, most importantly, the gun. "That'd be great, thanks."

"Just be careful not to damage any of the items. Those will find their way to families in need."

"Don't worry, I move like a cat."

Hatch climbed into the back of the van. Azul closed the doors. And in the seconds that followed, Hatch listened hard. Nothing. No click of the door's lock. No start of the engine. She didn't waste any time disrobing. Hatch ran a couple of the wet wipes over her body before slipping on the new clothes. The fit was good. The clothes had the rough feel of being air dried. She doubted they'd ever been touched by fabric softener.

She bagged up the dirty clothes and the pile of dirty wet wipes before exiting.

"A perfect fit," Azul beamed. He eyed the bag containing the clothes she crossed the border in and offered, "If you want, I can wash these for you. No trouble."

"Not necessary. I was just going to toss them."

"Toss them? Those stains can be washed out. If you're not going to keep them, I'd gladly take them," he eyed the bag's contents, "I'm sure I could find somebody who would benefit."

"I'm sorry. I wasn't thinking."

"No need to apologize." He stretched out a long arm and received Hatch's odorous offering and chuckled. "Maybe I'll even wear them? You look to be about my size."

He tucked the bag containing Hatch's clothes underneath an empty shelf and closed the rear doors of the ambulance. "Where are you heading now?"

"The police."

He looked concerned.

Hatch didn't want to involve this man in any way beyond their current exchange and so offered a dismissive wave. "No, it's nothing. I'm just looking for a friend of mine. Kind of a wild night." Hatch did her best impression of a party going American who let a night of drinking spin wildly out of control. Not convinced her performance was up to par, she hoped it would be enough to close the door on the conversation.

A question formed on his lips and she could tell he didn't buy her story, or at least part of it. But the question never came. Instead, Azul made another offer. "It's a couple miles walk to the station. I've got nowhere to be, and I would be more than happy to give you a ride."

He'd kept his word when she changed in the back, staying outside and keeping watch. Getting in a van and driving away was another crossroads in the establishment of trust. She shot a glance at the ambulance.

Her hand now clean, she shook Azul's. "Let's ride."

FIVE

Neil Taylor questioned Kyle Moss's decision to meet at the motel. As personal attorney for the Moss family and in particular Kyle, Taylor had amassed a small fortune in legal fees over the years. The perks of the job had enabled him to purchase a winter home in Aspen, Colorado. In light of recent events, it appeared as though their partnership was coming to an end and this meeting was likely to be a parting of ways.

The beige duffle bag filled with cash Taylor had been ordered to bring now lay at Moss's feet. Taylor now understood just how bad things had gotten. Kyle Moss's business with a multimillion-dollar human trafficking ring had backfired when a good Samaritan interfered and brought light on his involvement. Facing a life sentence in a federal penitentiary, Moss, through Taylor, made an offer of cooperation in which he stated he'd be willing to give a complete and total admission of his knowledge of the operations of the traffickers and the Fuentes Cartel behind its operation. It meant Moss would be naming names of some very bad people. All of this would be done in lieu of a jail sentence for the option of witness protection.

Taylor knew the truth behind the offer. Moss made it to postpone his arrest warrant and create a time buffer before his next move, which, if Taylor were honest, was totally insane. First thing his client had done, which made Taylor's job all that much harder, was run from the police.

Moss abandoned his palatial estate set against the backdrop of Camelback Mountain in the exclusive Hermosa Valley neighborhood of Phoenix. After that woman rescued his stepdaughter, Moss didn't stick around for the state police to arrive. Moss did what most criminals did when facing a lifetime of incarceration, he fled. He'd been in hiding since. Arizona state police in conjunction with the FBI were already actively seeking Moss for questioning. They were looking into the abduction of his stepdaughter after the do-gooder woman blew the whistle.

Then came the call. Moss reached out to him in the middle of the night. 3:47 AM to be exact. Taylor's hands trembled. Lack of sleep combined with the stress of the last five hours of running around after receiving his boss's instructions. Moss always knew this day might happen, a day when he had to cash it all in and disappear. For years, Moss had put cash into a storage locker an hour drive from Phoenix. The amount had reached a total of three-hundred thousand. Moss had given Taylor the address of the Sunnyside motel in Nogales, with specific instructions for Taylor to meet him there as soon as possible.

Taylor left his wife and three children, all of whom were sound asleep, to drive an hour outside of Phoenix to the location of the storage warehouse, load up the duffel bag, and then drive three hours south to the border motel where he'd been sitting for the last hour with the jittery Moss.

"Try to explain it to me again. Help me understand what it is you hope to accomplish." Taylor sipped at the tepid gas station coffee he'd picked up when exiting the highway. He felt the start of another migraine and hoped to be home in time to take his Ketorolac before it became debilitating.

Moss lit a cigarette from a pack of Camels set out in front of him. Taylor had seen Moss smoke on occasion, but never to the extent he was now. When Taylor first arrived, he tried to ventilate the room by opening the window, but Moss had nearly tackled him when he reached for the closed blinds. *On edge* would be an understatement. Moss looked as though he hadn't slept for a day or longer. Deep dark circles shrouded his bloodshot eyes as he stared deeply into Taylor's.

"No way I'm going to jail. And there's no way I'm brokering a deal with the FBI." Moss trembled. At first it appeared to be only in his fingers, but as Taylor looked at his boss, he saw the tremors spread across his body as if a low current of electricity were pumping through him. In fact, there was. It was called adrenaline.

"Two words: Witness Protection." Taylor offered.

"You really think they can protect me?" Moss huffed.

"Maybe. They've done it in other high-profile cases. Plenty of mob guys laying low somewhere." Taylor didn't know any of the stats on something like that, but he assumed.

Moss shrugged. "You think I'm going to be happy living in Mayberry and working in some office?"

"People do it all the time, Kyle."

"I'm not most people," he seethed. He then stretched out his arm and jingled the thirty-thousand-dollar Rolex. "I'm Kyle Freakin' Moss. I don't do that 9 to 5 bullshit!"

"You'd rather be on the run for the rest of your life?"

"Beats the alternative."

"And you trust these people?"

"I don't trust anybody, least of all the federal prosecutors or FBI investigators who will be looking for any reason to stick it to me. Besides, the minute I open my mouth, I'm as good as dead.

Taylor eyed the duffle. "And what's a quarter million or so going to get you really? How long are you going to be able to live on that?"

"Long enough. Plus, I was told once they sneak me across the border, they're going to set me up with them."

"You're going to work for the cartel? Doing what, exactly?"

"Doesn't matter. No choice in the matter. Mind's made up."

"And just how do you plan to get across the border? You've been flagged. The first thing the feds did the minute you ran was to put you on the no-fly list. It's not like you've got fake identification." Taylor thought about his last statement. "Wait, do you?"

"From this point forward, the less you know, the better. But let's just say, it's not that hard to border hop. Especially if you know the right people." Moss played with the cigarette in his hand as he surveyed the meager furnishings of the motel room. Twin beds, a dresser and tv, and the table where they both sat. "That's why we're here."

Moss sucked a long drag from the filtered cigarette. A curled bit of ash clung precariously from the burning ember at its end. He made no effort to tap it off, letting it hang there, until it was flung freely when he made an exasperated wave of his hand. "Why do you think I'm sitting in this shit motel, staring at you? They're going to meet me here. Before I called you, I called them."

"Wait. What? You called the cartel?" Taylor felt immediately uncomfortable with the thought of coming face to face with an actual member of the Fuentes Cartel.

"Of course, you think I'm just going to cross the border without some help?" Moss unzipped the duffel bag at his feet. He removed five stacks of cash, each banded and marked with 10K. "This fifty is for you, consider it severance pay."

Taylor thought about shoving the cash back across the ash covered table. But his conscience was silenced the second his finger touched one of the crisp, twenty-dollar bills atop the tightly packed stacks. Taylor also knew this would be the last stipend of money coming his way from his employer. Taking a page from Moss's book, Taylor realized the cash would make it easy should he need to go off the grid until the dust settled on this investigation. It wouldn't be long before the FBI dug into Taylor's background. He wasn't so sure how he'd look under the FBI's intense microscope.

Taylor grabbed a large paper bag from the nightstand. The bottle of tequila it had once contained was empty, the last glass half full in front of Moss. Taylor stuffed the cash inside and rolled it down making a paper briefcase. "How long do you have to wait?"

"They didn't give me a time. They just told me to come to the Sunnyside Motel and check into room number two. Somebody would be by to take me to the next destination."

"Did they ask you anything about the situation?"

"No." He smashed the cigarette into the top of the table and then tossed the butt to the carpet. He took a swig of the tequila sitting in a plastic cup in front of him. Cigarette smoke mixed with the booze gave his breath an unpleasant sourness.

"Then I guess this is goodbye." Taylor stood. This had to be, hands down, the most surreal business exchange of his professional life. He felt as though he were part of a noir novel his wife liked to read before bed. With it came a sense of exhilaration. A palpable fear combined to make an intoxicating elixir. He now understood the allure of the criminal world. There was some intangible high provided by living on the edge.

Even though he was actively involved in much of the criminal enterprises his employer had dabbled in over the years, all of Taylor's involvement to date had been from afar, working from his ornate office in downtown. He hadn't been in the trenches like he was now. Strangely, Taylor liked it.

As he stood ready to leave his former employer in the seedy motel and head back to his regular life, he wondered if he'd ever have an opportunity to experience anything comparable in the future. He scooped up the bag of cash with one hand and shook Moss's with the other, "Best of luck to you, Kyle."

"Same," Moss tapped out another cigarette from the crinkled pack.

Just as Taylor reached the door to leave, there was a knock. He leaned forward and peered out through the peephole.

"Who is it?" Moss asked in almost a whisper. He brought the new cigarette to his lips and paused with his thumb on the lighter.

Taylor looked through the fish-eyed leans of the peephole again. The man on the other side of the door wore a wide brimmed hat that obscured most of his face, leaving only the bottom of his pale chin exposed. A well-tailored suit draped loosely over his thin frame. In his left hand, he held what appeared to be a wide leather briefcase comparable in shape and size to a small dog carrier. The thing Taylor found most odd, was the fact the man on the other side wore gloves.

Taylor pushed back from the door and moved over near the table. In a low whisper he described their visitor.

"Let him in."

"I don't like it. You heard me? Right? He's wearing gloves."

Moss shrugged indifference. "Maybe he's real careful. Guys like this aren't going around leaving their fingerprints all over the place. Or hell, maybe he's a damned germophobe."

Taylor's excitement from the moment before, during the cash exchange, seemed less so now in face of the surprise guest. Panic set in as the realization that he, middle-aged attorney from Phoenix, was going face to face with a member of the Fuentes Cartel, one of the deadliest crime families in the world. He didn't like that but he hoped in the brief exchange he could pass by and out and leave this behind. Taylor vowed right there and then to pick a less dangerous path to his opulence. He certainly did not want another one of these experiences, in the future or ever. The exhilaration was replaced by the fear churning in the pit of his stomach.

He looked at the plastic trashcan by the dresser and fought the urge to fill it with the contents of his stomach, which at the current moment consisted of weak coffee and a sticky bun. Fighting to keep his composure, Taylor shifted back over to the door and unlatched the chain lock and released the deadbolt. His hand rested on the cool stainless steel of the knob for a moment before he opened the door to the man outside.

Taylor stepped aside allowing him access. Once inside, the man said nothing as he took three steps to enter the room and bring himself in front of the chair where Taylor had just sat. He placed the case on the dirty table, positioning it so the latch opening faced Moss. Taylor noticed the leather case had small holes along the sides.

Moss gestured to the door with his eyes. Taylor, taking the unspoken command, realized he'd remained frozen in place after opening the door and his hand was still on the knob.

"Please shut the door." The man in the hat spoke clearly and quietly.

Taylor's skin crawled. He clutched the brown bag a little tighter and it crinkled loudly. "I was just leaving."

"Shut the door." The volume and cadence of the man's voice was the same, but this second utterance had a coldness to it that caused Taylor to break into a cold sweat.

With the doorknob still in hand and the door wide open, Taylor decided to make a break for it. He felt the sun on his face as he stepped his left foot through the threshold. His right foot never felt the freedom of the pavement outside the door. The gloved hand of their visitor gripped him by the shoulder.

Taylor spun. Off-kilter, he fell backward. His body slammed into the door, closing it.

Looking into the man's eyes which peeked from under the brim, he could see two faded scars, small circles that looked like burst stars just under the man's right eye. It was the last thing he saw before the bullet passed through his head.

SIX

Azul pulled the ambulance to a stop in a strip mall parking lot. It sat idling in front of a Kenmore appliance store. Both businesses on either side were vacant. And from the looks of it, had been for a very long time. Hatch leaned forward and looked past her kind-hearted chauffeur.

Through the driver's side window, Hatch saw across the street to a building that looked more like a sandcastle than a police department. The light brown stone exterior blended into the dirt berm behind it. The sign affixed to the chain link fence topped with razor wire read, "Policia Municipal, Nogales." Beyond the fence, the steepled front with an arched, clear glass window at the center above the main doors looked more like a church than a law enforcement headquarters.

"Across the street," Azul pointed in the direction of a guard station by a pedestrian access gate, "at that little hut. You see it? That's where you check in. Tell them you're there to speak with one of the officers and they'll tell you where to go."

"Thanks." Hatched grabbed the door handle.

"Look, it's not my business—but if I can help..."

He let the question linger. Hatch noticed it was the third time he'd tried to bring it up without asking, but once again, Hatch offered nothing to satiate his thirst for understanding. Not that she didn't trust him. In their short time together, he'd proved that he was trustworthy. No, Hatch's disregard of his offer came from a different place. Protection. The people she was going after wouldn't hesitate to hurt anybody remotely connected with her and she knew this. The less he knew the better.

"You've been a great help, Azul. I can't thank you enough. I owe you." She took his hand in hers and shook it. "And I always repay my debts.".

"No need. The pleasure was mine."

Hatch exited, stepping on a half-eaten chicken wing overrun with ants. A nearby dumpster added its foul contribution to the weighty heat of mid-morning.

Just before shutting the door, Azul said, "You know where to find me, if you ever need me."

"You're right about that." Hatch chuckled and slapped a hand on the blue ambulance's side panel.

Hatch waited for a gap in traffic and then hustled across the six lanes to the sidewalk in front of the station. Out of the corner of her eye, Hatch watched as Azul pulled out of the lot and headed back in the direction they'd come from.

A short, fat officer crammed himself into the wooden guard shack after arguing with an older woman. Whatever her complaint had been, the officer met her with resistance. The squat officer folded his thick arms across his ample belly and struck a pleased look as he watched the woman turn and stomp off. Hatch took the slight incline in the walkway to the guard house and passed the irate woman who cursed in Spanish until she was out of earshot.

All the effort in thwarting the older woman's claim caused the floodgates to unleash. Sweat poured out of the portly man's forehead. The unfit police officer scrunched his brow at the sight of Hatch approaching. His face screwed up in a question mark when he realized she was American.

"Can I help you?" he asked in broken English.

"I'm looking for somebody."

The officer whose nametag read Torres cocked an eyebrow followed by a toothy grin. "Mexico is a big place."

"I'm looking for a girl. A teenager. Seventeen. I need to speak with one of your detectives."

He looked ready to gaff her off, just as she'd witnessed him do to the older woman moments ago. But instead, he surprised her. "In through those doors. That's the main lobby. Someone inside will help you."

She turned and started to the door when Hatch heard Torres say, "ID." She turned to see his opened moist palm. Hatch hoped she could avoid using any official identification, but time hadn't been on her side and she had not been able get a quality fake. Besides the hunter killer team sent to silence her in Colorado, nobody was officially looking for her.

Reluctantly, Hatch fished out her license and handed it to him. She was grateful he did nothing more than eye it for less than a second before handing it back to her with a clipboard. A ballpoint pen was attached to the metal clip by a rubber band. "Sign."

Hatch was grateful the officer didn't write it. In the best impression of the worst doctor handwriting ever, she signed it using a name combining a little girl she loved more than anything with the man who'd saved her life. *Daphne Nighthawk* was scribbled in the first available line. She handed it back to Torres. He returned the clipboard to the rusty nail without even looking at her signature mark.

Quietly grateful, Hatch pocketed the license. "I know it's not my business, but what was the deal with that woman?"

"You're right, it's none of your business." The guard retreated deeper into his shack like a turtle retracting into its shell.

Hatch walked away and into the main lobby.

SEVEN

She first heard the screams upon entering through the dark tinted glass doors of Nogales' municipal police department. The screams, more of high-pitched wails, reverberated through the open space of the lobby with megaphonic proportions.

Hatch spent time inside a variety of federal, military, and local police department lobbies across the US and overseas while serving as an MP. Combative people in the lobby were nothing out of the ordinary. The mayhem wasn't always caused by a criminal either. She'd seen plaintiffs become convicts when lost in the heat of the moment. The door closed behind her as she surveyed the chaotic events taking place.

A wild-eyed man was wearing nothing but a frayed pair of jeans wrapped around his ankles and exposing his red boxers. Once inside, Hatch waited for her eyes to adjust from the bright light of outside to the incandescent light of the interior of the lobby. In the clarity that followed, she realized he was not wearing red boxers. They were, in fact, white. The blood covering them gave them a red hue. The leakage stemmed from several long gashes on the combatant's head and skull.

He kicked wildly at the two officers restraining him. A handsome officer with an amused look on his face stood nearby, far enough away to not be directly involved in the melee. He gave an authoritative nod of his head to the bigger of the two cops holding the blood covered man. The larger officer drove a wooden straight stick baton across the top of the man's head. In the US, this type of blow would've only been authorized under a deadly force encounter. He delivered an additional blow that caught the shirtless man in the side of his neck before the fighting stopped altogether.

The two officers wearing the unconscious man's blood on their green fatigues dragged him away in cuffs. Something about not wanting to stay a night in a Mexican prison came to Hatch's mind. This experience reminded her of the truth behind its meaning. She hated to think of the conditions Angela Rothman was experiencing at this very moment.

The blood covered man disappeared behind a closed door and the hum of normalcy returned after a brief silence. The handsome officer remained behind. His entertainment gone, he turned his attention to Hatch.

Officer Munoz, identified by his polished brass nameplate, was of equal height to Hatch, if not slightly taller by an inch. His boyish charms were packaged into a man's physique. Munoz had chiseled good looks and a neatly gelled crewcut. His uniform was custom fit with tapered sleeves that rolled past his elbow, cinching tight underneath his biceps and engorging the veins on his clean-shaven forearms. The Nogales lieutenant looked to be no more than thirty. He smiled, broadly displaying his ivory teeth as he approached.

He pulled a pair of gold-rimmed sunglasses from atop his head and hung them from the outside of his breast pocket. Hatch met his gaze.

"American? Yes?"

"Yes."

"I'm Officer Eduardo Munoz. How can I help you on this beautiful morning in Nogales?"

"You and I have a totally different idea of beautiful." She gestured to the smeared trail of blood marking the unconscious man's path.

"Oh that?" He laughed. "That's nothing to be concerned with. Just a thief."

"What did he steal that would make him fight like that?"

"Does it matter?"

"I think so."

"He stole some fruit." Munoz's smile disappeared.

"Stolen fruit caught him a beating like that?"

Munoz shrugged. "At least we didn't arrest his mother too."

Hatch thought of the old woman's heated argument and wondered if she was the mother he was referring to when he leaned in close. She choked back a cough. His cologne smelled of vanilla, chestnut, and if she wasn't mistaken, a hint of clove. It gave him a sweet, woody scent as he spoke. "How may I be of service."

Hatch looked over to the main desk sergeant who was fielding a complaint, with a line three deep waiting. Lieutenant Eduardo Munoz was as good as any, and by the frazzled look on the desk sarge's face, might be the best choice. Munoz's proximity worried Hatch. She was in the lobby of a police department with a loaded pistol pressed against the small of her back. The borrowed clothes fit with just enough excess to hang loose enough to obscure the angular lines of the handgun's butt. She'd seen the beating they delivered the fruit thief and wondered what would be in store for her should they realize she entered a police department armed with a dead man's gun.

"I'm looking for a girl. She went missing a day ago." Hatch took a step back and pulled out her cell phone. She showed him a Facebook image of Angela Rothman. It captured the teen with her head turned. A sunset lit her red hair ablaze. It was a far departure from the last time she'd set eyes on the young girl.

"A missing girl." The lieutenant confirmed.

Hatch heard the sarcasm in his tone but didn't bite. "Her name's Angela Rothman. She's my niece. We got to Nogales two nights ago. We were supposed to head down to a family retreat at Copper Mountain today, but when I woke up, she was gone."

Munoz squinted at the screenshot. "You say this girl is your niece?"

The big officer who'd brutalized the apple thief reappeared from the door he and his partner had dragged the bloodied man through. Officer Rivera stopped beside Munoz and immediately inserted himself into their business. *Who's the cutie?* That, or something close to that is what Rivera chuckled to his lieutenant.

"This is Miss..." Munoz looked in her direction.

"Nighthawk."

"This is Miss Nighthawk. She's here on a family trip. Her niece Anna was gone when she woke."

"Angela," Hatch interrupted.

"Excuse me?" Munoz snarled.

Hatch saw through Officer Munoz's polished exterior. He was not a man who liked to be challenged, undoubtably worsened by the fact she was a woman. "I said Angela. Her name is Angela Rothman."

"My apologies. Yes, as Miss Nighthawk has just so kindly pointed out, the girl's name is Angela." Munoz put his hand on the bulky Rivera's shoulder. "Luis, I think you're going to need to write this down."

Rivera thumbed open a pocket and slipped out a small notepad. His meaty hands flipped to a clean page. "Go ahead with that name again."

Hatch repeated the name and she watch Rivera write it. He was slick, and if someone else besides Hatch had been there, they likely wouldn't have caught it. But she did. As Rivera looked up from jotting the name in his pad, he made a barely perceptible glance at Munoz. Something was off. *If something's not right, figure out what. If you can't, get the hell out of Dodge until you can.* Simply put, if something's not right, it stays that way until you make it so. Her dad's words always came back to her.

"I don't want to get your hopes up, but this town is home to thousands of lost souls. Do you know how many people go missing in Nogales per year?"

For all Munoz' talking, he never once asked for any details. Not even the basics like height, weight, and clothing. Nothing. Something's not right. One glaring possibility stared her right in the face. Munoz and Rivera never asked because they already knew. The how and why were still up for debate. But following her dad's advice, Hatch decided to get the hell out of that PD lobby.

Hatch pocketed her phone. "I've got to meet back with my family and check in."

"Are you sure?" Munoz gestured to a door, different from the one the bloodied man exited. Hatch had no plans of seeing what was behind door number two.

"I'll be back." Hatch took one step in the direction of the main doors.

"We'd have a better chance of finding her if we had some kind of incentive." Rivera brightened and rubbed his thumb against his fingertips in that greedy money-grubbing sort of way.

Munoz laughed. "For us to do our job effectively in our city, we find that if additional risks are warranted, then those risks come at a price. As municipal police officers, we are not paid nearly enough for what we are asked to do."

"You mean like beating somebody half to death because he stole a piece of fruit?"

"Every choice has a consequence." He closed the gap she'd started to create. The woody notes accompanied him. His hot breath kissed her neck as he whispered in her ear, "If you have a problem with how we do business, please feel free to take it elsewhere."

Hatch reeled against the overwhelming desire to slam the side of her head into the bridge of the lieutenant's nose before spinning on her heels and walking away.

Just before stepping back into the bright light of day, she caught sight of an odd-looking man sitting on a bench. A peacock trapped in a net; he wore an olive drab fishing vest over a brightly colored Hawaiian shirt. A straw-woven fedora topped off the ensemble. The peacock chewed the end of a cigar sticking out of the corner of his mouth and was taking note of Hatch as she made her way outside.

She walked back past the guard, through the pedestrian gate, and onto the sidewalk. Hatch had an idea of where she would go next and started walking back toward the heart of Nogales.

A couple blocks from the police department, Hatch caught sight of the peacock man again in the reflection of a store window. He was following her. And Hatch needed to figure out why.

EIGHT

Hatch stood in front of a strip club. The hand painted sign depicted a stripper's bare legs standing above a T-bone steak wearing sunglasses and throwing cash. The caption, targeted at Americans, was written in English and read, *Steak and legs! Get it by the mouthful!*

"Their steaks aren't bad, but you might want to skip the legs—especially the morning crew." It was the peacock man. She'd stopped and waited for him to catch up. She watched as he hung back, aside from his outlandish outfit, he moved in and out of the crowded streets deftly.

She turned to the brightly colored stalker. He tipped his fedora and smiled. "If you're looking for a nice place to eat, I could take you to a café not far from here."

"I think I'll take my chances out here."

He gnawed at the cigar in the corner of his mouth, exposing his yellow stained teeth. A messy salt-and-pepper goatee framed his smile. "I saw you at the station."

"I know. You're a hard man to miss."

"Miguel Ayala, I'm a reporter with the *Noticias Independientes Para La Gente*, the *Independent News for the People*. I know, it's a mouthful." He moved his hand to a fanny pack strapped to his midriff. Hatch's left hand instinctually moved toward the small of her back. It hovered an inch from the butt of the Glock hidden beneath the white shirt.

He unzipped the pouch and pulled out an official looking press badge with the man's picture. What lent credence to the pass was that it depicted a much younger version of the peacock man. Somebody using this type of subterfuge would typically use a recent photo. And the photo on the badge was at least ten years old and showed a clean shaven and less gray version of the man standing before her.

Sometimes the reward outweighed the risk. Hatch was in a foreign territory trying to recover a girl from traffickers and, right now, she was running low on leads. And a reporter might be just the right person to remedy that. If nothing else, Miguel Ayala, the Peacock Man, seemed good company in the interim, until she figured her next step.

He leaned a little closer. Unlike Munoz and his nutty vanilla aura, Ayala's was of coffee and stale cigar. He spoke in a whisper, "To be honest, I hate this place."

"Not a steak man, eh?"

He laughed. "I hate this place and all the others like it. But that conversation is one I'd rather have away from the little birdies that fly their messages back to their master." He stepped back and spat. "Take it or leave it. I'll be at Café de Rosa. Two blocks at the corner. Great coffee. And if I may say so myself, some pretty great company."

"I'll think about it."

And with a tip of his hat, Ayala pivoted and continued in the direction of the café. Hatch bent to check her laces. As she did, her eyes swept her perimeter. She watched for movement patterns outside of the flow. She looked for people pretending to be occupied. Surveillance is a cornerstone of any investigator worth their salt, but counter-surveillance was the real test. Harder than it sounds, Hatch was confident in her ability. She was also confident Ayala didn't have a partner and, more importantly, nobody else was following.

She watched as Ayala disappeared into the café's doors two block up from where Hatch stood. Satisfied it was safe to proceed, she stepped off in the direction of the Peacock Man, walking in a slow meandering, touristy sort of way. *Blend, even when you stand out*, one of her survival instructors always said to her. Hatch was already at a disadvantage in her ability to blend in with the crowd as she was an American female. This was only worsened by the fact that she was also a few inches taller than anybody else around her, including the men.

Two old men squabbled in rapid fire Spanish in front of the bodega next door. The clamor of their argument was washed away by the loud hiss of an espresso machine the moment Hatch entered Café de Rosa. The aroma of fresh ground coffee beans swirled in the air and carried with it a note of vanilla and honey.

Ayala popped his head up from his newspaper and set it aside as Hatch approached the small table in the back corner where he sat. She was glad he chose a table away from the windows, but bothered he chose to take the chair facing the door. That left Hatch with her back to the door. She compensated by adjusting her chair, blading her body to Ayala which enabled Hatch to keep the entrance in her peripheral vision.

A wad of dirty napkins stuffed under one of the metal legs acted to balance the table's wobble with little effect. Two cups of dark coffee appeared moments later. Ayala smiled.

"Were you expecting company?" Hatch returned the smile as she pulled the porcelain mug closer. The fragrant steam licked at her nostrils. "Pretty confident I was going to follow?"

"Confident, no. Hopeful, yes. I like to find the upside of down." He adjusted his gaze to the returning server. His smile widened. The cigar dangled loosely on the edge of his lip but somehow managed to remain in place as if sealed by super glue. "I also took the liberty of ordering two cups of atole. Ever had it before?"

"Can't say that I have," The cup set in front of Hatch was wider than the mug used for the coffee. In it was a thick, creamy liquid that looked like a cross between a vanilla milkshake and Quaker Instant Oatmeal.

"Well, you're in for a treat. It's my mid-morning snack. And it fuels me until lunch, sometimes dinner. It doesn't look like much, but it's quite filling." He leaned in, just as he'd done outside of the strip club. "Wanna know the secret ingredient here at Rosa's that makes hers so special?"

"Sure."

"Rosa uses *masa harina*, a traditional Mexican flour. Others have opted for store bought corn meal. Rosa also uses *piloncillo*, a thick syrup made from cane juice. Brown sugar can be substituted but here, tradition matters. And it makes a difference. You'll see."

"You seem to know a lot about this restaurant." Hatch sipped at the creamy mixture. She was shocked by its smoothness. It was sweet but not overwhelmingly so, with a hint of cinnamon.

"I should," Ayala spread his arms wide as he beamed with pride, "I own it. Well, I don't *own* it. My wife, Rosa, does."

"This is a great place. You'll have to tell your wife how delicious her atole is." Hatch had already worked her way through half the cup.

"Will do," he winked and then hollered something in Spanish toward the kitchen area. Hatch heard a female's voice return with *gracias*. "Done. Next up, let's talk about you and why you were at the police."

"I'm looking for somebody."

"I know. I overheard that part. It's why I followed you." "There are far too many eyes around the department. I wanted to wait until I was confident we were alone before I approached."

"Why were you in the lobby?" Hatch continued to scan the surroundings while being visually assaulted by Ayala's wardrobe.

"Waiting for my next story. That place is a treasure trove of leads."

"Looked like you had yours. The fruit thief took quite a beating in there."

"I know. I noted it. Even snapped a couple photos with my cell when nobody was looking. But that story won't print. Ever. Not here."

"Why not?"

"Because our media is tightly controlled. My editor would never accept a piece like that. Nobody would. It would literally be a death sentence."

"Then why take pictures?" Hatch asked.

His infectious smile reappeared. "Just because my paper won't run them doesn't mean there isn't somebody who will. A good pen name is a bulletproof vest for investigative reporters like me."

"How do you pick a pen name? If these stories are death sentences, wouldn't you be signing it for somebody else, then?"

"You're a smart person, Miss Nighthawk."

She set the atole down. And scooted her chair back.

Ayala must've read her body language because he quickly followed with, "Whoa, don't run off. I heard you give your name to Munoz back at the station. Bad dude by the way."

She settled. "Nighthawk. Just call me Nighthawk."

The inquisitive Ayala didn't ask for a reason for her naming convention, and Hatch didn't volunteer one. She exchanged the empty atole mug for the one containing her dark roasted coffee, still steaming.

"Your pen name question is a good one. And, yes, I too considered the potential fallout from naming a person. And, yes, it would be a death sentence. Unless that person was already dead."

Sadly, or ironically--Hatch didn't know which--she felt completely understood. It's a strange thing to be listed among the dead but walking among the living. It was the closest thing to being a ghost Hatch could imagine. Sitting here in the lively café with the quirky Ayala reminded her she was alive.

"So," Ayala continued, "years back I decided I would expose the truth no matter the consequence. To do that I had to come up with a way of protecting myself and my family from repercussions. I've crossed paths with many people I consider heroes in my fifty-six years of life. Many have become martyred by their cause. My stories are published using the names of the brave people who get one last chance to champion their cause. I honor them while honoring my code of bringing light to the darkness."

"These stories you write, do they ever go beyond Nogales?"

"All the time. Mexico is my jurisdiction. I go where the story takes me." He scooped the last bits of the atole up with a teaspoon. Setting aside the cup, Ayala focused his undivided attention on Hatch. "I think you have a story worth listening to. And I'd like to see where it takes me."

"Not much of a story. We came to Nogales on our family trip to Copper Mountain—"

Ayala held up a hand. "Not to be rude, but I'm going to stop you there."

Hatch was confused at the interruption and it showed in the expression on her face.

"I understand your need to be aloof with those cops. I get it. You don't trust them. And with good reason. You couldn't have lucked out with a worse person than Eddie Munoz. That's one bad guy. I've been looking into him for a while. He's a hard man to catch. Even in the lobby exchange with the poor man who was unnecessarily beaten, Munoz remained at arm's length, never actually dirtying himself with the act, always there but never directly involved," he stirred a spoonful of sugar into his coffee and continued. "But if we're going to have a conversation, a real one, then honesty is the only way to continue. If you're going to feed me the same story you did those dirty cops, then I would like to pleasantly break company and wish you the very best in whatever it is you're trying to accomplish."

He was curt, but courteous. Hatch appreciated his candor. "I see you're observant."

Ayala patted his fanny pack where he stored his press badge. "All part of the job." Punctuating his statement with a wink.

"And you're right." Hatch drank her coffee, the heat of it warmed the back of her throat as she made her decision. "I'll tell you what I can. Know that anything I hold back is done only to protect you. Because what I'm involved in, no pen name can protect you against."

A quiet intensity stirred between them. Ayala took out his notepad and pen. He cleared space and set them on the table. He clicked the butt of the pen, "I'm ready to listen, if you're ready to talk."

NINE

Hatch spent her second cup of coffee explaining a chance encounter with the teenage stepdaughter of multimillionaire, Kyle Moss, who sold her into slavery. And while trying to find her and bring her back home, Hatch had stumbled across an international sex trafficking ring, moving girls through Arizona into Mexico near the border at Nogales.

Angela Rothman had been one of these girls. She was suffering from a bout of Stockholm Syndrome. And in the brief opportunity to escape with Hatch, Rothman resigned herself to her captors. Hatch summarized a brief connecting of the dots bringing her to the here and now, sitting at a coffee table in downtown Nogales with the newspaper man, Miguel Ayala.

He set his pen down and looked up at Hatch. She eyed the journalist's shorthand. He used Hatch's fake initials to note any time she was involved. The D and N overlapped in Ayala's hieroglyphic note taking. The curve of the letters made it look as though they were in the crosshairs of a sniper's rifle. Maybe it was symbolic of her life. She hoped it wouldn't always be.

He took out his cell phone. "If you don't mind, I'd like to send some of this information you gave me to some people that I know."

"Can you be more specific?"

"I know people who might be able to help find her or at least give a good idea of where she may be." He tapped his journalist notebook. "You meet a lot of people doing this job, and a lot of those people find they like to share things with me."

"And why is that?"

"Because I'm a great dresser." He belted out a laugh. "Kidding. I guess I'd like to think I'm one of the good guys, Miss Nighthawk. Or at least I try to be. And I'd like to see if I can help you now."

"Mind if I ask why you do it?"

"Help people?" He chuckled softly as if the answer was obvious. Hatch had her reasons for what she did and was interested to know his. He grew serious. "Because it's the right thing to do. It's the human thing to do, something my father used to say. He believed every interaction had meaning. That nothing happens in isolation. How we interact with the world matters. I didn't get it then."

"And now?"

"Lots of things my father said and did make a lot more sense now that I'm older."

"That's why your father did it. But I asked why *you* chose this. Going against these people is dangerous business."

"Life is a dangerous business. You could get killed walking across the street. Choosing to use the life you're given to do something positive for others is an easy one to make. But you're right. I didn't answer your question. I'll answer it with a story. If you indulge me while we wait on my friend to get back to me, I'd like to tell you a fable my father used to tell before bed. It's a children's tale but I hope you see the relevance."

"Only if we get another round of coffee." Hatch smiled.

Their mugs were filled a moment later and after taking a sip, Ayala began his tale with a question. "Have you ever heard the one about the boulder and the troll?"

Hatch ran the mental library of her childhood children's books. "Nothing but the Billy Goats."

"Then you're in for a treat."

Hatch stirred in a scoop of sugar and gave Ayala her full attention.

"There was once a land filled with endless acres of fertile soil, but nobody in the neighboring village could access it because it was blocked by a massive boulder. Atop the boulder lived a huge, nasty troll and the brave few villagers that tried to cross never returned.

"Over time, their land no longer took seed and soon they began to starve. The smallest boy in the village, seeing his people's suffering, decided he needed to save them. He went to the medicine woman who gave him a seed. She told the boy that this seed carried a power strong enough to destroy even the biggest of stones. The woman told the boy to find a seam in the boulder and place the seed inside. The boy eyed the medicine woman warily and she whispered, 'The smallest seed can split the biggest rock'.

When the boy arrived at the base of the giant stone, the troll stirred and sat up. He beat his chest like a mighty gorilla and laughed. In a deep rumble, he told the boy, 'You're too small. Go back home before I make you my snack.'

But that brave boy walked over to the rock and stuck the seed inside a thin crack in the jagged boulder's surface. He stood back from the boulder and bravely looked up into the dark eyes of the monster above. He repeated the words the medicine woman had said to him, 'The smallest seed can split the biggest rock.'

The troll laughed at the boy and asked him what he had done. He answered simply, 'I will show you when the time is right. I will walk through the center of this rock and your taunts will fall on deaf ears.'

Keeping his word, he returned as a grown man with the rest of the villagers behind him. Where the boulder once stood was a massive tree. Thick viny roots created an archway between the split rock. The boy stood between the two halves of the split boulder and smiled upon his people. The tree had grown so tall it had launched the troll high up into the sky where his rants and protests couldn't be heard above the gusting wind."

Hatch took a sip of her coffee. It was no longer hot. She'd been so mesmerized by Ayala's retelling; Hatch had forgotten to even take a sip.

"That is why I do it, Miss Nighthawk. I want to be that seed for my people. Capable of splitting wide this terrible rock that is the cartel. I want to stand under that tree and call them forward."

"And as for that story you heard, I will say to you what my father said to me upon first telling it. *The story is a part of you now. Your retelling will not be the same, nor should it. The magic of this story is an experience now of your life.*"

Hatch finished off the tepid coffee, trying to imagine her retelling. Set against the violent backdrop of her life, Hatch couldn't fathom how she could ever make a parallel to Ayala's fable.

Ayala received an alert on his phone and looked up at Hatch. "It looks like we got some information on your girl. They're using a nightclub called Club de Fuego. It's on the outskirts, on the eastern side of Nogales."

Hatch jotted down the information on her napkin.

"I can come, or at least drive you."

"I prefer not. No offense, but I usually go these things alone."

"Here's my card. My number's on it. Day or night, if you need something, you let me know. And if you find her, let me know that too."

"Will do." Hatch stood up from the table and shook the man's hand. He noticed the scar but chose not to mention it. "I'm glad there are people like you out there. Continue being that little boy from the village."

He smiled. "Got any plan for how you're going to do this?"

"Name of the place is Club Fire, right? Maybe I'll just burn it down."

TEN

Rafael Fuentes watched the long-barreled shotgun draped across his father's support arm. Ever since the razor-sharp machete opened his mother's throat, Rafael eyed any weapon in his father's hand with concern. Concern that his father would turn on him without warning, as he had Raphael's mother.

Hector Fuentes' button-down white shirt was untucked from his khakis and flapped in the warm afternoon breeze. Heeled along his right side was his beloved Doberman Pinscher, Red.

Rafael always hated that dog. Though less leery now that he was older, he was terrified as a child. He rarely, if ever, put his hand near the dog. He had never bitten Raphael but had growled on several occasions.

Red was not a house pet designed for companionship. No, he was one of the several attack dogs guarding the massive compound's expansive grounds. But Red was different. When Hector was home, Red never left his side. Red was a killer. Just like his owner.

Hector yelled, "Up!" On command, one of his servants pulled the trigger on the target thrower and released two clay pigeons into the air. Hector swung the shotgun up and locked it into the natural pocket between his shoulder and pectoral. Steadying the muzzle with his supporting hand, Hector took aim. He fired, pumped it, ejected the spent casing, and repeated. The two clay plumes drifting like lost clouds attested to the accuracy of the volley. Hector lowered the weapon and ejected the second cartridge.

"I think I'm done for the day." The same servant who'd launched the clay pigeons now hustled to retrieve the long-barreled gun. A thin trail of smoke escaped from the ejection port and chased the departing man.

Hector turned to face Rafael. He ran his hand along the top of Red's jet-black hair. "It's all about the training. It's what I've been doing for you since you were born. Do you think this dog wanted to stand beside me when I fired those shots? Do you think he wasn't terrified of them? At first, yes. But now, barely a flicker of his ear. How did I do it? Training. Over time conditioning his mind much like I've been conditioning yours, to accept the duties and responsibilities of my position, should the time come for me to hand it off to you."

His father always spoke in rapid Spanish when giving life lessons. His speeches were always filled with questions. But Rafael had learned long ago, those questions, if answered, were done so by Hector himself.

It was assumed that Rafael, eldest son to Hector, would eventually take over the family business. But his father rarely spoke openly about Raphael's role in the future. And Rafael wasn't so sure he wanted it.

When Rafael was young, his father would say things like, "this will all be yours someday," as he pointed out a window overlooking hundreds of acres of property. But what parent doesn't say something like this to their children? Dreams of parents hold universal truths. But what father kills a mother and then asks his son to wear the crown? What kind of son would Raphael be if he accepted it?

"WE WILL NEVER SPEAK OF THE OTHER DAY WITH YOUR MOTHER. She will always be remembered for the life she lived, and not for her betrayal of me. But before we put it to bed forever, I want you to understand this, blood of my blood, my Rafa," Hector paused to kiss Rafael's forehead after calling him by his childhood nickname. Hector locked eyes with Rafael before continuing, "Betray me, and your blood will run down the back of Red's throat."

The dog licked its chops, running its tongue around the sharp edges of its teeth while making eye contact, or seemingly so, with Rafael.

"I would never—"

Hector held up a hand, his index finger pressing Rafael's lips closed. "Shhh. Words matter little, my son. Worth is only found in deeds. Honoring me and our family means doing whatever it takes. I keep the promise made to my father. And you'll keep the one you make to me. There will come a time soon where I will ask you to prove that you're ready to lead this family.

"The seat I hold is a fragile one, and people are always looking to dethrone me. My life might not be the one you envisioned for yourself, but it is the future I ask you to accept. You're a thinking man. And that's good. This family needs that. But it also needs a man of action. Our greatness was not built on charity and good will. Will you bear the burden and responsibility of carrying the Fuentes family into the future?"

Rafael opened his mouth to speak, not sure what he intended to say. His mind still reeling from his mother's murder. Now that murderer was asking Raphael to fill his shoes. Rafael was grateful his father continued his pontification.

"I know you've got the intelligence. Hell, you're smarter than me. That's not where my concerns are rooted. In the Fuentes Family we act. Are you willing to do the things that I have had to do to get us here? Because the only way we will ever be able to maintain our power is through demonstration of that power. Do you have the strength to plunge your blade into an enemy's gut when the time comes? Everything I've built, and my father before me, depends on the answer you give here and now. Are you ready to kill, if need be, to protect all that you hold dear?"

Rafael saw only his mother. But his mouth uttered words that betrayed his heart and he felt a piece of himself die as he spoke his answer. "I am."

"What a relief that is to hear, my Rafa. When your opportunity presents, be a man of action, act swiftly and decisively. Matters of life and death are not to be taken lightly." Rafael heard the words, but his mind kept taking him back to the sound of his mother's choked gasps in the minutes she sat dying while strapped to a chair.

One of the twelve cell phones neatly arranged on a nearby table vibrated. Hector's assistant answered and then walked it over to his boss.

"Sir, it is one of your *friends*." Even in open air conversation, surrounded by guards and a walled fortress and acres of land enclosed with the Fuentes compound, they spoke code. The veiled speech was done more out of habit, but there was always the looming fear a government agency or rival cartel was eavesdropping.

Hector took the phone. Rafael remained within earshot to pick up both ends of the conversation. If his father hadn't wanted him to hear, he would have sent Raphael away. The fact that he didn't meant he wanted Raphael to listen.

"An American woman by the name of Daphne Nighthawk was poking around the department lobby this morning." Both men stood shoulder to shoulder and listened as the informant spoke. "She's looking for that girl. The redhead we moved through here the other day."

"And where is she now?"

There was a long pause. "I'm working on that as we speak."

"I pay you good money to handle these problems. I might be forced to seek assistance elsewhere." The threat unspoken, lingered in the air.

"Mister Fuentes, I tried. I did. I offered to have her come in to make a statement. She got spooked and left."

"You should've stopped her. You're a big strong guy. Couldn't stop a little woman from slipping away."

"She's not little. And besides, that loony reporter was in the lobby again."

Hector sighed and pinched the bridge of his nose. "Find her. No excuses."

"And how would you like her handled?"

"I'd like to have Juan Carlos speak with her before she sets sail for the afterlife. Keep me posted." Hector ended the call and tossed the phone to his assistant who caught it in midair and then returned it to its rightful place. He then turned to his son. "Seems like your opportunity to prove yourself may rise quicker than I expected."

"Do you think it would be best handled by The Viper?" Raphael asked.

"He's returning from cleaning up that mess in Arizona. Plus, it gives me a chance to see you in charge. I'm leaving you as oversight on this problem. It should be a good warmup for things to come. How much trouble can one woman be?"

"I won't let you down." The words sickened Raphael. All his planned resistance to his dad's pressure folded the instant Hector confronted him.

"This will be your first test. And please, whatever you do. Don't fail me."

ELEVEN

The cigarette remained carefully balanced between Kyle Moss's trembling lips as he stared down the barrel of the silenced pistol used to kill his attorney, Neil Taylor, a second ago. Moss was paralyzed. Not frozen. Literally paralyzed to the point of needing to make a conscious effort to breathe.

The shot had been fired just as Moss lit the cigarette. Both his hands hovered just above the table as if somebody hit pause on his life. A fragment of Taylor's skull was stuck to his face, the blood and brain matter served as a glue, adhering it to the right side of his cheek. Kyle wanted to wipe it off. He wanted to put his hands down. He wanted to get to the gun on the bed. None of his brain's requests were being honored by his body. His state of disconnect left him rigid.

The black semi-automatic pistol in the killer's hand seemed to grow bigger with each passing second. The frozen Moss took shallow breaths of the smoke-filled air, waiting for the gunman to kill him. But as precious seconds ticked by, no shot came.

"You may relax your hands, Mr. Moss, but please keep them on the table where I can see them." The man in the dark wide brimmed hat and suit of matching color lifted the rectangular leather case, then set it on the table before him without moving the muzzle off its intended target, Moss's forehead.

A worn leather bracelet clung to the gunman's wrist just beneath his suit sleeve. A long rattlesnake's tail dangled freely from it. The sound of its rattle as the killer set the leather case down didn't bother him. But the rattle from inside the case nearly caused Moss to vomit.

"I don't understand. I called you." Moss found the courage to speak but the words came out in clunky spurts as if his mind were trying to assemble each word letter by letter before releasing them.

"You have stolen from Mr. Fuentes. I am here to collect that debt. Now let's get on with this unfortunate business. And who I am is not of consequence to you. And it will soon not matter to either of us that I tell you. I am Alfredo Perez, but few know it. To those who stare at the case, I'm called *El Vibora,* The Viper."

"Wait! What? Stolen? I didn't steal anything from Mister Fuentes. Absurd! Are you kidding me? Get your boss on the phone." The ice in his limbs began to melt away as his paralyzing fear gave way to anger. Getting the gun from the bed was becoming a more possible opportunity.

"Maybe your idea of theft is different from Mister Fuentes'. Was there not a contractual arrangement made?"

"Yes," Moss said. *Buy time. Get the gun.* He knew what The Viper meant by contractual arrangement. Selling his stepdaughter into slavery had turned out to be the worst financial decision in Moss's long list of mistakes. It had been a hail Mary pass to save a dying business. And it backfired catastrophically. The climactic end of that karmic fallout was standing less than six feet away from him and holding a gun.

"So there it is, an arrangement was made. Money changed hands. Deals were made. Deals were broken. I am the one who repairs the damage."

"It wasn't my fault. And I never stole the money. You gotta believe me!"

"It doesn't matter what I believe. The call was made. I am here. Nothing short of a miracle will stop what comes next."

"You don't speak like a killer." Moss felt the statement slip out. Even offered an apologetic look to accompany it. But it was true. His English was soft and fluid. Educated in the US. His skin was pale. Hard to tell if he was even Mexican. His dark wire thin mustache and wide eyes gave him a Doc Holiday sort of look. None of it mattered. Kyle couldn't help but stare at the ghost-like marks underneath his right eye.

"Do you know a lot of killers, Mr. Moss?"

"Well—eh—no."

"Well, I do. And one thing I can tell you is that each of them approach death as uniquely as a set of fingerprints." He moved his hand toward the leather case. Three brass snap buckles separated the serpent inside from Moss.

Stall. Business 101. "Look, I told whoever I spoke to on the phone that I was planning to wire the money back as soon as the Feds unfreeze my accounts. My attorney *was* going to handle that," Moss shot a glance at the recently deceased Neil Taylor, "but not to worry, I can hire another."

The gun remained leveled at Moss's head, but The Viper didn't continue his reach for the case. "Even now, facing the tragic consequence of your life's decisions, you still cannot speak the truth. Sad really, if you stop to think about it. But you won't have long to ponder. So, please make use of the time you have left on this earth."

"Why don't you just shoot me and get it over with?" Frothy spit shot from his mouth, knocking the cigarette onto his lap. The hot cherry embers burned into his crotch. Moss snatched it by the butt and dusted the ash onto the floor. "Why don't you just put that bullet in my head right now?"

"That is not how it works, Mr. Moss. My employer, Mr. Fuentes, believes in clear and objective standards for all his employees. A task is given, a task is completed. No excuses tolerated, not ever. A simple but effective business plan."

"What else can I offer you that you don't already know?"

"Excellent question, Mr. Moss. Now you're getting in the spirit of things."

Getting in the spirit of things? This guy's insane. But he's still human. And human beings have weaknesses. Those weaknesses can and should be exploited. See, you smug son-of-a-bitch, I'm a businessman too? Fuentes isn't the only one who knows how to go to war.

"It is important to my employer, and so it is important to me that I investigate how far we have to go until all loose ends are clipped."

"You killed my attorney! Was he a loose end?"

"Yes, as was your accountant and your security guard."

The room spun. "You killed Teddy?" His accountant, Clarence Park, was a good enough accountant, but Moss held no personal feelings for the father of four. But Teddy had been a childhood friend before Kyle brought him in to work the cush gig of gate guard at his Hermosa Valley estate. Not so cush now. Ever since that Nighthawk woman showed up and ripped a gaping hole in his life.

"By you calling your attorney and bringing him here, you just saved me a day of work. That leaves more time for you and me to get acquainted."

"I've got money." *What the hell does a cartel hitman make, anyway?* "The bag down by my feet has two-hundred-fifty thousand in it." He watched as The Viper shifted his head and eyed the duffle. *Stall.* "A quarter million dollars is sitting right there. Take it. All of it. Just leave me enough to get across the border."

The Viper was silent for a moment before responding, "What you see as a last-ditch effort to weasel your way out of another mess, I see as weakness. Even facing certain death, you still lie."

"Lie? There's two-hundred-fifty thousand American dollars in that bag. Why don't you open it and count it yourself if you don't believe me?" The stalling was working. The snake was in the case and the bullet remained in its chamber. Each minute alive fanned his hope of escape. His wife had called him a cockroach the last time he struck her.

Maybe he was a cockroach. And just maybe, under these circumstances, being a cockroach was a good thing. Hard to kill a cockroach. He remembered reading roaches could survive a nuclear blast. That's the kind of luck Kyle Moss needed right now.

"You're a businessman, Mr. Moss, yes?"

"Yes. Yes I am." He sat up a little straighter. Keep him talking. That's where deals were made. And he was a deal maker. Money is the universal language and Moss spoke it fluently.

"And in the business world, what happens when you underestimate your competition?"

"I capitalize on it." Moss replied.

"In your desperate plea to make a monetary trade in exchange for your life, you failed to consider a few very important things. To put it bluntly, you underestimated me."

"I think we're getting our lines crossed here. Not sure what you're getting at or what I'm missing. You said I lied."

"You did. You told me you had a quarter-million dollars for me. But there's three hundred thousand dollars in this motel room."

The color drained from Moss' face. His limbs were once again paralyzed. "I don't know what you're talking about."

"Even your voice betrays you. But yet you continue to lie. Were you going to tell me about the other fifty thousand? You offered me two-fifty."

"I don't know what you're talking about," he stammered the lie.

"Confronted with the truth that is quite literally at my feet, soaking up the dead lawyer's blood." The Viper kicked the brown paper bag toward Moss. *Count it if you don't believe me. Isn't that what you said to me?"

"How did you..."

"You weren't directed to come to this motel by accident. Who do you think owns The Sunnyside Motel?"

Moss scanned the room as if the drapes would have a tag that read *Owned and Operated by the Fuentes Cartel*, knowing full well the meaning of the assassin's comment.

"The Fuentes business model also doesn't rely on trust. It's not reliable. Who am I to say?" He cocked his head, tipping the wide brim of his hat to his shoulder. His facial expression never changed. The slithered tongued of the Viper's voice remained ever steady and had an almost hypnotic quality. "The motel may look cheap, and it is. But the surveillance system is first rate."

"You've been watching me?" Ice ran down Kyle's spine.

"Knowing that, would it change your offer?"

"I—well—of course." An empty offering. The leverage of advantage was lost. Moss felt the tipping of the scale. His ploy failed. Because he underestimated his adversary. *Business 101.*

"This is a special room. And it should have special meaning for you. Well, it would if you were a caring, compassionate human being. Which I can clearly see, you are not."

"Who the hell are you to lecture me about compassion when you stand over the dead body of my attorney while pointing a gun at my friggin' head! And that—that case! Are you insane?" Moss was unraveling. Sweat poured from his brow as he ripped a long drag from the cigarette.

"This is the same room your daughter stayed in after you sold her into slavery. The girl you failed to ensure was delivered to us without issue. Instead, you not only failed to deliver what was promised, your incompetence resulted in an additional loss."

"It was that stupid bitch! The Nighthawk woman. She's the one who ruined everything. That's who should be in this room right now sitting across from your damned snake in the box. She's the one you need to be looking for."

"I'm sure steps have already been taken to handle that situation. Regardless, it's of no matter to you." The Viper sidestepped a foot's distance, giving way to the growing pool of blood leaving the gaping exit wound in front of Taylor's forehead.

Moss shot a glance at the gun on the bed. He wasn't a gun guy. Actually he'd only fired it once. The day he bought it, he went to the range and put a box of ammunition through it. Shooting wasn't his thing. Concern crept in. *Could I dive the four feet to where it lay before the professional killer got off a shot?* Doubtful. *Even if I did manage to get to the gun before he fired a shot, what's the chance I can fire a shot before he does?* Slim. *And the likelihood that shot hits the target I'm aiming for?* No chance in hell. Moss could barely hit the paper target at five feet. And he hadn't been diving and rolling like a stunt double in a John Woo film. In his world of financial risk analysis, Moss weighed those principals against the circumstance he now faced. His calculation put his percentile of chance in surviving this encounter at zero. It was the first time Moss had been honest, with himself or anyone else.

The Viper's eyes followed Moss' and the path led him to the gun on the bed. "Survival's a curious thing. People think they are more capable than they are. Most go their whole lives thinking they will fight back if ever confronted with death and never get tested. I am in a unique position, one where I get to witness firsthand the answer to that question. Do you want to know the truth about people in those most dire of moments?"

Moss shrugged. His words no longer mattered. Stalling failed. A terrible trembling jackhammered inside him, spreading out from his rapidly beating heart. He read somewhere that often people falling from great heights would have a heart attack before hitting the ground. Moss imagined the feeling he was experiencing to be comparable.

Sun slipped through a gap in the curtain, finding its way under the brim of The Viper's hat. The beam stung his right eye and it immediately began to water. He pulled a handkerchief from his pocket and, with a gloved hand, dabbed under his eyelid. The gun moved off target while the killer cleared his vision. Moss saw his fleeting window of opportunity and chose to ignore it. Maybe a trained assassin in the same position could've seized the advantage. But he was not that person, no matter how much he wished he could be.

"Are you ready to honor your debt and obligation to my employer?"

Moss' answer came in the warm urine soaking through his jeans. The pungent liquid leaked steadily from the end of his pantleg, pelting the frayed carpet below.

The dripping was the only sound filling the stagnant air until The Viper unlatched the first buckle on the case.

The snake's rattle sang out its deadly hymn through the reddish-brown leather of the case, drowning out everything, to include the beating of Moss' heart.

TWELVE

Hatch found Club de Fuego easily, operating on the intel provided by Ayala. She'd turned down the quirky press agent's ride offer, not wanting to involve him beyond his initial help. From experience, Hatch had learned the assistance people provided her often had negative and potentially life ending consequences. She wanted his good deed to go unpunished. Hatch had, however, accepted his business card with the promise of calling him should the need arise.

In lieu of his offer, Hatch flagged a taxi and wasted no time heading out to the club. The cab driver looked as though he were a hundred years old and smelt of day-old wine. At one point, he'd dozed off at an intersection. Hatch banged the smudged plastic partition separating her from her sleeping chauffeur, rousing him.

The description Ayala gave had been spot on. He'd said it was on the outside of town. The club was literally at the fringe of Nogales' easternmost point. Just past the nightclub was a ninety-degree bend where the two-lane Nogales-San Antonio roadway snaked along in a southeasterly direction until it intersected with *Carretera Federal Numero Dos*, Federal Highway 2, in Rancho San Rafael. Highway 2 carved across Mexico's northern tip, stretching from the Gulf of California to the violent streets of Juarez.

Club Fire stood out against the desert canopy sprawled out in all directions. The drunk old coot of a taxi driver muttered slurred Spanish as Hatch closed the door. *Turno de manana.* The rest was incomprehensible gibberish, but those words she understood. *Early shift.* She didn't know whether it was meant as a question, joke, or neither. She took it to mean that a) this place moved girls, and b) she was ahead of whatever schedule the club operated. The time it would take for things to pick up was unclear. She felt the stink of the cab cling to her clothes as she watched the driver swerve his way back in the direction of Nogales' city center where she'd hailed him.

THE NIGHTCLUB WAS A CONVERTED WAREHOUSE. IT WAS TWO stories of black painted concrete. The only spot of color came from the large red swirled flame, the point of which nearly touched the flat rooftop. The flames resembled the symbol used for Cobra Command, the evil regime bent on world domination and G.I. Joe's nemesis. Fitting.

The curling outline of the flame was dotted in red light bulbs. Below the sign stood the main entrance comprised of two dual-entry doors separated by a couple feet of the painted brick exterior. The sun slapped its warm beams at the tinted glass face of the doors, painting a purple glow on the walkway in front. A place designed for night did not have the same shimmer in daylight.

A few men were hanging out by the far back corner of the building. Two of them had dark aprons on and the third older man had just carelessly thrown a dishrag over his shoulder and joined the other men in their cigarette break. Smoke encircled the huddled men, none of whom paid attention to Hatch as she walked away from the spot where the cabby had dropped her and away from Club Fire.

Hatch made a beeline for a broken-down water tower. A faded cartoon water droplet smiled down on her as she ascended the metal staircase. Pipes were connected to the warehouse at one point, and reached out their jagged, rust-covered limbs to dusty wind swirling the arid landscape.

The three men never looked up from their conversation. Hatch crested the top landing. The two-foot-wide grated walk that wrapped around the top of the water tower loomed twenty feet above the roof of the nightclub. The vantage point gave her a solid visual of the front and back, as well as the side closest to her. The far side, on the east side of the building, was completely shrouded from view. The rust-coated bolt squealed as Hatch lowered herself to the warm metal, taking up a prone position.

She settled in and waited for night to fall and the girls to arrive. Because as the driver so eloquently put it, the *early shift* had arrived.

THIRTEEN

The sun yielded to night, painting the sky in a dazzling orange blaze. A deep purple like that of the light bounced off the main doors and lingered before giving way to moonless black. The three kitchen workers had long since finished their smoke break. In fact, they'd had time for two more in the interim hours before nightfall. Headlights from the arriving patrons flooded the dirt lot behind Club de Fuego. Hatch remained in her sprawled position on the rickety landing.

She had made minor adjustments to her body's position during the five and a half hours she waited. These shifts alleviated the discomfort from the rough treads of the elevated walk where she lay. Being in one spot for long periods of time was a staple of her training and experience during her military service. *Embrace the suck*, ex-boyfriend and former Navy SEAL Alden Cruise's mantra, which he'd picked up while at the Basic Underwater Demolition/SEAL Training in Coronado. It was Hatch's next destination if she found Angela Rothman and punished those responsible for her abduction.

Rhythmic pulsing resonated through the concrete walls. The club's logo lighted edges flickered, casting their scarlet glow on the black backdrop, giving it the effect of being engulfed in flame. A pigeon stopped by for a visit. It rested its feast, a bit of bread from a tortilla shell, beside the heel of Hatch's boot. It went about picking at the morsel with no regard for present company, as if Hatch didn't exist. Fitting, since according to the police and medical reports out of Hawk's Landing, Colorado, she didn't. *Servicewoman's Life Cut Down During Home Invasion*, the title of the Denver Post article had read. In it her death was surmised in two sentences: "*Rachel Hatch, age 35, died in the fire. Cause of death is ruled asphyxiation due to smoke inhalation.*"

She watched the club's logo burn bright. She thought about the fires that had ravaged her own life, each one catapulting her life forward in a totally new trajectory. All different. One left her right arm permanently scarred. The second ripped her from her family and the one man she ever truly loved. The last stopped her from saving a traumatized teen from the monsters she currently sought. All of them led her to the here and now. Fractured points in time pieced together to form the mosaic-stained glass that was her life. Blood from the wicked and the innocent tainted each pane with its unique hue. Hatch looked out at the club and wondered what the next addition to her life's tapestry would look like.

A line formed and the parking lot filled rapidly. There didn't appear to be any type of dress code, which was good because Hatch didn't have too many wardrobe options. The people arriving, most of them at least, were well-dressed but casual.

Several large doormen controlled access to the club. Red velvet ropes now lined the walk leading to the two oversized door guards. They stood facing the crowd with thick arms folded across their broad chests. Their backs faced the second set of doors. Four polished brass stanchions connected by the same red velvet ropes quarantined off a six-foot space in front of the second doors. In the dark, Hatch could now see the neon sign above the door, which read *VIP*.

Two dark vans with blacked out windows pulled up, panel-side toward the back of the club. Each of the front passenger side doors swung open and similarly dressed men in black fatigue pants and t-shirts of matching color stepped out. She could see the glint of steel peeking out from the front waistband of the closest man. The armed men yanked the back doors open and barked commands at the occupants inside.

Five girls exited, three from the first van and two from the second. Both vans then drove off. They didn't go far, only pulling around to the back and parking away from the other vehicles in the lot. The two paramilitary men ushered the girls to the club's rear entrance, bookending the single file procession.

The girls' heads were down with their hands crossed in front of their midline in what looked like prayer. Plastic zip ties bound them together and told anybody paying attention the truth of their circumstances. But none of the employees lingering near the rear of the club even raised an eye in the direction of the slaves passing by. Likely, they were either complicit by their indifference or indentured to the cartel themselves. Either way, this backdoor entrance garnered no attention. Except from Hatch.

With their heads down, the girls' long hair obscured any chance of getting a visual of any of their faces to confirm whether Angela was among them.

As the last girl passed through, the cone of light projected out from the club's open door and Hatch caught a shimmer of red.

FOURTEEN

Hatch navigated the metal staircase to the sandy ground below. The abandoned water tower projected its shadow in the direction of the club painting an already dark path even darker. Hatch used it to approach the back corner where she'd seen the wait staff taking their smoke breaks undetected.

She stood still at the edge of the shadow. Hatch looked toward the growing line of people filling the red velvet roped corral. *Blend, even when you stand out.* His battle-tested life lessons served as his lasting gift. Her dad's words came back to her now with more frequency. The connection they'd shared in life only grew stronger in death. His guiding hand on her shoulder pushed her a fraction this way or that, enabling her to dodge some of life's hurdles. And in Hatch's life, those hurdles often came by way of bullets.

Hatch twisted the front of her white shirt into a knot above her belly, exposing the flattened hardpack of her abs. She flared the back, making sure the Glock's jagged lines remained obscured. Satisfied it was still safely tucked from view, she continued her rapid alterations. Hatch pulled down the sleeve on her damaged arm, masking the scars.

She mussed her hair. The dirt and grime she'd accumulated acted as a natural hair putty.

By the end of Hatch's makeover, she was a drunken party girl. Hatch stepped out from the shadows and began her wobbly stagger toward the back of the line. She kept her head down, avoiding the surveillance camera at the corner of the building as she came up behind two men, each reeking heavily of aftershave and marijuana.

Hatch maintained a light sway. Even with her head down, she could feel their eyes rolling over her body like she was a piece of meat. They said something in Spanish she did not understand. She hoped they didn't try to start up a conversation and was grateful when a loud group of party goers up ahead drew their attention.

Five or six American college kids were belting out the lyrics to a song Hatch had never heard. Based on what she was hearing, both in content and delivery, Hatch hoped she never heard it again. The men nearest Hatch laughed at the impromptu show and lost interest in her.

A stretch limousine rolled to a stop in front of the doors. The driver who exited, wearing a full suit, immediately hustled around the trunk and around to the back passenger door facing the club. He opened the door and stepped aside, allowing the occupants to exit. Two well-dressed men left the vehicle, one a dark-haired Hispanic male in his mid to late thirties, and the other an American of similar age with sun-bleached blonde hair. The American wore sunglasses. At night. His choice of accessory making the Cory Hart classic hit seem all that more ridiculous when observed in real life. They entered through the boxed off area marked for VIPs. The special treatment earned boos from the rowdy college kids who, in turn, garnered a nasty look from one of the oversized doormen.

The limo drove off. Hatch watched as the smaller of the two doormen waved a black and yellow metal detecting wand over each entrant. The cold steel of the Glock pressed into the small of her back dictated a different entrance point.

The line had continued to grow and now a young couple stood behind Hatch. She needed to get out of the line and find another way in. Then she saw it. The staff entrance opened and the dishrag man from earlier appeared still with the same rag as before, though this time slung over his opposite shoulder.

"Whoa," Hatch lurched forward, hopping out of line and covering her mouth. "Here comes dinner." She said this for anybody paying attention. The couple gave her wide berth and the aftershave-wearing weed smokers just shook disapproving faces as she hustled away in an overexaggerated stagger.

Techno music masked her footsteps as she closed in on her entrance point and the overweight chain smoker standing between her and Angela. Hatch fell against the wall. A small piece of broken plastic acted as a doorstop, keeping it ajar. The electronic repetitive four beat pulsed, assaulting Hatch's ears. The ragman turned in surprise. He spoke, but the club washed out any chance of deciphering its meaning.

Hatch let her head droop. It swung loosely as if dangling by a thread. His hand touched her shoulder and he worked to stabilize her against the wall. He continued to speak in Spanish. He was close enough for her to hear. And the words weren't kind and compassionate. *Drunk bitch* was thrown in somewhere. It didn't matter what he said or wanted. The minute he'd opened the door, he became another obstacle in a long list that stood in the way of Hatch and the girl she'd vowed to bring home.

If there'd been one lesson she'd learned from her father about obstacles, it was to overcome them by all means possible. He told her once, *no matter how remote, explore all avenues until you find a way around.* A young Hatch had asked, "what if you can't?" Her father's answer was, *then you kick it in.*

The smoke emptied from the ragman's mouth filling her nostrils as he put his other hand on her and shoved her hard. Two mistakes he made. First, pushing Hatch without blading his stance, leaving him completely off-balance. The second was putting a hand on Hatch in the first place.

Hatch capitalized on both mistakes in the seconds that followed. She spun her body redirecting the ragman's energy to the wall where

Hatch had been leaning. With both hands on Hatch, his momentum sent him headfirst into the hard concrete. She assisted the wall's efforts in rendering him unconscious by slamming her left elbow into the back of his skull. The ragman collapsed in a heap at her feet. Hatch used her body to temporarily block the crumpled man from view as she broke the lightbulb above the door.

Shattered bits of the popped bulb dusted the sleeping man. The only light now filtered out through the smoke-filled air of the club inside. The music pulsed on as Hatch cast a glance in the direction of the line. Nobody noticed the brief but intense moment with the ragman.

Nobody noticed as Hatch entered the club through the steel employee access either.

FIFTEEN

Hatch choked on the air. One of the cooks looked at her, conveying confusion and annoyance at her surprise arrival in the kitchen. Hatch threw her hands in the air and gyrated her hips with the music. She let out a loud, "Woohoo! Let's party!" In her best drunk-girl impression. Surprising even herself, she nailed the performance because the pout on the man's face instantly shifted into a gapped-tooth smile.

The cook ordered a busser to escort Hatch back to the main dance floor, but not before blowing Hatch a kiss which she playfully caught and stuffed into her pocket, staying in character until she was taken into the bar area. The busboy released his not so friendly grip and cast her back into the crowd of drunken clubbers.

Laser lights and smoke machines added their insanity to incessant vibrations echoing into the three-thousand square foot converted warehouse space. Nude girls danced in cages suspended at random intervals throughout the crowded space. The girls moved to the music's command, the drugs in their system undoubtedly contributing to their trancelike state. No Angela.

She continued her visual scan as she stepped further inside. A long bar stretched out to her right running the full length of the wall and dead ending on the other side where the front doors were located. Hatch pressed further into the room, slipping in and out among the undulating sweaty bodies lining her path.

The massive ventilation and air conditioning system centered above did little to alleviate the staggering swelter. Hatch's white t-shirt was becoming translucent, exposing the contours of her bra which a nearby club goer was admiring before getting jostled by a man of equal size behind him. The fight that erupted in the following seconds was like watching a silent western. Neither man backed down in the deafening drone. Without words, no resolution could be amicably agreed on for the accidental transgression and so the two men did what any neanderthal would do. Fight.

The man who'd been transfixed by the curvature of Hatch's breasts was the first to throw a punch. A wildly telegraphed right hook came in wide and should have been defended against. But it wasn't. The other man was so drunk, standing came at great effort and he was completely unprepared for the attack. And about five seconds late in his failed attempt to intercept the incoming fist that crashed into his nose.

Blood arced into the air and was caught by a yellow beam of light, giving it an orange glow before showering down on the man's girlfriend, who screamed. Bodies piled as more jumped into the fray.

Four bouncers, wearing skintight black t-shirts embossed with the red flame logo of the club, rushed the clump of people, and began indiscriminately delivering vicious beatings to anybody, man or woman, within the radius of fist or foot. Both men who'd initiated the fight, plus the blood-covered girlfriend, were pummeled until no resistance was offered. All three were dragged through the crowd by the four bouncers and tossed out through the main door.

The chaos was over in a less than one minute. Hatch had moved on, working her way toward the other side of the club floor. A closed door marked VIP cast its hot pink neon glow off the bald headed security guard blocking it. To his left was the disc jockey's massive turntable station where he was sending out his unique blend of music. The floor bouncers were now shooting the breeze with their doormen counterparts, celebrating their decisive victory over the drunk fools. In their moment of macho bravado, they'd left the floor unprotected, minus the one guard at the door. And with it, Hatch had a window of opportunity upon which to capitalize.

Hatch closed the gap, looking for her access point to the VIP lounge. Angela was nowhere to be seen among any of the working girls in the club. They had come through a back door which must have given direct access to this section. Weighing the odds, the door ahead held the best chance of finding Angela. Going head on with the guard would be futile. Even with the floor bouncers a distance away, she needed to come up with a less direct approach. She needed a distraction. And she found one in the unrelenting pulsing of the DJ's music.

The projector bolted to the ceiling above the DJ, casting the turntablist's teal spikey hair in prismed color patterns. A hypnotized crowd throbbed along as the beats directed them. A girl wearing nothing but a glittery thong shared the small, raised landing where the DJ spun his mix. He licked the sweat-soaked side of her neck as he changed out the record on the second turntable. She seemed not to notice or care that the wild music man had just treated her like a lollipop.

The landing itself was nothing more than a two-tiered scaffolding, not much different from those used for external repairs of buildings. The only glaring difference was this one had a large black sheet covering the crossed support bars underneath. A power strip poked out from underneath its mess of wires, looking like Medusa on a bad hair day, and spread out from the multi-socket outlet.

A sweaty male wearing a yellow mesh tank top, an homage to the outfits of the 80s big hair rock bands seemed a bit out of place amidst the crowd of hip partiers. He didn't seem to mind, partly due to the inebriated state he was in. He swayed more obnoxiously than Hatch had during her little act in the kitchen area. He gripped one of the support bars of the scaffolding, clutching it for dear life with one hand while eyeing the large plastic cup in the other hand that had gotten him to his current state. In the man's intoxication, Hatch saw opportunity.

Shooting a quick glance in the direction of the doorman outside the VIP lounge, Hatch confirmed his attention was elsewhere, on a large chested twenty-something bouncing in his periphery. The loud Americans who had been acting like fools in line moseyed up to the distracted bouncer. She couldn't make out what the tallest male in their group was saying, but the slow deliberate shaking of the guard's head told Hatch the request, presumably to gain access to the VIP area, was off limits. Fanning a wad of cash at the bald bull of a man only seemed to strengthen the resistance.

Bald Bull released his folded-arm, tough-guy stance, opting for a looser, albeit less imposing, stance. Hatch watched as the bouncer's right hand curled into a ball. The loud-mouthed American wasn't paying attention, turned to his friends and laughed. The American crumpled a dollar bill and tossed it over his shoulder. The wadded cash bounced off the shiny bald head of the infuriated door man.

The tall American never saw it coming. Bald Bull's rage spilled over, and although outnumbered five to one, hurtled his bowling ball sized fist at the back of the man's turned head. The impact flattened him against one of his friends. A churning swirl of wildly swinging arms followed as another pocket of violence erupted inside the club.

Bald Bull stood his ground against the crew of angry tourists. Several of the nearby locals jumped into the fight as the four bouncers who'd been celebrating now forced their way back through the crowd toward the latest melee.

The rumble continued as the tide shifted dramatically in the favor of the raging Bald Bull when his numbers increased by the arrival of the other bouncers. Devastating blows were delivered by the professionals, pummeling the younger, less experienced Americans into the ground.

Only ten feet separated Hatch from the unguarded door to the VIP access door and the chaotic free-for-all taking place in front of it. Using the unexpected disturbance to her advantage, Hatch slipped the full beer from the mesh-wearing drunk's hand. The amber liquid splashed down onto the power strip below.

A loud popping followed by crackling. The sound of the electrical fire replaced the blaring techno music. Acrid smoke rose in front of the DJ platform as the fire rippled along the network of cords until it reached the wall. In a matter of seconds, the wall behind the turntable, the same one where the VIP access door was located, ignited.

Fire licked its way up the wall. The topless girl next to the teal haired disc jockey screamed. Her pitched screech sent those in earshot into a frenzy of movement. Hatch was momentarily swept up in a sea of panicked bodies. She swam against the flow, and after wedging her way through, found herself at the VIP access door.

Bald Bull delivered a final devasting blow to the already unconscious American. He was now busy fending off the panicked crowd who saw the VIP room as an escape from the inferno. Nobody noticed when she checked the knob. Locked. She saw a key attached to a lanyard on Bald Bulls right hipline.

The fire tripped the circuit breaker and power went out as the overhead sprinkler system activated. Hatch felt the relief of the cold water raining down on her as she used the darkness to close the gap with the bald headed security man.

Hatch swept Bald Bull's legs out from under him. A quick stomp to side of the downed man's shiny head ended the fight. She pulled the lanyard and unlocked the door.

In the ensuing chaos, Hatch slipped into the VIP area undetected.

SIXTEEN

Hatch clicked the door closed behind her and slipped the Glock into her left hand. She focused her vision ahead while keeping her right hand on the doorknob. The contact with the door served as an alarm system of sorts, should the hulking Bald Bull try to barge in on her little rescue mission.

Light spilled under a door at the end of a hall leading outside. Only one other door existed in the otherwise barren hallway. The longer she stood in the dark, the better her eyes adjusted to it. And in her renewed vision, Hatch was now able to make out the darkened glass tubes of the blacked-out neon sign's letters. *VIP.*

The door remained closed and for a brief second, Hatch's heart sank at the thought that she'd missed her opportunity to recover Angela from her abductors. She released her contact with the doorknob, trading a known threat for an unknown one, and made her way toward the VIP lounge. She was a foot from the door when it opened outward, shielding Hatch from the person opening it.

"Back in a minute." was what she understood from the guard stepping into the hallway in front of her. It was the same guard who'd escorted the girls in through the back door of the club.

He closed the door, keeping his back to Hatch. And just as the obnoxious tourist had never seen Bald Bull's wild haymaker coming, the armed man in front of her didn't see Hatch's attack coming either. Although Hatch's attack wasn't an out-of-control limb wielding amateur hour as demonstrated by the bouncer. No, hers was a refined series of movements designed to incapacitate her opponent quickly and silently.

Hatch dispatched a violent three-move assault on the unsuspecting man, first stomping down on the back of his right knee and following with a debilitating brachial stun to the side of his neck with the butt of her Glock. Those two moves sent the medium sized guard into a heap. Her third and final move might've been overkill, but Hatch needed to ensure he'd be out long enough to carry out the next step. Snaking her arm under his chin, she cinched herself tight, restricting blood and oxygen for an eight count before releasing him back to the laminated flooring to resume his nap.

Hatch bound the man's wrists and ankles with plastic zip ties she found in his pocket, the same ones used to bind the girls she'd seen earlier. She gagged him and took the nickel-plated .45 from the man's waist and tucked it in hers. No spare magazines. Effectively pillaged in a matter of seconds, Hatch then dragged his unconscious body to the door leading back into the club and wedged him snug against it.

Satisfied her thug doorstop would hinder any attempts to enter the hallway, if only briefly, Hatch made her way back to the VIP access door. She checked the handle. Unlocked. She settled her breathing.

When Ayala had given her the limited information he had on Club de Fuego, there were no details beyond the location and general layout. Hatch was blind to what waited on the other side of the door. Only one way to find out.

The four girls in the room were already topless and were now in a state of suspended animation, frozen mid-dance as they stared at Hatch. She could see why, Hatch caught sight of herself in the mirror platform one of the girls was dancing on. Her shirt, still knotted above the waist and soaking wet from the sprinkler system, now had accumulated blood from choking the guard in the hallway. The gun in her hand finished off the deranged look as Hatch visually assessed her situation.

A Mexican businessman sat on a wide-backed dark leather chair with a cocktail in his hand, watching the half-naked girl standing on the mirrored platform in front of him. The other girls were standing nearby. Club Fire's VIP lounge was missing two things, Angela Rothman, and the Mexican's American counterpart. The only thing keeping her from crossing the ten feet of fuzzy purple carpeting, separating her from the room to the left marked *private,* was the other member of the security team from the van. His dark eyes peered out from under a black baseball cap. His hand was already moving toward the pistol tucked in his waistband.

A drink caddy with expensive bottles of liquor and wine were lined up behind glasses atop a polished silver cart on wheels, dividing the distance between Hatch and her adversary. Gunshots would alert the others. Gunshots would greatly reduce her chance of survival.

Her bootlegged pistol was already up and on target. The front sight post hovered over the Club de Fuego's red flame emblem stenciled into the form-fitting black shirt. She had him dead to rights. The security team member, who was of similar size and height as her, had his right hand tightly gripped on the gun tucked in the front of his pants. The white of his knuckles looked like big pearls as the fear seizing control of his mind increased the tension of his squeeze.

If this were game of slapjack Hatch would've won, hands down. Question now was, what to do about this paused standoff. *Seize the opportunity that presents itself and be ready because it may be the one you least expect.* Her dad's voice in her head brought an added layer of clarity to Hatch's already intense focus.

Keeping her weapon on target, Hatch thrust-kicked the metal cart, stomping her boot into the push handle and sending it torpedoing forward at the man. Instinct took over and he released his gun hand to stop the rapidly approaching cart. A moment later, the beverage tray slammed into his midsection with a crash.

Hatch was already pouncing as he cast the cart aside. She snatched a diamond encrusted bottle of champagne as the tray crashed to the floor beside them. Hatch swung for the fences and connected with the man's chin. The impact from the bedazzled bubbly spun him in a drunken pirouette and sent him into dreamland before he hit the ground.

Hatch searched his pockets just as she'd done with the man in the hall. Finding a similar cache, she secured the downed guard, zip tying and gagging him. She took the gun he'd unsuccessfully tried to pull on her, and instead of keeping it as she had the other, Hatch walked over to the half-naked girl standing in front of the businessman. He was still rooted in frozen terror on the seat in front of her and she handed the dancer the gun out of necessity. If she was to effectively clear the next room, she had to ensure the wealthy A-lister didn't escape and alert the others. His panic-stricken paralysis would only hold him so long.

The girl shook her head. Her eyes watered. "Please—no." Her broken English barely comprehensible through her ragged breaths as she tried to choke back tears.

"It's simple," Hatch pressed the gun into her hand, not wanting to give any more time to this debate, "if he moves, shoot."

The girl's trembling hand accepted the foreign object Hatch forced on her. She was scared. And Hatch didn't want her to pull the trigger. In fact, when she'd quickly assessed the four girls standing around the seated man, the girl Hatch selected was probably actually the least likely of them to actually use the gun. It was the reason Hatch chose her. Hatch couldn't afford to have the gun go off while she was searching the other room. On a moral level, Hatch didn't want to force this girl, who looked in her late teens, to shoulder the burden of taking a human life. Hatch had experienced it enough to know the toxic effect it had on one's life.

The gun vibrated in the girl's hand, but she managed to keep it pointed in the direction of the seated VIP. "He moves, you shoot," Hatch repeated before hustling off to the closed door of the private room. She'd kept her eye on it since taking out the guard and was surprised nobody came from inside to investigate the noise. Could mean a lot of things. None of them good.

The door was locked. *No matter how remote, explore all avenues until you find a way around. Sometimes you'll find the doors of life locked, and then what? Do you quit? Raise the white flag? No. You kick it in.* And that's what Hatch did.

She booted the door, striking with the heel of her boot just above the knob. Normally, she would've donkey kicked but didn't want to breach the unknown with her back turned, so Hatch opted for the traditional method of raising the knee and stomping out. Less reliable, but more tactical in a one-man, or one-woman, dynamic entry situation.

The door's frame cracked, and the free-swinging door slammed against the inside wall of the small room. The private room was nothing more than a sex closet, containing only a bed and a nightstand. Mounted by a series of hooks, the wall to the left was a sadist's dream board. Tasseled whips and rods of different thicknesses hung for a client's choosing. The American VIP member had opted for a long, pointed needle. Hatch couldn't fathom its purpose but assumed it had one because there was a similar tool on the wall rack. She knew the purpose for which it had been made was not how the terrified businessman now wielded it.

When Hatch entered, he was already tucked on the opposite side of the bed with the tip of the needle pressed firmly into the neck of the girl on the bed. The girl's red hair spilled across a pillow and in the dyed highlights Hatch saw it wasn't Angela. The girl's naked body was tied by bungee cords to the four black wrought iron posts rising from the corners of the bed. She was unconscious, or at the very least teetering on it. A teardrop clung to the end of her thick eyelashes and captured the light from the flickering candle on the nightstand, the only source of light for the otherwise pitch dark of the room.

The shirtless businessman exposed a corner of his shoulder. Hatch brought her aim to the small bit of exposed, sweat-covered skin showing from behind his bound hostage. The restraints binding her body made it impossible for him to completely hide from view. Whatever tv show this user of women had learned his hostage-taking skills from didn't seem to be working in his favor.

But there was still the possibility he could push the needle inside the girl's throat before she could kill him. Slim, but present. "You move and you're dead. Drop the needle!"

"I'll do it! I swear to God, I'll jam this thing so deep!" spit flew from his mouth as he spiraled out of control, "Get the hell out of here or I'll kill her!"

"You don't want to do this. Put it down."

"Hell no! You're just going to kill me." His eyes darted past Hatch.

"Nobody's dead out there if that's what you're looking for. I don't have all day, and the longer you take in making it, I can't guarantee this bullet here doesn't rip through your shoulder."

The frantic hostage taker tried without success to press himself further behind the girl, but to effectively hold the needle to her neck, he could not. And the effort left him in no better position than when Hatch first made the offer. *No gunshots*, she told herself.

"Let me tell you how this is going to go. First, I'm going to shoot you in the top of your right shoulder. It's not going to kill you, but the pain of it will make you wish it had. You will be in screaming agony in a matter of seconds. I will then fire a second shot after the first one moves you safely away from that girl. However, you will not feel this second shot because the jacketed forty caliber round inside this gun will pass through the front of your skull at nearly thirteen-hundred feet per second, killing you instantly."

Her aim never wavered as she negotiated the terms of surrender. He didn't utter a response. Hatch watched the businessman's shoulder rise and fall in rhythm with his breath as he weighed the offer. Hatch took the slack out of the Glock's trigger as her timeline in which she would make the decision for him rapidly approached.

The gunshot that came next cracked like a whip and caught Hatch completely by surprise.

SEVENTEEN

The shot hadn't come from her gun. It came from the other room. Hatch spun to see the source of the discharge. Smoke seeped from the end of the nickel-plated pistol, encircling the head of the tear-stricken girl who'd fired the shot. Her eyes apologized to Hatch as she and the other three girls made a mad dash for the hallway door while the expensive wardrobe of the dead man in the lounge chair absorbed the blood spreading out from the center of his chest.

The dying man's agonal breaths were drowned out by the wild scream from inside the room where Hatch stood. The shirtless American had launched himself into the air with the needle outstretched in his right hand looking like a pirate diving off the top mast.

Hatch sidestepped the poorly planned attack at the last second, allowing the deranged man's momentum to do the heavy lifting. His forehead struck the corner edge of the doorframe with a sickening thud. Until he let out a whimper, she thought the impact might've actually killed him. One solid stomp silenced any further resistance.

Hatch had no time to spare if that shot had been heard over the chaos of the club. There was a chance it wasn't. But Hatch didn't like playing those odds. In less than twenty seconds, she had stripped the guard of equal size out of his clothes. Seconds later, Hatch was now wearing the clothes of the man she'd bested with a drink cart. Hatch tucked her shoulder length hair inside the ballcap and cinched the brim down, hoping to block her face from view.

Hatch then set about undoing the knots and freeing the girl's hands and feet. "Gracias," she muttered. Her voice was stronger than Hatch expected, but then again if you're drugged and bound to a bed maybe it's best to put your mind elsewhere. Hatch spoke softly but firmly. She needed to get this girl out of the room, but she needed her functional enough so Hatch could address any threats.

"Do you speak English?"

"A little." The weakness in her voice was matched by the trembling wave of her hand.

Hatch was able to get the girl up. With each passing second her assailant's smashed face rested against the frame of the door, she seemed to grow a little stronger. Hatch got the girl into her old clothes.

"I'm Leticia," her voice a whisper, "but you can call me Letty."

"I'm Daphne. We can spend time getting to know each other later. What we need to do is get the hell out of here. And fast. Can you walk?"

"I think so."

Hatch assisted the girl to her feet. She wobbled but maintained her balance.

"Put your hand on my right shoulder. Do not pull or push. Only move when I move." Hatch laid out the ground rules. There was no way she could carry this girl and focus on their escape. But she also needed to keep her close so she could keep her safe. Knowing where she was relative to Hatch was critical should the battle erupt.

Hatch brought her gun up into a low ready, centering it near the Club de Fuego emblem above her left breast. She moved forward to the door leading to the hallway that the fleeing girls had left wide open.

To Hatch's surprise no security team members had entered. A moment later, as she stepped into the hallway with Letty in tow, she saw the reason why. Flames licked their way into the gaps in the door's frame. A heavy layer of smoke filled the top three feet of the hallway.

The thug she'd turned into a doorstop had inch-wormed himself away from the burning door. He looked in Hatch's direction. He grunted loudly. In the smoke, he must've thought she was his partner. His eyes widened when he realized the folly of his assumption.

Hatch turned and headed to the far exit at the other end of the hall. "Stay with me. Do what I tell you when I tell you to. Understand?"

Letty squeezed Hatch's shoulder weakly and nodded. Hatch opened the door and quickly scanned the exterior. Fire engines and police sirens could be heard approaching in the distance, but nobody noticed the open door. The few patrons passing by were in hustled jogs to the back lot. A passing car's headlights gleamed over Hatch just as she retreated inside.

Hatch took a moment to tuck the gun alongside the other one pancaked against the base of her spine. Walking with a gun was a surefire way to draw unwanted attention.

The two slipped out into the muggy night air filled with the biting acridness of the electrical fire now consuming Club de Fuego. They moved down to the far corner at the rear of the building. One of the vans had pulled up to the rear entrance. The other was still parked in the back corner of the lot, idling.

Hatch made sure her brim was pulled down as low as it would go. "Stay here. Don't move until I come back for you."

The young girl leaned against the painted black concrete wall. "Come back—please."

"Promise." Hatch patted the traumatized girl's hand before removing it from her shoulder.

She stepped around the corner, head down but moving purposefully to the passenger side of the van.

Unable to see through the tinted window, Hatch grabbed the handle with her right hand while simultaneously withdrawing the Glock. She slipped inside quickly and closed the door behind her.

The driver said something in Spanish before realizing the man he was speaking to wasn't a man at all. He never had a chance to unholster the gun strapped to his thigh. Hatch slammed the side of his head into the driver's side window with enough force to spider the glass. Had the thick tinted overlay not been affixed to the glass, it would've undoubtably shattered, drawing unwanted attention. Hatch delivered a follow-up blow with the metal slide across his exposed right temple, zapping the fight out of the man.

Hatch pulled him across the seat to her side. She then opened the passenger door and dropped him onto the ground. Hatch looked over in the direction of the awaiting teen. "Come! Now!"

Letty moved in a wobbly run, zig zagging her way, as Hatch climbed back in the passenger side and then pulled herself across to the driver's seat. She took a moment to look out toward the second van. It continued to idle in the back corner of the dirt lot, its driver unaware of his partner's fate.

She watched the driver roll up from the heap she left him in and scream something in Spanish as Hatch pulled away.

Club de Fuego burned bright, sending its gray smoke high into the dark as Hatch raced away. No Angela, and now with the addition of Letty, Hatch needed a helping hand. She hoped Miguel Ayala was still willing and able to offer his.

EIGHTEEN

Eddie Munoz arrived with thirty police officers who responded to the Club de Fuego fire. Although he wore the uniform identifying him as a ranking lieutenant, he didn't respond in his official capacity. He wasn't even technically on duty. His shift ended hours ago and he had been at a strip club on the other side of town when he got the call.

The call hadn't surprised him. He was called to handle all sorts of things for the Fuentes Family. He was their top guy in Nogales, serving both as enforcer and overseer for the operations within his hometown. He considered himself worthy of being at the head of the table someday. He often daydreamed about receiving the nod to come forward as next in line. If nothing else, as head of security.

Until that time when his talent and dedication were properly recognized, Munoz would continue to use his power and influence as a lieutenant to gather evidence, cover something up, and occasionally... kill. Tonight, his task had been simple. Gather as much intelligence about the person responsible and report back.

Munoz walked up on a cluster of Fuego employees, easily identified by their shirts' emblem. "Any of you have access to the surveillance system?"

A skinny man in his fifties put his hand in the air. "I'm the manager. But I can't access it remotely. I have to go inside to do that and the firemen already told us that nobody's allowed back in yet."

"Let me worry about what the firemen want. You see this? This highly polished brass bar trumps any of the firemen. Got that?"

The manager raised his hands defensively, "I'm just repeating what they told me."

"I know," Munoz gestured toward the smoldering building.

Munoz walked by firefighters working to control the blaze on the west side of the building, where the damage had been worst. Nobody had been killed or severely injured. Some suffered minor smoke inhalation.

A stocky fireman grabbed Munoz by the shoulder and spoke in the crackled voice of a chain smoker. "Can't go in until it's cleared."

Munoz looked down at the soot-covered hand touching the freshly pressed uniform and smudging the collar brass he always kept to a high gloss shine. He fought the urge to smash the back of his hand across the man's face. But all that was hidden behind Munoz' engaging smile. "Oh, thank you." Munoz simply brushed the fireman's hand away and proceeded in the direction he had just been forbidden to go.

A few minutes later, Munoz was standing behind the manager who was busy logging into the camera system. A men's room separated the office space from the rest of the club. The air stunk of the fire, but the manager's space had been untouched and ran on an alternate fuse box from the club. The fire had not corrupted the lines, and power had not been lost.

A raised monitor offered twelve greyscale perspectives of the club. Munoz received a quick tutorial on how to use the system, a simple mouse click function display on the monitor allowed for easy playback. And he began scrolling back in time to the starting point of the fire. Each monitor reversing in sync.

Munoz saw the flash on four of the cameras. He zoomed in. Two of the screens were too far away. Of the last two cameras, only one captured what Munoz was looking for.

He brought up the freeze-frame image to full size on the monitor. All twelve screens disappeared but one. Munoz stared at the face captured in the still shot. And he was shocked to recognize the person in it.

The woman who had come into the police department early that morning was now staring back at him. The security camera up above the DJ's turntable captured the face of Daphne Nighthawk.

He called a number and waited. Raphael Fuentes answered. Strange, because he had always been in the backdrop, hiding in his father's shadow. Munoz hadn't had many dealings with Raphael, and in the few times he did, it was never over matters of security.

"I needed to speak to your father."

"I'm handling this now," Raphael said.

"Then you have a problem."

"What is it?"

"It's not a what. It's a who," he continued to look at the woman on the screen. "The Nighthawk woman burned down the club. All five girls are gone."

"I'll handle it."

"Allow me."

"I'll be in touch." Rafael ended the call.

Munoz put the phone away and spent the next several minutes tracking the Nighthawk woman on her skillful rescue mission. He watched the pole camera capture the departing black van as it sped away into the night away from Nogales.

Munoz wasn't sure where she was headed. But he was sure a whole ton of trouble was heading her way. And he hoped to be a part of it.

NINETEEN

Raphael turned to his father, who was taking the first sips of his favorite brandy. It was all he permitted himself to drink after midnight. He said it left him with a clear mind in the morning. Rafael never saw the logic. It never bothered him before, but since the murder of his mother, everything his father did only further fueled the hatred Raphael felt for the man.

"Problem?"

"Daphne Nighthawk. The woman Munoz called us about just burned down the nightclub and freed five of our girls." Money and property were two things Rafael's father took very seriously. Raphael watched the ripple of anger pass across his father's brow at hearing the news.

Hector set his drink down and looked at his son. He was quiet, his reserved thoughts never permeating his facial expression.

"I think it's time for Juan Carlos and his men to take over." His father's native tongue always took on a lyrical note when he was pensive, as he was now.

"We need to think about this carefully. Having Juan Carlos hunt her down and kill her could possibly do more harm than good."

"Go on." His father raised a brow.

"Sometimes the heavy hand is not the way. Sometimes a more delicate approach may be advantageous."

"Delicate? Like a flower? Would you like to invite the Nighthawk woman to dinner so we could discuss her decision to burn down one of our nightclubs and steal five of our whores?" Juan Carlos Moreno strutted into the immaculate barroom in the west wing of the Fuentes palace in the desert. The room, designed to comfortably seat twenty people, felt empty with only three.

Juan Carlos was the only man Hector allowed to speak to Rafael in such a way. Not that he took advantage and abused that privilege, but the smug look on his face as Juan passed by and greeted Hector sure looked like he enjoyed it when he did. Rafael never offered a response to his father's top enforcer and personal bodyguard. Not out of respect, but out of pure, unadulterated fear.

Juan Carlos Moreno, a vicious man with a short temper, was feared by any who crossed him long before he ever came to work for Rafael's father. His reputation for the ruthlessness with which he dispatched his enemies grew by exponential leaps and bounds once he became head of security for the Fuentes Cartel. Moreno executed his orders with precision and violence, carrying out a variety of unsavory tasks for the family, and to this day, had yet to fail in that regard.

Rafael had borne firsthand witness to Moreno's ruthless delivery of his father's orders. The blood on the thick-necked man's hands could fill buckets. He was, in Rafael's opinion, the scariest man on the planet. Raphael hated any moment spent in Moreno's presence. Seeing Juan's face reminded Rafael of his tenth birthday, a memory he'd spent the years since trying to erase.

The scar rode down along Moreno's face at an odd angle, beginning at the top right side of his head two inches into his hairline, then spreading across his forehead until it stopped abruptly in the center of his left eyebrow. The day he received it etched a scar of equal size and proportion on the young Rafael's mind. He still felt its tingle as he recalled the memory of that horrible day.

On the morning of his tenth birthday, Rafael's father had the family barber come to the house for a grooming of all the Fuentes men, including Hector. Hector believed then, as he did now, certain events dictated perfection. Celebrating one's birth fell into that category, as did funerals. Maybe that's why the sight of Moreno now had triggered his memory. Rafael absently played with a curled tuft of his black hair. His mother's burial was in three days.

When the barber came, Rafael remembered excitedly waiting for a fresh haircut. As a kid, it wasn't the haircut he was excited about, but one of the few times he was guaranteed to spend time with his father. Up until the morning of his tenth birthday, it had been one of his most revered memories. Even the memory of preceding birthday mornings with the family barber were tainted in the darkness of that day.

Unbeknownst to Rafael's father, the barber, Gerardo Guzman, who'd been grooming the family for nearly twenty years, had been extorted by a rival cartel. They took his grandson as leverage. None of that mattered anymore. Anybody who was even remotely involved had been later hunted down and killed. Most at the hand of Moreno himself.

This was the day Raphael Alejandro Fuentes decided he would never grow up to be like his father. It was the wish he never told anyone, even his mother, when he blew out his birthday candles later that day.

Down the hall from the bar where the three men currently convened was the barber shop. His home had a two-chair barbershop built inside. Immaculate as it was, it was nothing compared to his mother's spa nestled against one of their three pools. Some days Rafael swore he could still see the blood stain on the barber shop's tile floor.

His father had been reclined in the soft brown leather of the barber chair with a warm, moist towel draped over his eyes. Rafael used to love the smell of the barber's foam. The fresh clean scent overwhelmed the air. He remembered watching his father in the chair and longing for the day when he could receive his first shave.

Guzman ran the length of the blade against the sharpening strap as he always did. Rafael used to love the thwack and swoosh sounds steel made against worn leather. He pictured the next moment with reverence. The image of Guzman's stoic face and sad eyes as he stood behind Rafael's father's foam-covered, exposed throat while holding the razor-sharp edge against the edge of his neckline. The image had come to symbolize a line of departure in which the course of his life was changed forever.

Moreno spent most of his life around death. Rafael had given much thought to what he'd witnessed that day and came to this conclusion. Moreno's experience enabled him to see in a way that few others could. Only a killer can recognize another by the look in their eyes. Moreno was as lethal as they come and saw a glimmer of himself that day in the sad eyes of the barber. But Guzman lacked the killer instinct. And Moreno could smell it on him.

The cat-like reflexes of Moreno saved Rafael's father that day. The straight blade razor nicked the skin as Guzman attempted the unthinkable. The hesitancy he demonstrated was not seen in Moreno's decision to act. He caught the barber by the elbow before he could work up the nerve to finish running it across the foamy throat of his employer.

The barber had proven desperate enough to continue his fight, as men do when life hangs in the balance, like that of his three-year-old grandson. All the want and will, when faced against a more skilled and determined opponent, means nothing on the field of battle.

Guzman ripped his arm free and made several wild slashes. But, like a horse swatting a fly with its tale, Moreno disarmed the barber with ease, sending the blade clinking to the floor. Rafael remembered the feeling of relief at seeing Moreno save his father. He also remembered how fleeting it was. A breath after the blade hit the tile, Moreno plunged a knife of his own, a long, eight-inch blade, under the barber's chin.

Rafael could see it now, just as he had at ten. The silent pause as the blade pierced Guzman's brain. He was looking into Rafael's eyes. The desperation of the preceding moment was all but gone. Only sadness was left. A teardrop and trickle of blood drag racing down the side of Guzman's cheek had been interrupted by the sudden jerking of Moreno's blade as he ripped it free. Guzman, no longer supported by Moreno's knife, dropped to the floor.

Juan Carlos Moreno never muttered so much as a curse when the blade cut him. As a young boy, Rafael had missed it. But in the lightning speed struggle, Guzman had somehow managed to slice Moreno's face. He merely grabbed a towel from a stack neatly folded on a nearby marble counter and pressed it firmly against his head. Moreno's soulless eyes watched as Guzman's body convulsed violently at his feet.

Hector promoted him to head of security that very moment. Moreno continued to fill that position to this very day. Rafael never looked at either man the same. After his father's recent pressuring of Rafael to follow in his footsteps, it looked as though his birthday wish ten years ago was not going to be a reality.

Rafael knew why Moreno disliked him and it had everything to with his avoidance of violence. Rafael had never even been in a fight. What kid would dare strike the son of Hector Fuentes? But that wasn't the reason. His younger brothers picked their fights. Moreno could smell it on him, just as he did that day in the barber shop. Raphael wasn't a killer.

Moreno only respected men of action. Rafael had never gained that respect. Although knowing his place within the rank and structure of the cartel, Moreno never openly challenged Rafael's suggestions, but there was an air of contention in the way he responded to them.

"Juan Carlos, I'm glad you're here. We've got a bit of a problem. The Nighthawk woman from earlier is turning up the heat. She's becoming more than an annoyance. Rafael and I were just talking about it."

"I'll grab my team and have it taken care of."

"Did you need to speak to her first?" Rafael asked. "Killing her without first knowing everything we can doesn't seem like good business to me."

Moreno grumbled something under his breath that sounded more like a growl. Looking at the scowl twisting the already twisted face of the bodyguard, Rafael reconsidered. Maybe he was growling.

"Father, years back you told me every life should be weighed in accordance with the value that life has to offer. If in that offering, value is found, then it should be explored. I wasn't sure of its meaning when you said it. Still not sure I'm applying it correctly here, but I think what I'm trying to say is, let's find this woman and see what she knows. There may be value in that."

Hector Fuentes nodded his approval. His face brightened. "My son is becoming a man. A thinking man, but a man, nonetheless. Juan Carlos, I would like you to listen to Rafael's thoughts on this matter. It's time he started to learn the family business and the leadership needed to handle situations like these as they arise. For now, we'll consider this an apprenticeship of sorts."

"As you wish," Moreno offered. No growl or hint of disrespect was present in the man's voice.

Hector wrapped an arm around his son's shoulder. "Let this be your first real test of manhood."

Rafael swallowed hard. He felt both men's eyes upon him. Juan Carlos, although shorter by about two inches, seemed taller. His intimidating demeanor added a few inches. Rafael felt like he was a little kid again in the barber shop watching the blood covered man stare down at the dead barber with a knife jammed inside, under his chin until it cracked the top of his skull.

"If you send a team out and dispose of her," Rafael was careful with his words, "we run the risk of bringing more heat down on us. We don't know who she is. She could be with the DEA or FBI. Who knows? Maybe she's with the CIA."

"Or maybe the family of that Rothman girl hired a private investigator? Who cares?" The disgust was inserted back into the tone of Moreno's words.

"Doesn't matter who. That's my point. If anybody knows she's here, we need to know. Because, if she goes missing, then more people come looking. Especially if she's got ties to a federal agency."

Moreno stepped one foot closer, his nostrils flared. "When I make people disappear, nobody knows where to look."

Rafael wasn't sure if the comment was made as a general testament to the man's skills, or a subverted threat directed at Rafael himself. Either way, he didn't like it, nor did he agree with it.

"That's not the point. I'm sure you can make her disappear so that nobody would ever find her, but if somebody knows that she was looking into us and they happen to have other resources like a federal agency, and she disappears off the face of the earth, then we can expect more visitors."

"Then, if you know better, tell me what you think we should do, Rafael," Moreno spat his name as if its taste in his mouth had soured.

"Eddie Munoz is already out there. He's got the authority to make any interaction with the Nighthawk woman to look like part of an investigation. She did just burn down a nightclub. I think it's a good idea if Munoz picks her up."

"And if she's with a federal agency?"

"We dust her off, say it was an accident."

"And let her live?" That part seemed a sticking point for the man who had chosen murder and mayhem as his life's calling.

"Maybe we hold her long enough, official-like, until we can get the Rothman girl sold off."

Moreno was quiet for a moment. It was Hector that spoke next. "Well, Juan Carlos, it sounds like you have your marching orders. Let me know when Munoz has our unwanted nuisance in hand. I'd like to have a conversation with this Ms. Nighthawk before we send her on her way."

Rafael gave a slight bow of his head and then departed the room, leaving his father to finish his brandy, while he went to find the woman responsible for burning down the nightclub.

TWENTY

Angela Rothman sat in a cell no bigger than the one from the previous day. But this one smelled different. Instead of the caustic paint thinner she sniffed for the better part of twelve hours yesterday, she enjoyed the fresh clean scent of citrus, though yesterday's cell was a whole lot quieter. Since arriving at her latest destination, there had been nothing but an incessant banging and clanging of bottles and a mechanical hiss and whir from outside the door. Having never seen the other side, she had no idea what was making the noise.

The zesty scent filtered through a small crack underneath the door and the light that accompanied it was the only light she had since arriving. Between the clatter from the other side of the door and the constant dripping from a broken pipe in the ceiling, Rothman settled into the sound providing her the only source of entertainment while she waited. Not that she wanted entertainment. She wanted saving. She wanted that tall woman, the bad ass who had almost saved her in Arizona, Angela wanted her to come here now, to kick through those doors and rescue her.

She regretted having dismissed Hatch's attempt. Angela wished she could go back in time. When she thought about the fire and her chance of escape, she could not understand why she resisted Hatch's help. She was out of her mind back then.

Thinking back on it, it was more of an outer body experience where she watched her actions, not fully in control of herself when it was happening. She regretted it, nonetheless. That wall of fire separated Angela from the only person within a thousand miles who seemed remotely capable of saving her. Angela knew well enough that it was unlikely the Nighthawk woman or anyone else would ever find her again. She passed the insufferable ticking of time by listening and watching.

Angela took in her surroundings like a sponge took in water. Not that any of it had proved useful so far. But if she survived, she'd get to finally tell her father that the four years of Spanish he made her take finally paid off. She kept quiet that she was able to understand the men who had been escorting her through this hellish nightmare. They spoke more freely than they would have, had they known she could understand them.

Sometimes she wished she didn't understand the things that they said. Most of the time, it was never good. Hope was fleeting, and she held on to her last thread of it with a death grip, hoping that something she heard would serve to benefit her.

She'd been treated like an animal since crossing the border. They fed her, or better yet gave her what could be construed as food. The slop was better than starving, but the last thing that had been on a metal tray slid under the door looked like it had come from a pig's trough. Angela had eaten it, every last bit, and took the time to lick the tray clean. *Gross? Yes.* But she needed to keep herself strong.

They were feeding her to keep her healthy enough to look presentable for sale value. She ate to be strong enough to fight back or escape when the time presented itself. Even in her starved state, the food turned in her stomach and the aftertaste in her belches almost brought it back up.

After every meal, she felt woozy and slept for an unknown amount of time. She was also aware that they drugged the food, so each time she ate, she worried that her chance of escape would have alluded her, but skipping the meal was a luxury she couldn't afford.

She always awoke after the meals with a knot in her stomach, just as she did a few minutes ago. She pushed the tray back under the door, which were Pencil's instructions. *When you finish, the tray must be returned under the door. The door cannot be opened if the tray does not come back out. You will not receive water if the tray is not out of the door.* Pencil's words were served with a side of onion soup, which is what the man's permanent body odor reeked of.

Angela, of course had to test the rule. She kept the tray, hoping to bash it over their heads if she could ever figure out how to undo the ropes from her wrist. The same ropes that forced her to eat off the tray like an animal. In the battle of No Tray No Water, the kidnappers won.

As of yet, nobody had bothered to clean the filth from her skin or offer her a change of clothes. She found a corner in every cell as her makeshift bathroom. If she ever survived, she would never tell anybody about the things she had to do, the smells she had to endure. Angela focused her mind on the scent of citrus, on the smell of freshly peeled oranges wafting underneath the door. She scooted closer, trying to blanket herself in the freshness of it.

Angela nicknamed the two Mexicans guarding her Pencil and Bigfoot. Pencil was a man of epically thin proportions. He was tall but made to look even more so by his lanky build. Every time he smiled, he revealed the discolored gold tooth in the front of his mouth. Upon first seeing it, Angela wondered if the gold was even real. She hated the way his buggy eyes poked out from the bony features of his face. She hated more the way he looked at her with those eyes.

Pencil's stare unsettled Angela. She felt as though she could read the thoughts running through the wiry man's mind, and she didn't like what she found.

His shorter and stouter partner she had named Bigfoot. Not so much for his size and bulk, but more for the thick wooly hair that poked out from his collar and extended down the length of his arm. The effect made him look more beast than man. While his thinner counterpart had a gold tooth, Bigfoot was missing most of his teeth and had a smile that would make a pro hockey player jealous. The scars decorating Bigfoot's face and hands spoke to the violence he'd both delivered and endured.

He was a nasty man. The words he spoke about the things he wanted to do to Angela made her sick with worry. It had been Bigfoot who'd delivered her the water after she tested Pencil's rule. He removed the bottle cap and spit in it before recapping it and giving it to her. He then made her drink it in front of him while he looked on and laughed himself red. Before all of this was over, she hoped to see him dead.

Her heart leapt at the sound of approaching feet. She'd come to recognize their tandem gait. Other people traversed the hallway, but nobody except for the two guards ever stopped or even slowed their pace while passing the door. The other people that moved by seemed to do so with purpose. Pencil and Bigfoot sauntered slowly as if time didn't matter.

What made Rothman's heart skip a beat wasn't the fact that they were coming, it was the hurry in their approach that had her concerned. They were stepping with a purpose. And with men like this, their purposes were never well intended.

Their shadows danced underneath the gap in the door. Rothman turned her ear and quieted her breathing. Her shoulders ached and her wrists were nearly worn to the bone. The cord securing them was a lot less painful than the cuffs they had used on her before, but the tenderness was unbearable. Long confinement in awkward positions didn't agree with her joints and muscles.

Angela heard the tension in the man's voice. Pencil's matched his look. He spoke in a choked squeak. Bigfoot, on the other hand, sounded like the low rumble of a diesel truck, but it was Pencil who spoke first. His panic-babbled Spanish was difficult at first for Angela to pick up, but she honed in on keywords and phrases and was able to make out most of what he said.

"I don't know how she did it," Pencil's voice was frantic. He was unhinged. He always had a nervous edge to him, but something was different, Angela could tell.

"One woman burned down the club and took five of our girls?" Bigfoot's voice rumbled. "I know one thing, if I was there, she'd be in a room with the red head there."

Pencil squeaked a laugh. "Maybe so. Doesn't matter. Not our job."

"I know, I know," Bigfoot said. "The orders just came in. Somebody paid a good price, and we've got to get our package in there cleaned up and ready to go."

Keys rattled against the lock. The shadows of her two captors crept inside as the door opened. Angela Rothman looked up into the light silhouetting their faces, and for the first time since crossing over into Mexico, she had her first glimmer of hope.

TWENTY-ONE

Miguel Ayala pulled up in an older model Nissan Sentra missing three of its four hubcaps. When Hatch placed the call to Ayala, the newspaper man answered immediately and had then given her directions of where to go.

Ayala had told Hatch to go to the San Antonio Nogales Road until it dead ended in a T intersection with Highway 2. He then instructed her to take a right and travel southwest on the two-lane highway for several miles until she came across the Mission of Guadalupe, a Christian mission devoted to caring for the people of the Rancho San Rafael region.

Hatch waited in the parking lot with Letty for over an hour before Ayala arrived. Hatch figured the van she'd stolen had some type of GPS transponder or way of tracking it. Even though she didn't locate one when she pulled to the side of the road after fleeing the nightclub, it didn't mean it didn't have one. Better safe than sorry. Plus, even without a transponder pinging their location, it wouldn't be long until the many eyes of the cartel spotted their blacked-out van.

Hatch was relieved to now be sitting safely inside of the Nissan while Letty slept curled in the backseat. Ayala must have been thinking along the same lines as Hatch because he'd picked a location in the opposite direction, where they headed now. They'd passed the T intersection on the left a few miles ago and proceeded in a north by northwesterly direction on Highway 2. They were a little over an hour into a four-hour drive before they reached Janos, a small town only a few hours east of Juarez. Ayala had a contact there who could help Letty get back to her family.

Hatch also figured it was a good place to regroup away from Nogales so she could figure out her next move and hopefully get word on Angela's location. They'd driven silently since leaving the mission's lot. Miguel realized both Letty and Hatch needed some time to recover both mentally and physically from the ordeal at the nightclub.

With three hours left in the drive, Ayala broke the silence. He leaned closer and in a low whisper said, "I drove by the nightclub on my way to meet you. When you said you were going to burn it down, I didn't know you meant literally."

"Truth be known, neither did I," Hatch gave a soft chuckle.

"Sorry about that information I gave you." Ayala's solemn tone was reflected in the man's face.

"The information you provided is the reason that young girl is sleeping soundly in back rather than tied to a bed. And you were right about the info." Hatch thumbed toward the girl in the back of the Nissan wearing Hatch's old clothes given to the kind-hearted Azul and now handed down to the girl. "She does have red hair—well reddish. And she's just as deserving of being saved as Angela. I just wish I could have gotten all of those girls to come with me, but..." Hatch let the rest go unsaid.

"Sometimes we can't save them all." Ayala guided the Nissan through a rough patch of road.

Ayala brought the shaking vehicle under control. A gold watch with an emerald green face jingled loosely at Ayala's left wrist. He caught Hatch eyeing it and turned it to her, bringing it closer to her face so she could better see it. "It was my father's," he said, happy to shift subjects, as was Hatch. "He was a good man, an honest man. He chose the path of peace and I, one of war. After I hung up my guns, I saw the value in his path and started wearing it as a reminder. Sadly, my father never got to see me change course. I wear it to honor him. It's like having him with me. Silly, I guess."

"Not at all." Hatch thought about her own father and how she honored him by living the code that he had taught her, *help good people and punish those who hurt them.* Easy to remember, harder to follow. Hatch's life's journey had proven that at least that much was true.

"I'm sure your father would be proud," Hatch said, bringing a smile to Ayala's face, "And I, for one, think the girl in the back would agree."

Ayala flicked his eyes to the rearview mirror at the girl on his backseat. "Ernesto and his wife will get her safely home. What you did back there was very brave."

"I couldn't have done it without you," Hatch replied.

"I'm hoping that Ernesto may have more information about the girl you're looking for. Just as the cartel has eyes and ears everywhere, so does Ernesto. And maybe one of them can point us in the right direction."

"Us? Look Miguel, I don't want to get you involved beyond what I already have."

"The minute I picked up that phone and got into this car to come get you, I knew what I was letting myself in for. The *us* part is not up for discussion."

"Alright." An extra set of eyes would've been beneficial at the nightclub.

Ayala picked up speed and they motored off into the dark unlit expanse of highway. "I just hope we're not too late."

TWENTY-TWO

Hatch finished the last morsel of the sweet cake Ayala brought for her and the sleeping Letty. It was made by his wife using a secret recipe, and one Hatch agreed was worth protecting. She washed the moist cakey cornbread down with a bottle of Propel Fitness Water. The blueberry gave the food in her mouth a funny aftertaste.

For a moment Hatch thought Ayala might've been moonlighting as a PR spokesperson for the water distributer. He prattled on about the bottle he'd given her, explaining that this particular bottle of the electrolyte-infused drink was low calorie and not zero calorie like their others. Ayala told her Propel made a zero-calorie drink, but that he drinks the Propel Vitamin Boost, which has ten extra calories from the organic cane sugar and Stevia it's sweetened with.

He had tapped his gut when he said it, laughing about not being the man he used to be. He later divulged his love of the water came from an insatiable sweet tooth. He used to drink lemonade by the pitcher full. His wife turned him onto the fitness water when she got tired of letting out his pants.

Hatch had seen it with some of her friends after leaving the service. They'd put on a few pounds, often proving true the age-old adage, *a good soldier makes a fat civilian.* She'd known more than a few hardened combat vets to add a little weight around the middle after separation. And then watched as they fought like hell to get back what was lost, often never quite getting to where they once were. Hatch had a different philosophy upon exiting the military. If you always maintain your readiness, you never have to get it back.

The last of the fluid hit her belly. Her stomach gurgled, expressing its discontent loud enough for the man who'd just generously provided a meal made at his wife's hand to hear she was still hungry. A low in a battle was always a time to refuel. And she needed more for the battle to come. She'd learned her threshold, after pushing herself under the most challenging of conditions. Through pain, Hatch found her limitations greatly reduced when she had fuel in the tank. Beyond the physical benefits, it helped with mental acuity, something Hatch valued above all else. She eyed the indicator light just illuminating the yellow E next to a gas can icon. Ayala shot her a knowing smile and rubbed the cracked seam of his sun-damaged dashboard.

"Don't worry. She'll get us there. That light usually gets me about thirty miles. Ernesto's is only about twenty miles from here. Eight miles beyond that is a small crop town with a gas station. I can fill it up after we get young Letty settled in."

They drove on for the next twenty miles and the Nissan held up. And as Ayala said, they'd come upon the turn off to Ernesto's home. He turned right off the main road, exchanging it for an unfinished road that led to a small house with a rickety front porch and a tin roof. The exterior walls of the house were a deep burgundy, and in the dark, Hatch couldn't tell if the color was from paint or rust. A railing extended along a short front porch that had several folding chairs scattered around a small table with a chess board in play. A hand-carved mahogany queen had the opposing king in checkmate.

An older man walked out of the front door of the house and stood beside a decorative wooden rocking chair waving happily. A strange sight to see after waking the older man who looked to be in his late seventies or early eighties. Most would be annoyed or at the very least groggy at the intrusion. But not Ernesto Cruz. He seemed as happy to greet this unexpected arrival as if it had been a planned dinner date.

Ayala approached, and the two men embraced in a quick and friendly hug, a gentleman's *bro hug*. Hatch reached into the backseat and laid a gentle hand on the sleeping teen. She felt the tension in the girl's muscles twitch, even before fully bringing the contact into her conscious mind. The girl's experience left her with the residual scars a lifetime of therapy couldn't erase, but at least she was alive.

Letty startled and launched herself up into a seated position while gasping. Hatch gave the teen a moment to adjust to her new and unfamiliar surroundings. Letty settled in and calmed at seeing Hatch's face.

"It's okay. That man over there is going to help you get home, back to your family. Do you understand? He's a good guy. Now let's get you inside and cleaned up." Hatch exited the Nissan and the girl followed. The air, even in the dead of night, was still staggeringly warm, but comparatively cooler than the daytime.

"Daphne, I want to introduce you to an old friend of mine. Ernesto Cruz, meet Daphne Nighthawk."

Hatch, following Ayala's energized introduction, gave a slight bow of her head and extended her hand to the man. Who in turn, disregarded it, pulling her in for a hug. "I'm sorry, Ms. Nighthawk. I'm a hugger."

He delivered his feigned apology in clearly understandable English. The words rolled off his tongue, making Cruz sound like Ricardo Montalban welcoming a guest to Fantasy Island. Hatch awkwardly accepted the man's welcoming. After the quick embrace, Cruz looked to where Letty was shrinking herself behind Hatch.

"This is Letty," Hatch brought the girl under her arm. Letty nuzzled in closer, accepting Hatch's kindness. "But she may not be up for any hugs anytime soon. This tough girl has been through a rough time."

"Of course."

Josefina Cruz stepped into view. Her English was not as good as her husband's, but it was easy enough to understand and Hatch was grateful. "Don't just stand there all night. Get in here and get something in your bellies. You've got to be starving."

Ernesto led them inside to the quaint surroundings. The entire house itself couldn't have been bigger than six hundred square feet, and even that was generous. The living room, and what appeared to be what doubled as an office, connected to a kitchen with a card table. Four chairs matched the table in color and design. A fifth chair, a metal folding chair, like the ones from the front porch, was wedged in. The out-of-place chair had a blue porcelain plate in front of it, as did all the other chairs encircling the table.

The smell of cooking onions alongside chopped potatoes and ham greeted Hatch's nostrils. Josefina went about cracking several eggs into the black cast iron skillet on the other burner. Hatch's stomach was having a conversation with Letty's. The incessant gurgling was starting to sound more like an argument.

"It sounds like we need to get somebody something to eat," Ernesto boomed.

"My friend, you didn't have to go through all this trouble. We're fine. I actually just gave Ms. Nighthawk some of my wife's bread," Ayala offered.

Ernesto cocked an eyebrow at Hatch and paired it with a quirky grin. "Did you try to get the recipe?" Without giving Hatch time to respond, he continued. "Nope? Even if you'd tried, he wouldn't tell. He never does. My wife's been asking for Rosa's cornbread secret for years. I think we'll move on to the next life before he tells. And he never comes around enough for me to get my fill."

Ayala jogged back to his Nissan and returned a moment later holding a brown box stamped with a rose and the words *Rosa's Café* on top.

"I said I wanted the recipe."

"You said, you wanted the recipe because I never come around enough to keep up with demand. Consider this box the first of many personal deliveries. It has been too long." Ayala's chuckle was joined by Cruz and his booming laugh which shook the tin in the roof above.

Cruz opened the box and inhaled deeply. Hatch found herself leaning in for another sniff of the sweet cake bread. Letty just stared into the kitchen at the sizzling food on the stove top. "I'll take this as a temporary concession. And only under one condition." Ernesto said.

"And what's that?" Ayala asked.

"You stop chewing on the end of that cigar."

"Now why would I go and do something like that?" Hatch watched the men in their strange yet familiar banter.

"Because your lips are going to fall off with cancer. I've told you this a thousand times."

"You smoke."

"That's different."

"How so?"

Cruz pawed his chin. "Because it's in and out of my mouth. Doesn't just hang off my lip like a wet dog turd."

"Ernesto Cruz! A child is present," Josefina barked from the kitchen.

"I said turd. Not shit." Cruz winked at Letty. A weak but genuine smile broke the girl's placidity.

Cruz chuckled and offered his closing remarks. "But you breathe it into your lungs."

"True."

Hatch watched the stalemate unfold before her eyes in what proved to be one of the most bizarre debates she'd seen in a while. Each man kind-heartedly at odds with the other.

"It is good to have you in my home again friend. And Josefina and I are overjoyed at the company you've brought." Cruz walked the group further into his quaint home.

"Enough of your talking. Ernesto will have you standing there all day. Now, grab yourself a seat. The food will be ready shortly."

Hatch pulled out the folding chair and sat. Letty took up next to her, staying on her right and keeping herself close enough that the hairs of her arm tickled the scar tissue of Hatch's. The girl was latched to Hatch like a newborn puppy to its mother. The contact didn't last. As soon as huevos rancheros hit her plate, Hatch went to work devouring the meal. She finished her plate quickly and washed it down with freshly brewed coffee made by Josefina. The air still held the hint of the fresh grinds used to make it, although the scent of the recently cooked breakfast overwhelmed it.

With bellies full, the conversation shifted to Letty and her circumstances. Letty ate slowly and quietly. By the time Hatch finished her plate, Letty still had barely eaten four, maybe five bites. Whatever drug they'd been giving her had begun to wear off and she was starting to feel the effects of its withdrawal.

Ayala began, "Ernesto here kind of runs what you call an underground railroad of sorts. He, and many like him, have formed a pact, an alliance, to work together, to use their skills and the resources at their disposal, to help victims ravaged by the cartels.

"Young girls like Letty aren't the only ones forced into servitude. Older men and women are used as mules to bring drugs across the border, oftentimes inside their bodies, hoping that their age and infirmity cause inspectors and border agents to pass a blind eye over them. At least those agents who haven't already been bought and paid for.

"Whole families were often brought in to work their drug labs, often in some type of repayment for ferrying another family member across the border, their lives spent working off a debt they'll never be able to pay off.

"You see, slavery is still alive and well here, although people don't see it. All they see is the drugs and the money and the shootings. We fight against an enemy who is as powerful as it is extensive, but we do not stop.

"And every man, woman and child, like young Letty here, that we can return back to their family gives me hope that someday we can beat back the cartels, and take back Mexico, bring it back to the strong and vibrant country it once was, so that the strengths of its good people outshine the darkness of the few."

"How will you find her parents? She said her family's house was burned down. She was taken from one of the shelters where they displaced her. She doesn't know where her family went from there, and that was three years ago." Hatch asked.

Ernesto did not direct his answer toward Hatch, but instead toward Letty. "My dear, we are very capable of finding people. I don't want to bore you with what I did in my previous life, but don't let these frail old man's hands fool you. I used to be able to run with the best of them." Ernesto gave a playful wink. Hatch only guessed at the man's inference, maybe a reference to some type of military or paramilitary organization. Not relevant. What was, was his ability to get Letty home. "I can find anybody, given enough time. Speaking of time, I know you all have been on the go for a quite a while now. How about you get cleaned up and off to bed for a bit?" Ernesto said to Letty.

"If you go down that short hallway there, one door will lead you to a bathroom with a small shower. I've set out a stack of towels and a change of clothes. We keep a stockpile of clothes. You should find something that fits." Josefina eyed the clothes hanging off the younger, smaller girl's body, and then looked over at Hatch. "There should be something for you as well, if you need."

Hatch took stock of her Club de Fuego shirt and matching cargo pants, the benefit of its wearer's unwilling donation. "Thank you for the offer, but I'm fine."

She felt the girl beside her tense up. Hatch leaned closer and said in a voice only Letty could her. "If it would make you feel safer, I can stand outside the door while you shower and change. Is that something you want?"

"You don't have to stand outside. I'll be fine." Her voice was even lower than Hatch's, a whisper of a whisper. "Thank you--for everything."

Letty pushed her seat back and stood. Just before making the short trip to the bathroom she turned back toward Hatch. "I know where she is."

Silverware stopped banging against the blue porcelain plates where the last scraps of food were being scooped into awaiting mouths, which hung open as the girl's softly spoken words grabbed the attention of everybody at the table. "I heard you talking before I fell asleep. I listened to what you said about a redheaded girl. You thought I was her. You came for her, but you got me instead."

Hatch said, taking the girl's hand in hers, "you're right. I was looking for someone else when I found you. And I'm glad that I did find you. But you know where Angela Rothman is?"

"The other day, she was with me and a bunch of other girls. We all got shipped off in different directions, but when they took her away, I heard them say where they were sending her."

"Where?" Hatch edged forward in her seat.

"They said they were taking her to The Last Stop."

"Is that a place? Like a restaurant?" Hatch surveyed the rest of the group's faces and saw no sign of recognition.

"It's not a restaurant. It's a juice factory. These people move us around all over the place. Some of them get nicknames. The Last Stop is what we call the Solarus Orange Juice factory."

"You mean my favorite juice, the one with the wacky orange walrus as the mascot? Really? The cartel takes everything I love. My wife never lets me have it often because it's got too much sugar. Now it'll never touch my lips again." Ayala looked as though he was going to burst at the seams.

"The two taking her away were talking about it. They didn't know I heard, but I did."

"Just like in the car," Hatch whispered. Letty smiled. "But I still don't understand. They move girls out of the juice factory?"

"You could say that. I've never been there myself. If I had, I wouldn't be here with you now. They call it The Last Stop for a reason. It's the last place they put us before we are sold to an outsider. Girls who go there are never seen again."

"What do you mean?" Hatch said. "Will they kill them?"

"It's less than two hours from here." Ayala popped his head up from his phone with a determined look on his face. He turned the phone to show them. Sure enough, just off Highway 2, south of Juarez by about thirty miles, was the Solarus Juice Company. A digital pushpin pointed to the location. "There's only two factory plants in the country and the other one is three hundred miles south. I'm guessing a Juarez cartel would want to use a Juarez juice factory."

"Then we better get a move on," Hatch took Letty's hands in hers. "These good people are going to take care of you now. Trust them and do what they say, and you'll be home before you know it."

A tear cleared a path down the girl's dirty face as she locked her arms around Hatch's neck and hugged tightly. Hatch held Letty until she released her grip. It felt good. Although much older, holding the small girl's frame in hers reminded Hatch of her niece, Daphne.

"Thank you," Letty whispered before she walked to the bathroom.

Hatch watched the waif of a girl slip inside the bathroom and close the door before turning her attention back to her hosts. "I can't thank you two enough for your hospitality." Hatch took her empty plate over to Josefina, who'd already finished rinsing the two heavy cast iron pans and was toweling off one of them. "And for the amazing food."

"I hate to eat and run, old friend," Ayala said. "But it looks as though Daphne and I have somewhere to be."

"Just make sure you don't take so long in between your next visit. We miss seeing your face."

"I think you miss my wife's cornbread."

The two old friends embraced in a goodbye hug. Hatch, more prepared this time, accepted hers as Cruz pulled her in, and after getting to know the man, accepted it far less awkwardly than she had when first arriving.

Josefina had packed a couple water bottles and some fruit into a paper sack and handed it to them. As they said their final goodbyes and turned toward the door, headlights penetrated through the curtains. The light was accompanied by the crunching of tires over the unfinished roadway leading to the front of Ernesto's house was followed by the sound of brakes.

"Ms. Nighthawk, you're too pretty a lady to be out here causing this kind of trouble." The voice of Nogales Police Lieutenant Eduardo Munoz broke the silence of the heavy night air.

TWENTY-THREE

Hatch had peered through a slit in the curtains and saw that the light coming through was generated by two vehicles. Both of the older model Crown Victoria Interceptors fanned out in front of the Cruz residence bore the emblem of the Nogales Municipal Police.

"Is there a safe space we could shelter, aside from the bedroom and bathroom in the back?" Hatch looked across the table at Ernesto.

Letty changed into the better-fitting clothing that Josefina had provided, bypassing the shower, and was now standing in the hallway. Josefina ushered the girl to their version of a safe room, a trapdoor in the floor of the hallway covered by a musty throw rug. Wood stairs led down to a poured concrete basement with canned goods lining the walls. It was a food pantry, but in a pinch, it would have to do.

"I'll let you know when it's safe to come out." Hatch offered a hand to Ernesto who began his descent into the cooler space below.

"You're not getting in?" Ernesto asked. Josefina and Letty were nestling themselves into the far corner. Josefina offering a motherly embrace to the terrified teen.

"Somebody's got to put the rug back over." Hatch winked.

"I can do it," Ayala stopped with one foot in the steps going down into the cellar.

"And then what?" Hatch said. "Wait for them to enter? So they can torture you until they get what they want?"

"What's your plan, then?"

"One that doesn't involve any of the things I just said."

"That wasn't an answer." Ayala, the wordsmith, countered.

"I can tell you this, you're a lot more valuable to me down there. You're going to be the last line of defense."

Ayala accepted his new role and descended the wobbly steps to the uneven basement floor below.

"Any other way out? Windows, doors, anything besides what I can see?" Hatch called down.

Cruz rubbed the scruff at the bottom of his chin. "If you're talking about them getting in, then the front door is the only way. If you're talking about getting out, then that bathroom window might work. It's going to be tight, but I think you'll fit. But I beg of you to stay with us, down here, where it's safe."

"Nothing's safe unless I can stop those men outside from entering." Hatch lifted the hinged door in the floor and prepared to close it.

"Be careful when you get out the window. My bicycle is beneath. It's a broken heap that I've been meaning to fix. Just be careful to avoid it. Otherwise, you're likely to make a lot of noise."

No further protest was made. Hatch closed the door to the cellar and covered it with the rug, ensuring that the dirt line on the floor matched the carpet. If she was compromised, she wanted to give them the best chance of survival.

Hatch moved quickly using the toilet seat to access the small window and Ernesto was right. It was a very tight fit. So tight in fact that she had to take both pistols out of the small of her back and then Superman her way out of the window holding both guns in front of her.

She wriggled herself forward to her midline using her back and core muscles to hold herself as erect as possible before lowering herself.

Hatch folded down, bringing the guns in her hands closer to the ground so she could drop them while minimizing the noise.

After momentarily freeing herself of the weapons, Hatch pressed the palms of her hands against the burgundy wall, which upon touching it, she realized it was paint the color of rust and not rust itself. A second later, Hatch propelled herself out of the window like she'd been fired by a cannon, sailing over the broken bike. She turned her shoulder in before hitting the hard dirt, using the momentum from her launch to tuck into a roll just as she passed over the handlebars. Hatch righted herself and immediately grabbed both guns, scanning her surroundings for any potential threat. Finding none, she moved to the left and found cover by a tree.

In the dark gap between the crossing headlights of the two police vehicles stood the barely visible Lieutenant Eddie Munoz. Even now, he struck the same cocky pose, his muscular arms folded neatly across his chiseled chest. He continued to bark at the front door of Ernesto's house.

"You've gotten yourself into a whole mess of trouble with people that don't like trouble. I'm here to sort all of that out."

Hatch saw what he meant by "sort out". She counted a total of four men, all outside of their vehicles. The driver of the vehicle closest to her was a fat man who she had never seen before, but he wore the uniform of the Nogales Police. Munoz was next, standing to the right of an opened passenger door shielding his torso and lower extremities. The driver of the far vehicle stood a few feet away from Munoz, leaving his door open. The two doors, Munoz' and the other driver's, nearly touched ends. The fourth man was barely visible except for his hand reaching out into the light. In it, he held a pistol. They all did. All the policemen had their weapons drawn and pointed at the front door of Ernesto and Josefina Cruz's house, except for Munoz. He remained still with his arms folded.

"You've taken something that belongs to us," Munoz continued as if he was on the podium pontificating a speech to the masses. "Did you not think we'd find out? First, you burned down one of Mr. Fuentes' favorite nightclubs and then you relieved him of his property."

Hatch understood why men like Munoz used words like property or package. Men like Munoz didn't see girls like Letty or Angela as human beings. These girls in their possession were commodities to be traded and sold, to be discarded when used up. Nothing more. From the looks of the way Letty was being treated or about to be treated in that room at Club Fire, she appeared to be heading toward the discard pile.

What bothered Hatch was how quickly Munoz and his goons had been able to track them down. Munoz did not seem like the brightest in the bunch when she'd encountered him in the police department lobby. Yet, here he was, standing outside with a smug look.

"Mr. Fuentes keeps tabs on all his property."

There was the word again. The gears shifted in Hatch's mind and now she had a better inkling as to why or possibly why. Maybe they had tracked the transponder to the mission where they dumped the van and picked their trail up from there, but it seemed doubtful. She'd kept watch the entire way and saw no tail. But he'd managed to show up, in spite of all that.

"The kindness of my offer will only last a very short period of time. The clock has started. I'm going to give you a minute to think about it. At the end of which, I will help you along with your decision.

"There's two ways this can go. In the end, it doesn't matter to me or my men which you choose. The result will be the same. You're coming with me, and the property taken from Mr. Fuentes will be returned to its rightful owner. When those two things happen, I will determine how I handle the three others who chose to help you. But hey, I'm a reasonable guy. And I'm sure I can work something out."

The fat cop to his left laughed. Munoz leaned over and said something in Spanish that even if she could hear, based on the speed at which Munoz spoke, it was doubtful she would have been able to comprehend. But the message was clear.

The heavyset police officer moved off into the darkness, stepping wide, careful to avoid the cone of light flooding the front porch. He began making his way around toward the back.

Hatch pulled her weapon tight to her chest and readied herself for the man who stalked toward the tree she pressed against.

TWENTY-FOUR

The large Cypress painted her in its dark shadow, further masking Hatch's approach under the cloud covered moon above. The man positioned on the back corner of Ernesto's house had radioed to Munoz, letting him know there was no back door access. She heard Munoz's response and understood enough of it to know he told the fat policeman to hold the corner and wait.

He took an interest in the window she'd just escaped from and walked to it. Standing beside the bike she'd soared over, he looked up and lowered, but did not holster, the semi-automatic pistol in his right hand. He was shorter than the bottom lip of the windowsill by a few inches. He forced the balls of his feet to endure the brunt his weight as he pushed himself up on his tiptoes.

The large man wobbled on his stilted toes as he peered in the window. He holstered his weapon to pull out the radio positioned behind it on his patrol belt. The heavyset cop didn't have a lapel microphone attached and had to unclip his radio each time he needed to use it, which this time, he didn't get to do.

While the officer was engaged in a tug of war over his radio with impressive girth spilled out atop of it, Hatch struck the butt end of her pistol against the base of his skull. He fell to ground knocking over the bike she'd narrowly avoided. It clattered loudly in the silent countdown Munoz had given.

Hatch quickly used the man's two pair of cuffs to bind each wrist to his opposite ankle, the crisscrossed shackles rattled as the unconscious man now lay hogtied where he fell. She stuffed his wallet in his mouth and unholstered his pistol and tossed it in the bathroom window. Hatch hoped, should she not make it, the gun would provide Ayala and the others another option before submitting to the hitmen. Hatch hoped they never had to find it.

The gun landed softly on the towels Josefina had set out for Letty. Hatch rounded the other side of the small house, staying out of the light emanating from the patrol cars parked in front. She used the trees as cover while she snaked her way through the darkness, leading up to the other men holding the good people inside hostage.

When she heard Munoz speak again, she realized he hadn't heard the crash of the bicycle, or at least made no mention of it when he spoke next.

"You have offended the courtesy of my offer by not accepting it." He sounded genuinely disappointed. Maybe this tactic had worked in times' past. But to lay one's self at the feet of their killer is what sheep do. And she was no sheep. Rachel Hatch was a wolf. And wolves don't lay in wait. They hunt.

"Sadly, Miss Nighthawk, we must do it the hard way. I take no comfort in saying this, but you have chosen a painful death, one that will go on hours longer than it should, and one that you could have avoided for the innocent people inside." Munoz signaled silently with his hands, directing the two remaining men to enter the front door.

The man closest to her, the one Hatch had intended on taking as her own hostage, rounded the front of the vehicle he'd been standing beside. He walked through the headlights and met up with the other officer. The two formed side by side and moved in step toward the front door.

Hatch changed plans on the fly when she saw Munoz was intently focused on his two henchmen going forward at his command to do *his* dirty work. The intersecting paths of headlights was a tactical move used in felony stops conducted by law enforcement officers. The cones of light from the use of high-beams, spotlights, and takedown lights work to blind those on the other end. That part was apparent. The *why* was less apparent. And Hatch, having spent fifteen years in her capacity as an MP, knew the answer. In that answer came her next move.

The overlapping light between the two vehicles in a felony takedown serve a very important purpose. It created a black hole. Officers used the void to place cuffs on suspects. It is done in that dark space for one important reason. Nobody on the other side of the light can see what happens. It keeps the bad guys from knowing what's happening. For most, seeing their thug friends disappear is scary as hell. Or so she'd heard from the numerous criminals she'd done it to. And though the man only a few feet in front of her wore the uniform of her brothers and sisters in blue, he did not honor it. He was a criminal. And the criminal was standing directly in the black hole.

Before he had a chance to even unfold his arms, she had kicked hard at the back of his legs, buckling the man. Hatch caught him mid-fall and just before he struck the ground, she spun him to the side to keep him off-balance while she threaded her arm under his right armpit.

A fraction of a second passed before Hatch had Munoz locked against her body. His right shoulder pressed firmly against his neck was countered by Hatch's forearm squeezing the other side. She locked the choke hold in place using just her right arm, the palm of which was pressed flat against the right of her own neck.

This maneuver did many things at once. By controlling Munoz' right arm, he was unable to access his gun. Leaning him back against her body kept him off-balance enough that she could maintain effective control while enabling her to keep him in front of her as a human shield with her Glock pressed against his left temple.

"Tell your men to come out and drop their weapons. Do it now."

The stink of his cologne tickled her nose as she whispered into Munoz's ear.

"I would, but they won't listen."

"You're their Lieutenant, of course they'll listen. Now tell them to stand down."

"They'll kill me just to get to you. Nobody fails Mr. Fuentes." The macho bravado she'd seen in him before at the police department lobby was all but gone. Strangely, it wasn't fear replacing it now. It was peace. Munoz surrendered to the acceptance of his death with an almost enviable serenity. The road he'd taken in life to bring himself to this point had finally reached its ultimate and expected trade-off, as deals made with the devil typically do. Maybe when Munoz signed his soul away, he had also resigned himself to this outcome long ago.

The two officers Munoz had sent inside now stood on the front porch with the door opened behind them, their guns pointed out into the light, blinded by their devices, and momentarily frozen by the invisible adversary who hid behind their lieutenant holding him hostage. "Nobody inside boss," one of them said.

"'Take the shot," Munoz yelled in Spanish.

The two men, suddenly aware of the shift in power, widened their stance and took aim but did not fire. Not yet at least.

"Kill her," he hissed. The words never getting past his lips as Hatch constricted.

The men on the porch had yet to move. Instead, they peered out into the light and shifted their weapons in several different directions. They didn't know where she was.

Hatch made herself as small as possible behind Munoz who was of similar height and size. She prepared for the eventuality that once the rounds started firing, she would move Munoz forward and try to flank around to one of the vehicles. It wasn't a perfect plan. Lots of variables. Lots of places for Murphy's Law to insert itself.

Coiled. Ready. Hatch breathed in the muggy air tainted with the cologne of her hostage.

The first bang came, followed immediately by another. And neither came from a gun.

Both armed men were now face-down on Ernesto's yellow porch. Standing behind them, or more appropriately above them, Hatch saw Miguel Ayala and Ernesto Cruz holding up heavy cast iron pans like baseball players, celebrating an over-the-fence home run. The two men broke into a bit of a jig.

Munoz cursed at the sight of his two men being handcuffed together by the two older gentlemen.

Munoz, realizing his fate was back in Hatch's hands, made a last-ditch effort to break free by bucking hard.

Hatch felt his movement in his muscles before he made it. She began her counter before he attempted his attack. With the forward threat neutralized, Hatch stowed her gun and used her left arm to lock in the back of Munoz' neck. The interruption of the blood and oxygen to the brain caused the corrupt lieutenant to drop to the ground.

When consciousness returned, Munoz was cuffed to the open door of the police cruiser he'd arrived in.

"You might as well kill me." He spat blood into the dirt.

Hatch felt the cold steel of the Glock against her back and seriously considered taking the dirty cop up on his offer.

"They'll never stop. You know that," he continued through ragged breaths. "After I'm gone more will come."

"How did you find us?" She had other ways of extracting the information, but time was of the essence.

"I told you, Mr. Fuentes tracks his packages." He smiled. It was the same smile he'd given her when he first saw her walk in through the doors of the Nogales Police Department. The glaring difference this go round, his bright white teeth were now painted with his blood.

"The girls, like the one in that house and everything else the Fuentes family claims as their own, are monitored. It didn't matter that you ditched the van at that mission parking lot, though it would have been a lot easier had you not. It would have saved us a lot of time. We were tracking the van, not the package. Once we realized what'd you done, we activated a different tracker."

"Where is it?"

Munoz shrugged. "I don't know. Some doctor puts them in."

"Then a doctor will take them out," Ernesto said walking up on the man with his frying pan weapon still at the ready. The seventy-seven-year-old looked ready for another round.

"What are you going to do with me now?"

"Don't worry. If what you said is true, and Mr. Fuentes tracks his packages, then I'm sure someone will be along to find you soon enough." Hatch walked away, back towards Ernesto's house.

"You're already a dead woman! Do you hear me? A DEAD WOMAN!" Munoz called out.

The black hole swallowed Munoz as Hatch walked into the light. She thought about the words. There was more truth to that statement than he'd ever know.

TWENTY-FIVE

They filled up Ayala's yellow Nissan, just as it started to sputter its final protest. Hatch gave an uneasy smile, still unnerved from the gun battle they'd narrowly avoided at the hand of the pan-wielding hero in the driver's seat. A man who, by his own admission, was accustomed to covering the violence of the world but unaccustomed to experiencing it firsthand.

"See, I told you we'd make it." His voice still quivering as the adrenaline dump he'd received during his moment of triumph had begun to recede within his system. Homeostasis would be reached again, but only after he'd crashed. The trick in combat was to keep the crash from happening before the battle was fully won. And they were still far from done. After filling up, they set off toward the Solarus Juice plant.

Ernesto and his wife Josephina had loaded their small Jeep with supplies, as much as they could comfortably fit and still leave enough room for Letty. The trio headed off in the opposite direction of Hatch and Ayala. It hadn't taken Ernesto long to find a doctor in his inner circle willing and able to find and remove whatever tracking device was implanted in Letty. And hopefully keep the cartel's henchmen at bay.

It was as good a plan as they could muster in the time they had to create it. With Letty's information, Hatch knew this next stop might be their last chance to recover the abducted teen.

With two hours to go until they reached their destination, Hatch realized she'd lit a fuse when she started the fire that burned down the aptly named club. And once lit, she feared it wouldn't end until the cartel had their pound of flesh. She felt the bright sparkle tail of the fuse chasing her now, and as she looked in the rearview mirror for headlights, Hatch half expected to see glowing embers chasing close behind them.

"You look worried," Ayala said.

"I am. This might be my last chance to save her."

"*Our* last chance," Ayala corrected with a smile.

"You know that I couldn't have gotten this far without you."

"If this is going to be one of those 'I can go it alone' speeches, you can just save it. I'm in this until the end. Whatever that means. And trust me when I say this, I understand what's at stake when I say this to you." His face warmed. "Daphne, you can get it out of your head that you're doing me a favor by leaving me behind. Because you're not. This is my home. I may not be as tough or skilled as you, but I am damn well not going to sit down and let the cartel, or anybody else for that matter, sell a little girl into slavery if I can help it. And without question, this is something I am willing to give my life for, just as readily as you."

"Partners it is."

"I just wish I'd brought Josefina's pan with me."

"You were really brave back there. The way you and Ernesto took out those two guys was nothing short of amazing. It's going down in my book as one of the coolest endings to a hostage standoff that I've witnessed in a long time. Plus, you saved my life."

"Seemed like you had things well in hand. Ernesto and I just sped it along. I'm just glad it didn't end in a shootout. I think even those men we hit with the frying pan would agree with that one."

"Not when the cartel learns of their failure. All we really did was prolong the inevitable. I'm just holding out hope that we can put a little bit of time between us and whoever else they send."

Her last statement ended their conversation as both occupants of the little yellow Nissan hummed along the darkened roadway.

"You know, you never really answered my question back there." Hatch broke the silence with a change in topic.

"Which one?"

"At your cafe, when I asked you why you did this, why you help people and put yourself out there with so much at risk."

"I did answer you."

"You told me that wonderful story your father told you about the seed and the boulder. That's true. But you never really answered."

"This is true. Let me see if I can remedy that for you as best I can. Maybe you could rephrase your question?"

"What specific moment in your life put you on the path you're on now, one where you're willing to risk everything, including your life, to save people you don't know?"

He smiled broadly before answering. "You say I don't know these people, but I do. Just as you do. As my father said, at our most basic essence, we are all human. We are all the same. And therefore, I feel a sense of connection with everyone. I may not always understand the reasons for why they do what they do, but I have to believe, at the very core of human nature is goodness. With that said, when people ignore the goodness in their heart and do harm to other people, I agree there needs to be people like you in the world too. Your purpose comes from a place few can understand. But I'd try, if you're willing to tell me."

Hatch thought about the defining moments in her life that had led her here. And the point and purpose it had given her life. In a lifetime of defining moments, one stood out above the rest, one responsible for permanently redirecting the trajectory of her life. The devastating nature of her father's death at the young age of twelve had forever changed the course. All things led back to that morning in the mountains when the gunshot stole her father from a young Hatch.

"My father was shot and killed." Hatch left out the details because those details got people killed. It was the reason she left Hawk's Landing. And indirectly why she was here, with the pan-wielding-peacock man.

Hatch refused to burden Ayala, or in any way connect him to her past. The results could be life altering. Hatch was still looking over her shoulder for the people who might never come or might already be on their way. It was a torturous way to live. But she had no choice in the matter, and much like Munoz had resigned himself to his fate, Hatch had done similar with hers.

"'That must have been terrible. And that's what drove you to, as you say, 'help good people and punish those who do them harm.'"

Hatch nodded. "So now you know my story. What about yours?" Ayala adjusted himself in his seat and looked at the speedometer as if doing a time distance equation to gauge if he had enough time to tell the story. He cleared his throat and began. "Five years ago, I was embedded doing a journalistic piece on a Mexican special forces unit like your Navy SEALS. Unlike your military, who only operates abroad, ours takes direct action within our country. And with the cartels running amuck, our military are fighting a daily battle waged on the city streets and country hillsides of my beautiful Mexico. I followed them on raids and was writing a piece documenting all the efforts on the war being waged against the cartels."

"I accompanied them on one raid on a particular morning. They said it shouldn't be too dangerous, and that I could come along if I wanted an opportunity to be with the team when they entered. In the back of the group, of course. Not that I'd want to be anywhere else, even if they offered. The back was plenty fine for me.

"Getting a firsthand account of how they operate was a rare and unique opportunity. And I seized it, if not a bit reluctantly. The target of the investigation was a low-level drug dealer in the Fuentes cartel's distribution chain, just above your common street pusher. He had no record of violence, which for a drug dealer in Mexico wasn't common, which is the main reason I was authorized to attend the raid. He was deemed a minimal risk operation. The unit commander was interested in getting the story of his specialized unit told. He felt it would assist his psychological campaign, helping him strike fear into the enemy. The commander was an enthusiastic man and one whose passion and pride for his unit was unequaled. It became a perfect storm of sorts. And though I didn't know it at the time, I was in the eye of a hurricane. And one I fear still has me spinning.

"I was partnered with a strong young operator by the name of Arturo Sanchez. They assigned him to be my shadow to protect me throughout the execution of the raid. He was not very happy with his assignment, to say the least.

"Sanchez was one of their top men. But the unit commander wanted their best with me to ensure my safety."

"Makes sense."

"Sanchez and I were in the back of an eleven-man line of heavily armed men. They used flash bangs and other devices to break into the house and surprise its occupants. Arturo Sanchez and I were the last to enter.

"Upon completion of the initial sweep of the house, they had located and detained the wife of the drug dealer along with her young daughter, who was roughly the age you were when you experienced your traumatic event. The little girl was sobbing uncontrollably.

"But what I remember most about her were the drawings. The walls of her room that she shared with her parents were covered in the little girl's artwork. Each picture was of a single flower. Her artistic ability was not that of a girl her age or even one twice it. She glowed."

"Glowed?"

"Sometimes I forget myself. My father's words slip out of me sometimes. *Glowed* was a term he used to describe a person whose inner beauty shone so brightly it cast an aura around them. My father claimed to be able to see. And until that day, I thought it was just one of the oddities I'd come to expect from him. But on that day, I saw it. I felt it. If nothing else, I understood what my father's word meant.

"Was that little girl adorable? Sure, but what child isn't. Was her artwork amazing? Absolutely. Maybe it was the fact she was standing there amongst those soldiers in all their gear, with their rifles and armor, while the girl wore nothing but a long nightshirt that went past her knees. Maybe in contrast to all the darkness around her she became the light.

"I know what you're thinking. *Did she really glow?* I'll say to you what I've said to the countless others with whom I've shared this story over the years. Her name was Maria and she glowed brighter than any to come before or after."

"What happened to Maria?"

"Upon the initial sweep of the house, it appeared as though the husband wasn't home. As the team was assembling to do a secondary, more detailed search, the drug dealer emerged from a trap door in the floor, not unlike the one at Ernesto's house. He fired his gun wildly as he came up.

"I remember the sound of it passing by my ears. That strange zip and pop is something I had never heard before, and to be quite honest, something I never hope to hear again. Arturo Sanchez, standing next to me, fired three rounds, killing the man instantly.

"The wife, upon seeing her dead husband, left her daughter's side and launched herself from the couch. To say she was enraged doesn't do justice the viciousness with which she attacked. Make no mistake about it, she was intent on killing the men responsible.

"Sanchez was already moving to intercept the attack. He told me afterward, years later when we reconnected, that he intended to shove her back to the couch. That was before she grabbed the pistol from her dead husband's hand."

"In a tragic chain of events, Sanchez discharged his weapon, only firing one round. It killed her instantly. The mother and widow collapsed on top of her dead husband. The sounds of her death still haunt me. The sight of their young daughter Maria painted in both her parents' blood.

"In the shock and aftermath that followed, the blood covered Maria disappeared from the soldiers tasked with keeping an eye on her. And I've been looking for her ever since."

"Any luck?"

"Sadly, no. I do see her in the faces of the girls I help, like Letty. Hoping one day I will learn that little Maria is alive and well, and that her beautiful flowers continue to cover the walls of wherever she is now. Most of all, I pray with all my heart that she glows."

"Think of all the good you're doing in the process."

"Take heed of your own words, Daphne. Young Letty has a new chance at life thanks to you." He looked down at the fluttering arm of the speedometer as if willing the car to go faster. "Now let's see if we can do the same for Angela Rothman."

With only a few hours of darkness ahead of them, Hatch hoped that at the new day's end, Angela would be safe, and Hatch's promise to the young girl would have been kept.

A sign rose in the distance. The twenty-foot, bright orange of the Solarus Juice Company's walrus painted on the sign above the factory beckoned them forward.

TWENTY-SIX

Miguel pulled the Nissan to a stop in a lot across from a high chain-link fence. Topped with spiraled razor wire, it stretched around the 8,000-square-foot warehouse. On top of the building sat the twenty-foot lighted billboard depicting the orange sunglass-wearing walrus, holding a cup of orange juice and wearing a satisfied smile.

The lights and activity around the warehouse stood out around its dark surroundings. From an outsider's perspective, it looked to be nothing out of the ordinary. Most of the employees wore powder blue coveralls and hard plastic helmets painted white.

"What's the plan?" Ayala ducked down in his seat, shutting the car and headlights off.

Hatch took a similar position and cranked her seat back, enabling her a clear line of sight with minimal exposure. She looked over the cracked desert of sun-bleached leather in Ayala's old Sentra. She scanned their surroundings, waiting for an opportunity to arise, and a plan to form.

Workers moved about the concrete campus surrounding the building. Hatch watched the men come and go using a pedestrian gate alongside the main truck entrance. It was located fifty feet in front of where they were parked. A dirt path had been worn through the weed-laden patches of grass, leading from the parking lot where they sat to the gate. A gray rectangular keycard fob access panel was attached to a cylindrical metal pole. No physical security was present at the pedestrian entrance. There was a gate guard positioned in a guard shack on the other side of the truck entrance, but he was not inspecting employees who entered the facility, just the trucks passing through. Hatch watched several employees come and go from it, using their badges, all of which were attached to lanyards on the lapel of their pockets.

The way Hatch saw it, two major problems stood in her way of infiltrating Solarus. First off, every employee she'd seen pass within view, in the time they'd been parked, was male. And secondly, they were all Hispanic. She absently ran her hand over the pale skin leading up from her right wrist, feeling the raised roadmap of scars leading to her shoulder, and looked over at Ayala, her big-hearted justice-seeking sidekick doing his best impression of every cop from any '80s television cop stakeout.

He gnawed nervously on the end of his cigar when he caught Hatch looking at him. "What are you thinking?"

"I'm thinking, I don't think I can get in there, not without raising a thousand alarms and bringing more heat down on us than we can bear."

Miguel let out a sigh. "What do we do now then?"

"I said, I didn't think *I* could go in there."

Ayala swallowed hard and looked a shade lighter than he did a moment before. "I don't think I'm capable of that."

"People are capable of a lot more than they give themselves credit for. You told me about the story with the rock and the troll. Be the brave boy that splits it in half and walks your people to the other side."

And with that, Ayala's color returned, as well as a competent, but nervous smile. "Just tell me what to do and I'll do it."

"First thing we need to do is get you a change of clothes. Covering that awful Hawaiian shirt might be the second-best thing I do today."

"Second best?"

"Because today, we're going to bring Angela home."

"Optimism shines light on the prepared."

"Another one of your dad's grains of wisdom?"

"Nope. That one's all mine."

"I like it." Hatch opened the door to the Nissan and slipped into the darkness.

An older white model Toyota pickup pulled into the lot and parked a few spaces from the Nissan. She made her way toward it, staying in a low crouch and moving along the back end of the vehicles until she came to the space between the driver's side door of the pickup and the narrow avenue of space created by the Subaru it was parked next to. The employee never saw her approach because he was bent inside the cab of his truck and looking for something, cursing under his breath in Spanish.

Hatch struck him hard with her left forearm, the bone driving into the side of the man's neck. The brachial stun rendered him unconscious without serious damage.

She stripped him of his clothes, hog-tying his hands and feet together with some rope she'd found in the bed of his truck. She stuffed one of his socks in his mouth to keep him from screaming and slid him across the bench seat of the Toyota before locking him inside.

A moment later, she was back inside the Nissan.

A glisten of sweat formed on her brow. She held out her offerings to Ayala who took them with a surprised look.

"I think they should fit. I'll give you a moment to get ready." Hatch stepped back out of the Nissan and ducked low, posting up alongside the front wheel of Ayala's weather-beaten Sentra.

She looked at the factory. She thought about Letty and the nickname given to the walrus-endorsed juice company involved in the trafficking of girls. *The Last Stop.*

Ayala sat in the driver's seat wearing the subdued powder blue of the Solarus factory worker. He nervously grinded his teeth across the chewed end of his cigar, the only visible remaining trace of his loud ensemble.

Hatch's best chance of slipping in undetected now rested in the hands of an untrained civilian reporter with an unhealthy attachment to Hawaiian shirts.

TWENTY-SEVEN

Ayala stood on the outer edge of the trail leading from the parking lot to the pedestrian access gate, and beyond that, the Solarus Juice Company. Even though the cool night still prevailed over the coming day's sun, Ayala was already sweating profusely. He tried to sound macho back there in the car when he agreed to do it. The Nighthawk woman had proven her bravery and now it was his turn, but as soon as he'd moved off in the dark, he unburdened himself the fear he'd been holding back in one long body tremble.

Gaining his composure with a long deep inhale and equally long exhale, he set his eyes on the gate and the task ahead. The man pictured on the ID card clipped to his left pocket bore a striking resemblance to Ayala. The excitement he'd experienced at first noticing the resemblance was dashed the moment he stepped from the car.

In his other breast pocket, his cell phone's circular eye of the camera was just barely visible above the top off the pocket. The Bluetooth device nestled in his right ear came to life with the sound of Hatch's voice.

"Tip your head down and to the right. There's plenty of cameras, but the one closest and angled to get the best possible shot of your face is located on the back corner of that storage shed, just beyond the gate."

"How did you see that?" Ayala whispered.

"I ate my carrots as a kid. Now, no more talking. We went over this."

"Thanks for reminding me." Ayala tried to laugh but his nerve-wracked body released it like a hyena's cackle.

Ayala remembered he'd been given strict instructions from Hatch.

This is a one-way radio system.

I am the only one who speaks.

The moment I say move you move.

Hesitation will kill you.

Do not die.

Do not get captured.

In the event you are compromised, I will come for you.

He remembered the intensity in her eyes as she spoke to him. She'd managed to tune out the entire world around her. Hatch's face had been eerily calm, almost serene, as if the impending threat of death held no burden. In that moment, Ayala remembered the cyclonic events that forever changed his life and the conversations he'd had with Hatch about hers.

Looking at Hatch in that car, just before he exited for his rescue attempt, he remembered thinking, *Hatch wasn't in one of those* calm before the storm *moments*. She was calm because she was the eye of her own hurricane.

This is a one-way radio system.

Those were Hatch's exact words. He hadn't even made it to the first checkpoint before violating the first rule. He hoped to keep *Do not die* off the table for the foreseeable future.

He shook off the mistake and focused. Ayala's shaky hand extended the key card from the attached lanyard. He pressed it against the access pad. *Here goes nothing,* he thought, instead of saying, proud of himself for remembering.

The delay between the red light flipping to green and the door making its electrical buzzing release sound seemed like an eternity to the impatient Ayala.

"I've got eyes on you until you get to that door over there on the left. And don't worry. Once you're inside, I'll still have eyes by way of your cell phone. It should work just as long as the connection holds." There was a pause. In it, Ayala heard Hatch sigh. Her exhale, amplified by the small wireless earbud in his ear, sounded of rushing water crashing over wet stone. The sound of it reminded him of that day by the river. The other day his life changed forever. The story he never told the woman watching on from the passenger seat of his Nissan.

Ayala had wanted to tell her. And had planned to after they'd finished eating their meal at Ernesto's house. But then Munoz and his goons showed up. The rest is history. But still, Ayala hoped to live to tell her about it.

There were similarities and differences, both in the circumstances of their childhood, and how each handled fallout. Both lost a parent at a tender age. Both marred by the wounds of their experiences.

Ayala couldn't remember a time when he didn't hate the sound of rushing water, but he still had one photograph, warped and faded with time that depicted a young Ayala at, age ten. It had been taken by his uncle who was excited to use a camera he had just bought. He had the photograph tucked in a shoebox with other old memories collecting dust. But no other memories collected were as important as the one in that picture. Because it was taken the day his mother died, not one hour before her death.

Ayala's father had always wanted to take them to the Rio Grande but getting from Nogales to the eastern side of the country without a car would take them a lifetime. He never figured it would happen, but a month before his eleventh birthday and to his family's surprise, his father got them there. His uncle married into money, and to show it off to the family, offered to take them in his new car.

Ayala's mother was sweet and kind, everything a mother should be. He had no bad memories from his childhood. He lived in a cluster of homes on the western side of Nogales, away from all the riffraff of downtown. They didn't have much. But nobody did and so it didn't seem to matter as much. Crime was minimal there, and aside from struggling to keep a chin above poverty, Ayala's family could be described in one simple word: happy.

His father wanted to take the family to a section of the river that was calm. His uncle, being one to live a bit more on the edge, and also the person driving, had opted for a bend in the river called The Devil's Hand because of the twisted shape of the enormous boulder jutting out from the riverbank.

The entire way to the river Ayala's uncle went on and on about The Devil's Hand. He said the boulder pinched the river tight. The following bend created a brief, intense section of rapids. His uncle thought it would be a great family photo.

He tested the camera, using Ayala as his first subject. The first of two photos taken that day was now tucked away in a shoebox buried in his bedroom closet. He'd thought about throwing it away, but each time he held it in his hand, he couldn't bring himself to do it.

After his uncle tested the camera and was satisfied he understood its function, he called the family together. He placed them between the enormous Devil's Knuckle and a smaller, but still quite large boulder on the other side. The gap between was littered with rocks of all shapes and sizes but was wide enough for Ayala, his parents, his new aunt-by-marriage, and his uncle, who'd managed to figure out how to set a timer on the camera and actually be in the picture himself.

Ayala remembered, as a young boy seeing his uncle dashing toward them along the slippery rocks, how truly amazing the technology was that allowed this moment to occur. The second picture taken that day did not capture Ayala's happy family in a neat row bookended by enormous boulders on each side. His father had whispered in his ear, telling him how much the boulders looked like the ones he envisioned in the childhood story, the one with the troll. Ayala also remembered the pained expression streaking across his father's face as he spoke the words. He had apologized later in life, and thankfully before his passing, to his father for not seeing what his father saw that day. His answer had been simply stated. *We see what we need to see, when we need to see it.* Ayala's apology and his father's forgiveness washed away the guilt of it, his father's voice still resonating its calming tones even these many years later.

What had been captured by the second photograph had, in fact, been the opposite of what the five family members had envisioned on the bank of the raging Rio Grande. Ayala's uncle lost his footing on a wet rock while sprinting to beat the ten-seconds he had to close the distance between the camera and the assembled group.

Traction-less loafers and wet rocks proved a deadly combination. His uncle's right foot shot out behind him just as he neared his family. Out of an instinctual counter move, Ayala's uncle shot out his left arm. Ayala's mother, who was beside him and holding his hand, took the unintentional left hook delivered by his uncle.

To this day, he wakes sometimes to the sensation of his mother's hand in his. He cherishes those fleeting moments because of the moment that created it.

Ayala's mother fell back, striking her head on a knot of stone protruding out of the giant boulder. She fell into the river. Ayala remembers the splash and rush that followed. Because he too was swallowed up into the tempestuous whitewater. His mother's grip had brought him on a similar path, but being much shorter, he missed the jutting rock that had rendered his mother unconscious.

He rode atop her lifeless body for a moment before the churn of the water upended him and separated him from his mother. He held onto her hand, but the grip of her fingers faded until they were no more. Unable to keep hold, his mother slipped away. Ayala never saw her again except for when they'd buried her after finding her body twenty-seven miles downriver from the small town of San Antonio del Bravo.

The violent water swallowed him only to spit him back out a second later. The air turned to cold froth and Ayala choked it down. Without knowing which way was up or down, and with a lungful of water, Miguel Ayala, boy of ten, had resigned himself to his impending death. As darkness edged its way into his periphery and as the Rio

Grande roared, Ayala felt a tugging. It was distant at first. Becoming clearer as he broke the surface of the water again, but this time to the panicked eyes of his father who had jumped in to save him.

His father, a kind, thoughtful man became a man of action that day. He jumped in fully clothed to save them. He later told Ayala that he had tried to save his mother too. But she was too far downriver and was bleeding badly from the head. The water damaged his father's watch, grinding its gears to a halt the moment he jumped in. His father never got it fixed and chose to wear it every day as a reminder of what happened.

Ayala now wore that watch. Ayala found his uncle's old camera many years later and with it discovered the second photograph taken that day. And to this day, he kept it tucked inside his left breast pocket, believing the brightness of his gaudy Hawaiian shirts helped brighten the dark memory of the photo.

He wanted to share these things with Hatch and hoped someday to have that opportunity. But first, he had to survive the next few minutes. The crashing wave of her exhale receded, followed by a word of encouragement. "You can do this, Miguel." The rest was up to him.

He got to the door, another access pad with a red light just above the height of the doorknob and off to the right.

"Same as before," Hatch said in his ear. And same as before, the key card granted him access. He hesitated. Hatch's voice sounded in his ear. "You can do this, Miguel. Remember when you entered that house of a known drug dealer with members of the Mexican Special Forces? You faced fear then, and you can face it now."

Ayala took Hatch's words in stride as he stepped inside. Ahead of him, three steps led up to a landing where two armed security personnel stood, wearing dark black uniforms. They both had guns but kept them holstered on their waists. Each bore a tired expression.

One of the men, the lankier of the two, lazily balanced his chin on his fist in a thinker's pose. But instead of thinking, he looked more like a man trying to find a way to sleep standing up.

The squat hairy man next to him popped his knuckles while he passed an eye over Ayala. This man didn't look at Ayala in the manner of a professional, instead acting more like a school yard bully. He wondered if they spent their day intimidating all the workers like that. Ayala thought the answer to that question might make a good piece of journalism. He put a mental pushpin in his idea board, wishing he could pull his notepad from his fanny pack stowed in the Nissan and jot it down.

The one not trying to sleep gave Ayala a quick eye, but only for a moment before turning back to his partner and attempting to engage the man in whatever conversation Ayala's entrance had interrupted.

Past the man, Ayala stopped. He slowly turned his body with his hands on his hips like he was Superman overlooking a crowd of adoring fans. There was a crowd, but they weren't adoring fans. They were employees dressed like him moving about the floor of the orange juice bottling plant. Ayala's slow turn gave Hatch the needed surveillance information to make her best guess of where he needed to go next, which he heard through his earpiece a moment later.

"To the left, there's a door with that restricted access symbol over it. You see it? The yellow and black one."

He turned to the door, acknowledging he saw it without speaking. Hatch got the message because she continued a moment later.

"That's going to be our best guess now, and we'll go from there. I don't see a lot of activity by that door, so when you approach it, do so confidently, in a manner that won't draw any suspicion."

Ayala moved across the floor, doing his best to look as though he belonged, nobody in the cluster of workers on the main floor noticed or cared. Ten feet from the door, a security guard was dressed in similar colored overalls with a badge attached to his chest that looked like it was taken from a child's costume. He was not armed like the other two at the door. And unlike the two men in black, he did harbor ill will in his eyes. In fact, he gave a nod and slight tip of his hard hat in Ayala's direction, who did likewise in return. The two moved on at an equal pace, but in different directions.

"Excellent," he received Hatch's compliment as he got to the access door.

The red light went to green.

Ayala opened the door and slipped inside as the passing guard disappeared with its closing. Ayala faced a long, narrow hallway, several doors on both sides, and waited for instructions on what to do next.

TWENTY-EIGHT

Angela sat in her dank cell, absorbing the world around her that was ticking by in a timeless fashion as she waited in anticipation of the next time the door opened. The bucket of cold water was now filled with her grime, or at least what she could get off with the dish sponge they'd given her to wash with. The sponge, once yellow, was now smudged a dark brown and set next to the bucket.

Angela had been given specific instructions from Pencil. The bucket and sponge had to be in the corner visible to the door when it first opened. He said they would open the door a crack and if it was not, they would not come in until it was placed in its proper place. Angela didn't want them in the cell, and so did not listen to the instructions.

An hour, or what felt like an hour, had passed since the thin sliver of light cut a path into the dark and Pencil's beady eye poked about, and when he didn't see the bucket and sponge, he shut and locked the door. Before his and Bigfoot's clamoring footsteps faded completely, she heard him yell back to her in English, "You just added an hour. Next time we come back, the bucket better be in the corner or your time will add up to a day. Not sure you're gonna last that long."

Angela knew there was no point in testing the veracity of the lanky captor's threat. So far, he'd proven to be holding strong on the one-hour thing. She thought about trying to figure out a way to attach her new clothes to her old clothes and knot the makeshift rope to the handle of the water pail. Angela had spent much of the time since the door last closed imagining if the rope-bucket-weapon would even work. After running several scenarios through her mind, none in the past hour seemed viable. The game was over. Her last-ditch hope of escape rested in a bucket and a heap of clothes piled in the corner in sight of the door.

She reluctantly accepted that this would be, as Bigfoot put it, the last stop on a long and winding road through this hellish nightmare. She kicked herself for ever listening to the woman at the bar, the woman with the long, jet-black hair who'd convinced her she was special. The same woman who would, after making promises of fame and fortune, walk Angela to the SUV where her kidnappers waited.

The hallway had been quiet since they'd left. Angela remained tucked into a ball, her shins held tight with her arms. With arms wrapped, she began rocking. The hard, foul-smelling floor of the cell waged a continuous battle against the scent of citrus emanating from beyond the door. Angela edged closer to the clean smell but kept a few feet between her and the door.

Facing the coming darkness, she worked to call forth her brightest memory. She had been stubborn, even at nine. Angela had taken a strange vow of silence made in a written decree to her parents in which she stated that from that point forward, she would only communicate through written word, and never speak again. She was young and full of childlike curiosity, and after watching The Little Mermaid, decided to try to understand what life could be like without a voice.

Angela's maintained her stubbornness for three months. Those were three very long months for her parents, she remembered. Looking back now, it saddened her to think she lost out on three months of speaking with two people she loved more than anything else in the world. What she wouldn't give to have that time back now, knowing deep down, it was likely her parents would never hear her voice again.

But she didn't recall the memory to reflect on the negative, but instead on the moment she cherished as her all-time favorite. It was that drawing. Angela wished to see it one more time.

Her mother was in the kitchen making dinner while a young Angela was drawing in the living room, using the early evening's sunlight to warm her as the first snowflakes of winter began to fall.

She loved to draw on those days, she still did in fact, but it wasn't the memory of the drawing or the setting that made her happy. The reason Angela chose this memory to be her last before she gave herself completely away to despair was that while drawing, her father had been watching, unbeknownst to her. And being the loving, caring man that he was, and still is, wanted to communicate so badly with his daughter who had taken mute.

He crawled up alongside her, choosing not to speak, choosing not to write words, and picked up a piece of scrap paper. In a moment of artistic inspiration, her father, a man who had never drawn a thing before or after, picked up a brown crayon. The minutes of doodling quickly revealed why she had never seen him draw before.

The image was of a gas pump. The pump handle waved and the pump itself had circles for eyes. It looked more like a triple decker upside-down ice cream cone that had been in the sun for about a week, than anything resembling the image her father had drawn. It was the fact that, knowing he couldn't draw, he did, and he did it for the sole purpose of reconnecting with his batty, awkward, nine-year-old-daughter, who'd gone adrift.

The sight of that pathetic brown cartoon gas pump forced a laugh so deep and hearty from Angela, the sound of it had surprised her. Something broke loose in that laugh. Whatever darkness made her go mute, the sensation of the rumbled giggle obliterated its hold on her. And she silently wished it could work its magic one last time and take her away from this awful place.

Angela closed her eyes. When she woke, her surroundings had not changed. The leaky pipe above pelted out its metronomic beat on the cold concrete floor stained with dirt and excrement. Air that smelled like oranges floated in, accompanied by the whir and clang of the machines outside the door.

In the cold dark space, Angela let the memory of her father's love warm her. The cold immediately returned with the sound of a door closing from the hallway and the rapidly approaching footsteps that followed. Footsteps that did not belong to either Pencil or Bigfoot.

These were hurried, purposeful steps, and they came to an abrupt halt in front of her door. The shadow of the man behind it swallowed up the light.

Angela convulsed in fear as she prepared for the door of *the last stop* to open for the last time.

TWENTY-NINE

Ayala fought to control his breathing as he stood outside the door. Hatch identified it when he had entered the hallway. She was looking for a room that was separated from other rooms, somewhere where they could keep people and keep them away from others. When Ayala nearly gagged on the smell upon approaching it, Hatch knew she had been right. Her only worry now was that either Angela wasn't in there, or never was.

"Why do you think any one of these keys you took from that guy's belt are going to work on this door?" Ayala asked in a hushed whisper.

Hatch had not scolded him once for speaking inside the hallway. She told him it was permitted only in a whisper. And used only when absolutely necessary.

Ayala's question was unnecessary but he was glad when she decided to answer it instead of admonishing him for breaking radio silence to ask it. Ayala was nervous. He assumed Hatch could see his tremors from the camera nestled in his pocket as she watched him from the phone in her hand. She needed to keep him calm. Best way to do that was to keep him talking.

"Your ID badge says manager, right?"

Ayala recalled when he'd tried to lighten the mood and compensate for the nerves rocking his system by making a joke about being promoted. It had given them both a little chuckle, and the release had helped him in those final moments before he left Hatch.

Ayala began rifling through the keyset looking for one that would match the keyhole in the door. He felt like he'd been standing in the hallway jingling keys for way too long. A key floated by the eye of the camera as Ayala unsuccessfully tried it in the door's lock. He exchanged the key for another, taking the new one in his fingers and leaving only two more.

Hatch continued to speak. "My guess is that if you can find a key that fits and opens that door, it might shed some light on how complicit the Solarus Juice Company is in their knowledge of the girls kept in their facility. If I'm wrong, the keys won't work, which means the cartel may be using the space as a front without the knowledge of its employees.

"But I'm counting on the other, a much darker probability, that the girls they run through here, some of them at least..."

Hatch presumed Ayala was about to tell her the odds had just slimmed a little further, but just as he started retracting the key, it caught and the door unlocked.

The hallway's dim light captured the pale features of the red-headed girl Hatch had shown him a picture of. She looked nothing like the girl in the photo. Angela was smeared with dirt around the edges of her hair like a charcoal drawing left out in the rain, though her clothes, a blue t-shirt and worn jeans, were clean and looked out of place amid the filth. It made sense when he saw the soiled heap near a pile of human waste.

He expected to see relief in the girl's face, instead it was twisted into a snarl and had been since the moment Ayala entered. Hatch watched the image of Angela edging herself back in a strange three-legged crab walk on account of the bindings on her wrist. She moved toward the back wall and pressed herself firmly against it.

"We have to move quickly, please," Ayala said in a hushed whisper. "Let me cut those bindings off."

The girl was crumpled awkwardly now against the back wall with her bound hands. She was having great difficulty righting herself.

Ayala edged forward and pulled out a knife. "Listen, I'm here to help." He tried to get close to the rope, but Angela squirmed. She was terrified, and rightfully so, but Ayala knew he needed to get her under control so that he could free her hands. He looked at the blue uniform he was wearing and down to the knife in his hand. Then Ayala remembered what Hatch said about the key. If the managers had access to the room, they're also a part. And Ayala couldn't fathom the trauma this girl had faced by seeing him wearing the exact same uniform he now wore. Angela thought he was one of them.

"Take me off the Bluetooth. Put me on speaker." Ayala did as he was told and took a step back from the girl, keeping one eye on the open door. "Angela, it's me, Daphne."

Angela stopped moving immediately. Her eyes darted around the room as if waking from an awful dream.

Hatch's voice crackled, cutting in and out. Ayala spoke in the most soothing and reassuring tone of voice he could muster considering the stress he was under. "Please, you have to trust me. I'm not one of them. I'm here to help you. Daphne Nighthawk is in the parking lot outside this place right now. Isn't that right, Daphne?"

Silence followed. He pulled the phone and saw it had died. His crap charger in the Nissan had left him with a low battery. With Hatch no longer his eyes and ears, Ayala set out on his own.

Angela calmed some after hearing Hatch's voice. The knife in Ayala's hand had not been used against the girl and with each passing second, she seemed more receptive to the idea of accepting his assistance.

The girl turned and exposed the bindings on her wrists without the fidgeting and movement of before. Ayala used the blade that Hatch had given him to saw through the cords, releasing her damaged wrists. She gently waved them in front of her. The wounds left by the bindings were too sore to even rub. Ayala had no medical training but had spent enough time documenting tragedy to know the gash on Angela's right wrist would definitely need medical treatment.

He outstretched an open hand to the girl and guided her up from the cold, damp concrete. "Please, we must hurry. We have to get going."

"You're not going anywhere."

The light from the hallway was blotted out by the shapes of two men of opposite proportions, but both equally terrifying.

THIRTY

Ayala turned to face the two brutish men, putting his body between himself and Angela. Being a man who preferred doing battle with the pen rather than the sword meant the knife Hatch had given him quivered in his hand.

The two men laughed as they closed in on Ayala and the girl. The short, hairy one pulled a pistol from his waist and pointed it at Ayala, the blade now seeming a foolish choice, wishing he had opted for the gun but knowing that it was against his nature to use one.

The knife in his hand now was drawn instinctively, but he knew he didn't have the will to use it as he looked down the barrel of the gun pointed at his head. That's why when it left his hand and slammed into the side of the brutish, hairy man's neck, Ayala looked on in shock.

Blood spurted and death called him to the cold, stained concrete floor. A single round left his gun as he convulsed and hit the floor. The round slammed directly into the forehead of his lanky partner, sending blood and brain matter into the high corner of the ceiling.

Angela stood over the burly man, gurgling blood through both his nose and mouth, a result of the knife punched directly through his neck.

His left hand fell away from his throat and into the blood pooling out from the hole created by the knife still embedded in his neck. Angela stood over him and didn't move again until the gurgling stopped altogether.

Ayala looked at the girl, who, only moments before, was tucked in the corner. In the wake of the violence, Angela's face calmed and for the briefest of moments, she looked like the girl from the photo, at least in her eyes. The fire of life breathed back into them by the death of these two horrible men.

Rothman followed Ayala out into the hallway. The two crossed the main floor at a good pace, somewhere between a speed walk and a jog, trying to move quickly without drawing attention. With the two guards he'd seen at the front door dead, the main exit was clear.

Ayala and Angela exited the warehouse and broke into a brisk jog as an alarm sounded from inside the building they had just left.

HATCH WAS NO LONGER IN THE NISSAN. SHE'D LEFT IT SOON after Ayala entered the building. In his absence, Hatch had been gifted a powder blue uniform in similar fashion as the first. Her hair tucked up under the plastic helmet as best she could manage, making her look more masculine, just as she had done when infiltrating Club de Fuego. Hatch now lingered at the top of the footpath leading to the factory gate and was nearing the pedestrian gate access when Ayala burst through the door. Angela was close behind. They broke into a sprint when the alarm sounded. The guard from the truck checkpoint ran in the direction of the warehouse and the escaping duo. Hatch slipped her gun out, the coveralls making the simple task harder. As she brought the weapon up on target, the guard ran by Ayala and the girl without a second look.

Hatch was already in the Nissan with the engine running. She'd left the passenger side doors open and a moment later the seats were occupied by Ayala's and Angela's bodies.

"I can't believe you came back for me," Angela squeaked the words out as tears ran down her face, marking a clean trail through the filth acquired by her experience in captivity.

Hatch pulled the yellow Nissan out of the lot and onto the dirt road leading back to the main highway.

The headlights in the rearview mirror grew brighter.

"Don't thank me yet."

THIRTY-ONE

Miguel's beat-up yellow Nissan protested Hatch's efforts to push beyond its capacity. Her knuckles were white as she worked two-handed to maintain her grip. Getting it under control, she looked at Angela, who was terrified, curled in a fetal position and rocking, her eyes wide with terror, her moment of exhilaration at being released by the rescue were instantly dashed by the pursuers now chasing them, only a few miles behind.

"Miguel, I'm going to need you to take the wheel."

"What?" He put his hands up. "How?"

"It's going to have to be quick. Hold the wheel. We're going to slow down. You have to keep it steady. I'm going to come across behind you, and you're going to go in front of me. I'm going to see if we can put all those propel waters to work."

Ayala's face suddenly brightened with the challenge. A few minutes of wild jostling, and the Chinese fire drill was complete without either of them leaving the car.

Hatch spun in her new seat, turning to face the rear windshield of the sedan, using the head rest as a supported firing position while she brought the Glock up and took aim at the headlights behind them.

"It may not even be them," Miguel whispered in a worried hiss.

"We'll know the second they start shooting."

Miguel seemed be able to whisper to his Nissan because with him at the helm, it quieted enough that Hatch could hear the murmured whispers repetitively spoken by Angela in her curled position. She understood the two words she was saying repeatedly. *Kill me.*

Hatch released her grip on the back seat and reached her hand out. The old scars of Hatch's battle torn arm rested atop the girl's trembling arm, being careful to avoid the area of Angela's wrist damaged by her restraints. The physical contact seemed to be working because Angela stopped the rocking, and she grew quiet.

"I know you're scared."

Tears streamed down Angela's face, cleaning paths through the grime still clinging to her skin. "I'll never go back there. Do you understand me? You have to promise, don't let them take me again, even if that means killing me first."

"I'll promise you this, the only way they're ever going to get to you, is if they've gotten to me first. And I don't plan on dying today."

Miguel jerked the wheel hard to the right, taking the poorly constructed road that led down into a shanty town. Hatch was thrown to the right, catching herself by the headrest before falling between the seats.

"Sorry for not giving the warning. I saw it last minute."

"Where are we?" They sped by stacked rows of broken-down homes.

"These are the towns they give the workers who work their fields. They pay them next to nothing if anything at all. Most are working off a debt they'll never pay off. Look at the houses around you. They're built from junkyard scraps."

Few people were out to see the Nissan race down their quiet village streets. He'd taken several rights and lefts, and then slowed at Hatch's request, and cut the lights. The Nissan's motor made a loud clicking sounds as the engine began to cool.

Less than two minutes passed before the darkness was shattered by the reaching glow of the approaching headlights silhouetting the uneven lines of the village. Menacing shadows outran the light, as if to warn of the intentions of the men behind them.

Hatch directed Ayala into a driveway off to the right, leaving their headlights off and only braking hard at the last second before cutting the engine. Once stopped, Hatch jumped from the vehicle and ran through the garbage-littered yard to Ayala's trunk where she'd seen a tattered green sleeping bag when she'd deposited the supplies, including a cache of guns collected from the dirty police lieutenant and his cronies, and a medical kit donated by Ernesto.

She pulled out a five-inch folding knife and cut at the seam of the sleeping bag. Hatch spent several precious seconds tearing at the sleeping bag to widen its reach before throwing it over the back end of the Nissan. The poor condition of the sleeping bag exposed part of the yellow through its thin membrane and worn holes visible from the street. As best she could, Hatch battled to subdue the hideous yellow metal from view, but the Nissan fought back, just as its owner's Hawaiian shirt did, poking its way out from the collar of the blue coveralls he was still wearing.

Hatch looked for something else to cover the back of the car when an old woman appeared out of nowhere. It was a rare occasion when somebody snuck up on Hatch, and the eighty-something year old in slippers and a long pink tank top as a nightgown had somehow managed to make a very short list. The discolored blotches made the tattered clothing look more like a tie dye, rather than the faded and tattered covering that it was.

The old woman's thin arms rested atop a wooden cane, holding up her bony figure on unsteady wobbly legs. Her hair was the color of smoke, blowing in every direction. She winked at Hatch and said something rapidly in Spanish that Hatch could not understand. Watching the exchange between the two, she thought of the story Ayala had told her about the medicine woman that had given the boy the seed.

"She wants to help us. She said to follow her."

The street filled with the light of the approaching vehicles. She followed the smoky haired woman as she disappeared inside the door to a two-story house, hopeful that they had not been seen, and that their vehicle had not been spotted.

As the door closed behind her, Hatch heard the squeal of brakes and knew that that had not been the case.

THIRTY-TWO

The three of them followed the wispy trail of the woman's hair up to a second flight of stairs, which led to a laddered access way to her tin roof. She never spoke. Not a word. Not to Hatch, not to Angela. The only utterances were in Spanish to Ayala when first offering her assistance outside.

The old woman quickly went about removing the padlock, which had been hanging in an unlocked position prior, and pushed open the door. A jerry-rigged door-catch, consisting of nothing more than a bungie cord and a whole mess of duct tape, kept the outward swinging door from slamming into the tin roof which would have alerted the men hunting them. Hatch was grateful that did not happen, and equally grateful for the woman's assistance.

The wild-haired woman shooed them onto her rooftop. Hatch looked down at the woman as she pulled it closed again. Before it shut, Hatch took one moment to admire the woman, who would forever be engrained as the Medicine Woman from Ayala's childhood story about the seed and the boulder. She was glad to have given the moment due pause, because in return she received the old woman's dazzling smile. Another wink and the door closed completely. This time when the padlock was returned to the hinge, Hatch heard the accompanying metallic click as she locked it, followed by the creak of her footsteps as she descended to the lower floor of her home.

Hatch only had the one gun. She carried it now in a low ready, bootlegged position by her left thigh as she turned to the hunched reporter and teen huddled close beside her, both faces offering the same question through terrified eyes. *What now?*

She had intended to go back for the sack full of weapons confiscated from Munoz and his men. Hatch had given a gun to both Ernesto and his wife Josefina in the hopes neither would have to use them. The rest were stowed in the trunk of Ayala's car, parked on the other side of the roof. No more than fifteen feet separated them from the car. But it might as well have been fifteen miles because of the cartel men sniffing around below.

The four armed men standing between them and their only transportation were now going house to house, looking for them. The terroristic nature of their questioning could be clearly understood in any language, even if their words weren't.

Hatch watched from above and hoped they wouldn't see the yellow of Ayala's Sentra peeking out from under the tattered sleeping bag blanketed over it. But she knew better. Everything now was not a matter of if, it was a matter of when and where they would be when it happened.

The three of them were pressed flat on the tin roof, cool to the touch having not yet been kissed by the morning sun. They were looking over a tight alleyway on the opposite side from where the Nissan was parked.

The gapped space measured no more than ten feet across. Hatch looked at the weakened Angela to her left, and the older but agile civilian reporter on her right and wondered if they'd be able to handle the jump and landing needed to get from where they were to where they needed to be. Hatch tucked the weapon inside her waistband and cinched her belt down as tight as she could, locking it to the small of her back, while being careful to adjust the hard angled steel of the weapon off the center of her spine and keep it in the upper part of her buttocks where her lean body had the most padding.

A commotion broke out below from within the Medicine Woman's home. The wild-haired, kind-smiling woman who hadn't uttered a word since bringing them through her tiny two-story home, more a one-story loft, could be heard loudly fending off the men with verbal assaults delivered in rapid-fire Spanish. Only two words Hatch could clearly hear, probably because they were said with such frequency, but she didn't recognize the words. *Perros del diablos.* Dogs of the devil. *Devil Dogs.*

"What'd the woman whisper to you when she invited us in?"

"Just told us to get inside followed by some mumbo jumbo."

"What was the mumbo jumbo?" Hatch asked as she quietly pushed herself up into a low crouch.

"She said she looked out her window and saw glowing woman by her baby cypress."

"Glowing woman?"

"I know, like I said, mumbo jumbo."

Hatch tried to make sense of the Medicine Woman's words as she stood and silently directed Ayala and Angela to do the same. Glowing woman? Then it made sense. She'd been flapping the shredded sleeping bag when the moon had finally broken its way through the cloudy pre-dawn sky above. The green of the makeshift blanket must've caught the light in a way that gave her a glow. Regardless, if that had been the reason for her opening the door and extending her bony hand in kindness, then Hatch glowed.

The Medicine Woman continued her verbal onslaught against the Devil Dogs as Hatch herded Ayala and Angela toward the center of the roof. Glass shattered in the chaos beneath their feet. Hatch imagined it had been thrown, and that whatever was used to make the loud crash had hopefully found its mark in the face of one her aggressors, because the next thing Hatch heard was the gunshot that silenced it all.

"Ready or not, we're going to have to jump."

Hatch expected resistance but got none. Adrenaline fueled them, generated by the imminent fear of death.

"Miguel, I'm going to need you to go first. You have to be on the other side to make sure Angela lands okay. She's very weak and might not be able to catch herself if she's unable to stick the landing."

Ayala nodded and set his gaze on the seven-foot tin runway between him and the edge. He took in air through deep and rapid inhales. Hatch was worried he was going to hyperventilate and pass out before even making the jump.

"It's ten feet across. I know that seems like a lot. I'd never ask you to do it if I didn't think you could make it. You don't jump and you know what's waiting on the other side of that door."

"I know all of that. I just can't seem to make my legs move."

Hatch knew what he was going through. Her father had tested her on that ridgeline and pushed her through the fear. "The distance seems impossible, but that's because you're not taking account of the six foot drop to the roof on the other side. It will carry you further than the ten feet you need."

Ayala's breathing became more settled as did his focus. "Where'd you learn that? Some top-secret killer school?"

"Mr. Henderson's tenth grade geometry class."

"I finally can tell my friends I used not only used my Spanish, I also used math to survive this crazy crap."

Hatch could tell the girl's awkward chuckle that followed melted away some of the fear and replaced it with determination.

"Don't choke up on your run. You hit the edge at full stride and launch off that edge. Do both of you hear me on this?"

Both nodded in unison.

"When you hit the other side, it's important to remember to bend your knees. You don't want to land straight legged. And if you don't stick the landing, then, as best you can, go with the momentum and curl yourself into a tuck, and roll out of it."

"I'll do my best." Ayala stripped off the blue coveralls. He reappeared as the Peacock Man in his bright yellow Hawaiian shirt overlaid by the green fishing vest. The gnawed cigar remained tucked in the corner of his mouth, during this quick change. "If this is going to be my end, then I want to look good when I do it."

Hatch heard the men below making their way to the second-floor landing. It wouldn't be long before they'd be checking the roof, door locked or not.

"I don't know anything about tactics, so please forgive my question. But if we run hard, as you're telling us to do, won't that alert those men on the floor below to our whereabouts?"

"Yes. But in a matter of minutes, maybe seconds, that's not going to matter anymore, because those Devil Dogs will be breaching that access door either way.

"The way I see it, we either make a run for it and take our chances on the unknown that comes from that. Or we stand here and wait for them to come. And I already know the probable outcome that would result from that." Hatch spared them the obvious.

"And once Miguel starts running, I want you right on his heels." Hatch directed her attention to the frightened teen who in turn nodded.

A bang of metal on metal sounded from the door below. The breach had begun. And, like a sprinter at the sound of a starter pistol's pop, Hatch watched as the newspaper man ran the length of the tin roof. He hit the edge and did exactly as Hatch instructed him to do.

Hatch looked on in awe as Miguel Ayala, the Peacock Man of Nogales, pushed hard while flapping his arms wildly, and flew.

His flight path was not perfect though, and upon hitting the roof on the other side, Ayala also managed to snag himself on the clothesline stretched end to end. The line slingshotted Ayala back in the direction he had just come. It looked as though somebody had hit stop and rewind. It would've been almost comical had he not been heading directly into the path of Angela who was rapidly approaching on a collision course.

Ayala caught himself by grabbing the pole of the clothesline, immediately halting him and avoiding the impending impact with the teen.

Angela had not stepped with as much force. Either she was too weak from her ordeal or too tired. The why of which didn't matter. What did was the lack of kinetic energy created had not been enough to boost the girl's light frame enough for the distance. Angela was on a racetrack to the ground after missing the second roof by a foot.

Ayala sprinted forward toward the falling teen with no regard for himself. His arms stretched out like a wide receiver going for a game-winning touchdown pass. The clothesline that had tossed him around was now in shambles strewn about the roof. Ayala's foot tangled in the line just as he caught Angela by the waist. The rubber-coated wire of the clothesline acted as a safety harness and stopped Ayala from going over the side. The girl now clutched his neck and held on for dear life.

With great effort, Ayala pulled Angela onto the rooftop. Hatch looked on and was sure Ayala would later tell his beautiful wife Rosa about how the extra vitamins in his Propel Vitamin Water was what gave him the needed strength to pull off such an amazing feat.

Hatch held her run until Angela dangled from the side. Precious seconds were lost in the process. With the girl safely cleared from the laundry-strewn landing pad, Hatch took her first step when the door beside her burst wide.

The Glock was still ratcheted against the small of her back. In preparation for the jump, Hatch needed her hands free for the landing. Left hand, moving on instinct, swept to her back. She felt the familiar cold of its steel in her hand as three men fanned out in front of her with guns drawn and aimed.

The fourth man exited after the others and was holding a cloth to his face. The blood covered rag pressed against a gash on the top of his head, presumably from whatever the Medicine Woman struck him with. The blood ran down his forehead. The river of red was slowed by the cloth, but a narrow stream trickled its way down and connected with a nasty scar running diagonally across his face.

Hatch was caught in mid-draw. These men were not the amateur enforcers Munoz brought with him. These three men were skilled operators.

When facing death, embrace it with open arms. For it is a friend who's been with you since the beginning and now you finally get to greet each other face to face. Do it with honor. Do it with a smile on your face. Her father's words sang to Hatch as she approached her end as her father had taught her to do long before he hoped she'd ever need to use it. Hatch wasn't sure of her thoughts on what happened when she crossed over to the other side. But she did believe without question that when she did, she would see her sister and father again. She thought of them both now. And the image of them in her mind helped honor her father's command.

Hatch looked past the gunman, locking eyes with the scarred man who stood behind them, and smiled.

Hatch refused to close her eyes. A decision she'd long ago made. Hatch wanted to face her killer as the reaper's scythe swept the life from her body. She felt it only fair to embrace the way she used death's gift to fill the cages of hell.

The smile hadn't ended with the consequence she'd expected. The firing squad held their position. And Devil Dogs' scarred master gave no command to do otherwise. The only change was in the man's face. Cruel intentions lay behind the eyes as he returned her smile with one of his own.

"I am Juan Carlos Moreno. I serve at the right hand of my employer, Hector Fuentes, and he has requested the company of your presence."

Hatch weighed her life in Shakespeare's simple yet eloquently put soliloquy on death, *"To be or not be."* The answer to which was a simple one.

Being interrogated by the world's most dangerous cartel leader was still a hell of a lot better than being dead.

Hatch released the Glock. The rough texture of the weapon's grip left its imprint on the palm of her left hand that was now raised in line with her right as she surrendered to her enemy. This would be the first time Hatch had been taken hostage. But the bank robbery in San Antonio was very different from the circumstances facing her now.

"On your knees."

No opportunity for heroics, Hatch complied.

"Turn around and put your hands on your head."

Hatch looked in the direction of the rooftop Ayala and Rothman had escaped to. She was scanning the debris field of laundry fluttering in the warm breeze whispering of the approaching heat of day and was relieved the two were nowhere to be seen.

An unnecessary pistol whip was delivered to the side of her head by one of the men who wielded the cold hard steel like a blackjack. Hatch's vision blurred and she fell forward onto the tin roof.

And just before she disappeared into the dark, the light of the moon danced across the top of a yellow Nissan, as it slipped away undetected.

THIRTY-THREE

The stagnant water a foot below Hatch's head captured the image of her blood-soaked face. The butt stroke to the side of her skull had bled steadily, as evidenced by the amount that was dried and caked across her face. It had clotted while she was unconscious.

In the few minutes since her vision had cleared, she'd taken the time to assess her circumstances. She was suspended over a round metal kiddie pool, the kind Hatch had seen in the black and white westerns her dad watched when she was young. A belt connected the top of the chair to a bolted hook on the wall behind her, keeping the chair and Hatch, who was strapped to it, held firmly at a forty-five-degree angle to the water below.

The tight restraints bit into her flesh at her wrists and ankles, the worst of which had cut open her right wrist, adding what would surely be new scars over the old one. The ripples made by her steadily dripping blood carried away the grotesque image of Hatch's face.

Warm wet blood slickened her wrist where it escaped from her body, lubricating the cord just enough that Hatch felt it budge. Her hand was now an inch freer than it had been a minute ago.

There was no clock on the wall, or at least none she could see when craning her neck. Hatch knew a countdown had begun. To whose end was still up for debate. Under the current set of circumstances, Hatch did not feel the odds were in her favor. But Hatch had surprised herself in the past, so didn't count herself out of the game, just maybe down a few points. With Ayala making touchdown receptions, maybe Hatch would get her turn in the endzone. And if she did, she hoped she or one of her teammates would send the big yellow goal crashing down on top of Hector Fuentes' skull.

Beside the metal pool lay car batteries and the black and red leads coming out of them were dangling loosely near, but not clipped to, the pool. The dim light of the room taunted Hatch and warned her of terrible things to come.

She continued to work at the restraint on her right wrist before she heard the door behind her open and close.

A metal chair dragged across the concrete floor and came to a stop just in eyeshot of Hatch's peripheral vision. Moreno's scarred face was now tinged an orange hue. Hatch thought of the oversized walrus championing the cartel's juice company. In her mind, the orange sunglasses-wearing tusked creature became synonymous with the beast of a troll described in Ayala's fable.

"Miss Nighthawk, you have been quite troublesome for my employer. And as angry as he is with you for what you've done to his nightclub and how much you have taken from him, he would like your audience for a brief moment of your time. Before the last sands of your hourglass add to your life's pile, Mr. Fuentes would like to ensure when I arrange your disappearance, that nobody else comes looking afterwards to finish the trouble you started. It ends, here, today, with you. My employer believes, all truth lies just beneath the surface of a person's eyes. And before I dispatch you, he wants to look you in the eye himself."

Hatch thought of the people she would leave behind and those who would undoubtedly hunt for her until they found word it was no longer necessary, just as she had done with Angela Rothman. She thought of

Savage, and how she wished the smell of his licorice overpowered the funk of the room she was in now.

She gave the man nothing in return. She would not entertain the whimsy of a murderous cartel thug, nor the wishes of his master. Hatch would face her end the way she had faced everything in her life up to this point, head tall and eyes front. She would give this man, and any to follow, no satisfaction to the contrary.

"You don't feel like talking. I understand. I think you will find you and I are a lot alike. I can smell the military training coming off your sweat. Did a little digging. Nothing came up under a Daphne Nighthawk. I think I can safely assume that's not your real name. But not to worry, I have other ways of digging. They're just a bit more painful." Moreno winked. "I'm very thorough. When we're done here today, there won't be a piece your life that I haven't peeled back and exposed."

The thought churned in her stomach, souring the bountiful meal she received at Josefina's hand. She thought of her family, of her mom, of Daphne, of Jake, and the last face to cross her mind's periphery was that of Dalton Savage. In running from Hawk's Landing, Hatch had effectively traded one threat for another. *Was there ever a time when they'd be safe?*

"Mr. Fuentes is in the other room finishing up his breakfast. It may not look like it by this room, but it is one of his favorite restaurants when he ventures out to be among his people." Moreno's reverence for Hector Fuentes went beyond the norm, speaking of him as God or a holy man, whose power and influence extended into the very soul of the cartel leader's top enforcer and personal bodyguard.

The door opened again.

Hatch shifted her gaze to the man in the thousand-dollar suit who dabbed a silk napkin against the corner of his lips before repocketing it. He walked with an air of confidence that identified him to Hatch before he offered his name.

"I am Hector Fuentes, head of the Fuentes cartel. I have forgone my second cup of coffee to come sit here in your presence. This may mean nothing to you. But my routine is everything to me. And I love my second cup of coffee. You must imagine how important this conversation is for me to miss its flavor in exchange for the foul stink of your blood. The answers you give matter, so do not be hasty and ensure you choose them with the care and consideration of somebody who understands that they might end up being your last. By the looks of that arm of yours, I think this is something you understand. Am I correct to assume this?"

He looked down at the pool of water accepting another droplet of Hatch's blood and Fuentes smiled. "And the answers you give do not determine whether you live or die. That ball was in motion the minute you crossed my path in Arizona. The way you answer my questions and the information you provide determine how you die. And trust me, when I say this, Miss Nighthawk, or whatever your name may be, death is an ugly thing and can be experienced in many ugly ways. Ways which I'm sure, even with your experience, would shock you to your soul. Let's hope we do not need to explore these options in search of the truth. Yes?"

Hatch spit the blood that had pooled in the lower portion of her lip into the water below, scattering her bound image in the ripples that followed. "Better men have tried."

"We'll see about that, but one thing's for certain. As foolhardy as it is, I respect your will to fight. I think Juan Carlos will put that statement to the test. You should pray it's not your last."

THIRTY-FOUR

The interrogation lasted less than thirty minutes. They had moved Hatch to a chair and bound her arms. Hatch now had a large fire poker sticking out of her left hand. The thick fire poker's light black coating was now stained in the red and brown of new blood over old. The fire poker entered through the web of flesh connecting her hand's index finger and thumb and the pointed end broke through to Hatch's palm and rested, painfully so, against the handrail of the chair.

Juan Carlos Moreno, the man who introduced himself as Hector Fuentes' personal bodyguard and head of security, worked the long metal fire poker like the joystick to an old Atari. Every time he asked a question, he would shift the fat fire poker in a different direction, twisting her flesh and trying to pry tendons away from her joints.

This was a different technique than she'd experienced before, but these were different men. One thing was a constant in all the survival training Hatch had endured: disconnecting the mind from the experience was the best weapon in defending against it. Truly taking on a transcendental state allowed the mind to drift to a safe place where pain didn't exist. This was a hard thing to do for most people. Hatch did it now with a large fire poker buried in her hand.

She was somewhere else now. Not in whatever room this was, wherever it was. Hatch felt the cool breeze spread across her face, replacing the sensation of the dried blood. The fire poker holding her left hand in torment was now replaced by that of Savage's strong grip. Hatch stood at the ridgeline behind her childhood home of Hawk's Landing, set against the Rocky Mountains of Colorado. That same hill where her father had challenged her to face her fear of heights. The same hill where she opened her heart to Dalton Savage. It was a good memory. It was a good place to be. Hatch bathed herself in the perfectness of the moment.

Juan Carlos manipulated the painful joystick one more time, Hatch felt it, winced at its sting, but managed to stay beside Savage just a few moments longer as the sunset danced colors of purple and red across her mind's eye, replacing the bruises she'd endured. And this time, her recall had no rattlesnake to interrupt their kiss.

Her lips were pressed against Savage's. She could still taste the licorice on them when she opened her eyes and looked down at the water below. Blood stung her eyes, further blurring her vision. The water held her reflection for the brief pause between red droplets. In its momentary stillness, Hatch saw herself. And for a moment, she was that twelve-year-old-girl again. It held for the briefest of moments before the next drop shattered it, further muddying the stagnant water with her blood.

Juan Carlos released the fire poker and sat back in the chair he had first taken up when he arrived. He looked at his employer. "She's not going to break. I've never seen it. A strong woman."

"Your mother was a strong woman." Hector Fuentes was talking to someone else in the room. She blinked to clear her vision. During the torture, and her altered mental state, somebody must've entered. The man standing next to Hector Fuentes was a younger, leaner, version of the drug kingpin. "Wouldn't you agree, my son?"

His son, who looked more like a boy, nodded. Hector Fuentes now spoke to his son and not to Hatch, as if she was not in the room, suspended in a chair, moments from her own death.

Hector put a hand on his son's shoulder. "Men of power wield their power firsthand. Strength comes in those moments when the unthinkable must be done. I know death does not sit well with you, my son. It never has. But if you are ever to hold your place at the head of this family, you must make death your ally. You will need to use it your advantage. And with that, today you will prove your worth in that regard. And in that demonstration of strength and will, you will show me you're worthy to be my heir."

He pulled out a long machete with a twelve-inch blade and black handle. Hector shoved the handle into his son's right hand, firmly, and then squeezed the shoulder he held, and pulled his son tight. Then he looked over at Hatch. "This woman here has stolen from us. And you know how I feel about thieves within my organization. Not only has she taken from our family, she has burned down one of our nightclubs. Even now we're looking for the girl that she freed.

"This cannot go unpunished. Rafael, I give you my blade, just as my father gave it to me. I offer it to you with the same message he had before commanding me to use it.

"Our blood is our oath. May we spill our enemies' first. Use this blade to take this enemy before you. Look into her eyes. See into her soul. In there you will see the answer. And when you do, use this blade to bring honor to the Fuentes name, and take your rightful place beside me."

Hector Fuentes stepped back. Juan Carlos Moreno connected the battery to both ends of the metal pool. The rusted clip clacked loudly and sent a spark through the air. Then Juan Carlos moved back a few feet, standing beside his boss.

Rafael Fuentes stood to the right of Hatch. He gripped the machete with two hands, both of which were trembling. He raised the machete high in the air like a lumberjack ready to swing an ax.

Hatch furiously worked at the bindings of her right wrist. Millimeter by millimeter she worked to release her right hand and had gotten it to her first knuckle when the machete began to fall. Hatch refused to close her eyes.

Instead of severing Hatch's head, Hector Fuentes' son had shifted direction at the last minute and pivoted to the two men looking on. In a flash of movement, Rafael crossed the distance and swung at his father with the machete in his hand and buried it into the side of his father's midsection, just below the rib cage.

The attack had been more of a slash than a thrust. Juan Carlos moved forward, knocking the blade free, and plunging one of his own under the chin of Rafael Fuentes. It was a long blade, maybe eight inches long, the point of which came through the top of Rafael Fuentes' skull at the same time Hatch freed her right hand.

The machete had helicoptered to a stop underneath the right side of her chair and was within arm's reach.

Juan Carlos Moreno was busy tending to his master as Hatch quickly cut herself free of the remaining bindings. There was no way she'd be able to cross the distance between her and Moreno before the cartel enforcer would get the drop on her.

With Moreno momentarily distracted, Hatch was already in motion and running for the door. She'd just passed into a short hallway which led to a kitchen. One of the bodyguards was leaning against the ordering counter and flirting with a waitress when he noticed Hatch.

She slammed the machete down, severing the man's gun hand at the wrist. The blade impacted with such force it stuck into the wood of the counter. The handless cartel man staggered back in shock. With his only hand he held the severed wrist up. Blood sprayed into the face of the waitress he'd been flirting with. She screamed, drawing attention from the crowded restaurant. Hatch grabbed a frying pan, still hot with the sizzling spiced chicken, and used it to finish off the guard with a blow learned from Ayala and Ernesto.

The bleeding, and now unconscious, guard fell aside as Hatch ran out into the street when the second shot hit the wall next to her. Shouts of angry men accompanied the smell of onions chasing Hatch out of the café and into the morning's light.

A moment ago, she was with Dalton Savage on top of a Ridge line in Hawks Landing, Colorado, preparing to say goodbye in her mind to the man she loved most. Now she was given a new breath of life. And she used it.

Hatch sprinted into the street, trying to put as much distance between her and the café as possible. Tires screeched nearby. Yellow filled her blurred vision.

As her eyes cleared, Hatch saw the beat-up yellow Nissan Sentra.

"I like your choice in weapons." Miguel Ayala gnawed on the end of his cigar while wearing the same Hawaiian shirt with the same yellow pineapples. And Hatch couldn't be happier to see all of it.

Angela sat in the passenger seat. Hatch pulled the door handle, and it came off in her hand. She heard Ayala muttering something about meaning to get it fixed as Hatch raced around to the other side.

Hatch's body hadn't even hit the seat when bullets began to strike the back of Ayala's sedan. She pulled the door closed as she landed on the frayed leather bench-seat covered in the shattered bits of glass from Ayala's back windshield.

The little yellow Nissan, old and tired and now bullet-ridden, pushed forward by will of its driver while Hatch remained low in her seat as she took stock of her injuries.

"Where to now?" Hatch asked.

"The river."

THIRTY-FIVE

Ernesto took solace in the fact that he had gotten Letty to his doctor friend, who'd agreed to meet them at the same mission where the black van had been dumped. He'd thought it would've been safe since the cartel henchmen had already been through the lot.

It hadn't taken the good doctor long to find the small microchip, no bigger than a cellphone sim card, embedded in the girl's calf, just above the ankle. After patching her up and cleaning her properly, another member of their team, a man who was known locally throughout Nogales as Azul, met them at the mission.

She departed in his blue ambulance ten minutes before they returned, and thirty seconds too long for the doctor, who was in mid-embrace when the bullet passing through his skull showered Ernesto in the good doctor's brain matter before slipping from his grasp to the gravel lot.

At least he died quickly. It was a thought playing on a constant loop in his mind since he and his wife, Josefina, had been captured by Moreno and his goons.

He refused to give the sadist any information about Letty, and he needed to hold out if he could give her and Azul as much of a head start as his waning life would allow. It was a long ride to Vera Cruz, where one of Ernesto's connections had run down Letty's mother. Through the grapevine, she had expressed her gratitude and excitement at the prospect of seeing her daughter again, who'd she'd given up for dead since three long years had passed since she disappeared.

Mexico was a big place, but it can become very small when somebody like Hector Fuentes decided they needed to find you. There are few rocks one can hide under. Unable to use his right shoulder, Ernesto leaned to the left, dipping his cheek to it, and clearing away some of the blood leaking from someplace he couldn't see or differentiate from the other wounds he'd sustained since making Moreno's acquaintance. His right shoulder had been dislocated and they'd spent countless time twisting it into unspeakable positions, using a tire iron as a fulcrum.

He'd heard his wife's screaming die out ten minutes ago. They were torn from each other the moment they entered the building, a dingy place smelling of day-old fish, that Moreno and his men were using as an impromptu torture chamber.

Ernesto's last image of his wife was that of her tear-soaked face as she spoke the last words he feared he'd ever hear pass over those lips, *por siempre nunca es suficiente*, forever is never enough.

Her words left her lips, those same lips he'd shared sixty years of conversations with, spoken over sixty years in the home they shared for the entirety of those sixty years of love that blossomed some sixty years ago with a simple kiss…on those lips.

He called out his response, repeating the words spoken before the end of every day. This being their last, Ernesto held onto the memory of the first time he'd laid eyes on his beautiful Josefina, and not the bloodied image hauled away by their captors.

He remembered the first time they'd held hands, replacing the snap of his finger when he refused to answer any question regarding the whereabouts of Hatch, Ayala, Angela, or Letty.

Ernesto thought of the time when he tried to impress his Josefina with his horse-riding skills having never ridden one in his life. As Ernesto tried to leap onto the saddle, he overestimated the amount of effort and had launched himself onto the saddle and over the other side landing awkwardly on his ankle and spraining it. He called that memory forward to erase the moment of Moreno plunging a hot poker into the bottom of his left foot.

He held the last memory the longest. His body numbed to the abuse. Ernesto felt himself above it all. The last memory had been holding back the emotionally crippling pain of the building probability that his beautiful wife's beautiful heart stopped beating ten minutes ago.

Refusing to accept it and wanting to stay with her for as long as forever took, he called to mind what happened to the young seventeen-year-old-Ernesto after he fell off that horse. Because it had been in that moment, sitting in the hot midday sun while rubbing his sore ankle near a pile of hay that smelled strongly of horse manure, that Josefina had come to his side.

He remembered, to this very breath, the electric sensation passing from her lips to his as she leaned in for their first kiss.

He remembered breathing her breath as their mouths worked awkwardly, as teenagers experiencing their first romance.

He remembered everything and held onto it all for as long as humanly possible while he waited for the answer to the question he refused to ask. *Is my Josefina gone?*

"Ernesto, my friend, we are going to continue our little conversation, you and me. You're going to tell me where you shipped Mr. Fuentes' property, so that he can properly recover it."

Ernesto heard the words but could no longer make out the mangled face of the man speaking them. It was to start again. The knife was in Moreno's hand again. The last time he'd used it, Ernesto nearly bit off his tongue while he endured it. He could not endure it again. And so, Ernesto Cruz asked the question that came out as a final declaration.

"I can't hear my Josephina anymore, and I fear that you have taken her from me. If this is true, then there is nothing further for us to discuss, for it is you that has taken something. You have stolen my purpose for living. You ripped out my heart, the moment you touched my wife. When the fires of hell lick at your feet, know that my wife and I are sailing high above, where we can no longer smell the stink of the world that you have poisoned."

Moreno coughed up a smile that was more a sneer and played with the knife in his hand. Ernesto could no longer make out the blade's sharp point.

"I free you to go be with your wife."

The blurred image of the knife dancing in front of Ernesto's face disappeared. A second later, the stinging in his hands and the pain in his body disappeared completely, as Juan Carlos Moreno used the same blade that killed Raphael Fuentes and buried it in similar fashion.

Moreno wiped the blood from his blade on Ernesto's shirt, before picking up his cell phone and making a call. "It was just the two old ones."

"Make the call." Hector Fuentes coughed into the phone and then hung up.

THIRTY-SIX

Jose Machado walked through the front door of his small ranch-style home set on a ten-acre plot of land in the countryside, forty miles south of Juarez. It had once belonged to a tobacco farmer and his wife before Jose's employer acquired both the farm and farmhouse after being slighted by the couple in a business deal. Machado, one of his employer's most trusted employees, was given the keys to the house so that he could oversee the land and its harvesting. Or better yet, that's what he told anybody who asked.

It's what he told his daughter, although it was a lie she had begun to silently question recently, noticed by Machado in the looks she gave when he added his money to the stack behind the false wall in the pantry.

To most, Machado was known as *Fumar*, Smoke. He was given the moniker on account of both his profession and his light-skinned complexion. To others, he was known by another name, one whispered on the breaths of dead men. To those who had met him at their life's end, Jose Machado was known as *El Vibora*, The Viper.

He dusted the top of his hat and hung it on the coatrack near the door. The smell of eggs and peppers greeted him, and it pleased

Machado to know Maria was awake. At seventeen, she tended to him more as a wife than a daughter, but only in the platonic sense of domestic responsibility. It was initially why he'd taken the girl. But over time, he'd come to see her as more than a servant girl.

The girl he'd saved from the hellhole of a life that she was destined for five years ago had become in time as much a daughter as any flesh and blood ever could be. Machado, unable to father a family of his own, found himself a bachelor, but Maria completed him, gave his life a purpose beyond its purpose, and a new perspective.

He rounded the corner of the short hallway and entered the kitchen where the smell intensified. He was pleasantly surprised by the plate of Chorizo cooling on the stove. Maria cracked an egg into the pan just as Machado walked in. She breezed across the kitchen floor as if walking on air. Then, with the grace of a prima ballerina, simultaneously dropped the eggshells in the trash and laid a kiss upon his cheek before pirouetting her way back to the stove.

"My flower," he said. "It smells delicious."

"Have a seat, papa. I'll have a plate to you shortly. It's your favorite."

There were four seats at the small round table, but they typically favored only two. He sat in his and only had to wait a moment before Maria brought the plate. She nudged the drawing she'd been working on. From the looks of it, it was a lily blooming in springtime with the last droplet of morning's dew dangling at the edge of its light purple petals.

When Machado found Maria those five years ago, the home she was in was littered in the drawings, as was his now. Every time he returned from one of his "business trips," she greeted him with a new illustration, sometimes several new ones depending on how long he was gone.

Machado waited patiently until Maria was seated. The two let the food cool. And in the quiet that settled over the table and its occupants, the two took hands and prayed. His arms were almost as thin as the girl's across from him, one of the lasting effects leftover from a rattlesnake bite he'd received as a child.

As a young boy, Machado's bird-like physique cost him ridicule and abuse in both verbal and physical forms. That was before they saw past his pale, lanky body and hunched shoulders, making him look more vulture than boy, and saw that he was not actually a vulture at all. But instead, a viper.

Machado felt then, as he still did now, that in the brutal moment when the rattlesnake seared him with its venom, a transfer had occurred. In that transfer of blood and venom when the two were joined, Machado believed a communion between man and serpent took place. His destiny had been laid at his feet on his fourth birthday.

His first memory outside of the infantile amnesia boundary line in his memory was of the time he was bitten by the rattlesnake. He believed that day marked his spiritual rebirth into the world. His re-emergence came with its own personal spirit guide whose menacing rattle and slithering tongue called to him and showed him his path, one he'd been walking since that day.

It is why Machado still wrapped its leathered skin around his. The rattle of the snake that bit him still dangled its warning loosely outside of the white button-up dress shirt, cinched tight at the collar by the turquoise bolo necktie his father had worn, and the sun-faded black blazer and wide-brimmed hat of similar color and wear. Two of the items he wore had cost the life of their wearer. No matter how hard he had scrubbed, Machado couldn't get all of the blood out of the cracks and crevices of the snakeskin and necktie. And in just the right light, he could still see the stain of it. The bloody talismans served as an important milestone in Machado's life. It's when he, at the early age of nine, first killed a man.

A thief had broken in through the window in his family's home and slit his father's throat while stealing a necktie he wasn't even wearing. The thief then killed his mother, but not before the horrible things she had to endure while laying in her dead husband's blood. Things Machado endured while he watched, hiding in the hallway pantry across from the opened door of his parent's bedroom when the burglar first entered. He'd tried and failed to block the sights and sounds.

On that day, Machado felt that he had died. The serpent whose blood pulsed through his veins swallowed his soul whole.

And on that day, a boy of nine gave himself over to the snake's power. He no longer hunched his shoulders to hide himself as he skulked about. He stood erect. He remained thin and pale. And the hat kept the promise his father had made when giving it to him. The shade continued to shield his trigger eye from the light.

The neighborhood boys stopped teasing after seeing the young Machado wandering the streets draped in his dead father's clothes. As he grew into those clothes, so did the stories of his legend.

The shake of the rattle dangling from his wrist drew an unholy fear. When he was young this had not been so because he wore it for its intended purpose, using it as a belt. As he grew past the belt's last notch, Machado, refusing to separate himself from the talisman, wrapped it around his left wrist. And there it had remained.

He secretly found amusement in the truth that what people feared most about him was built with love and worn in honor of it.

Machado found the snakeskin in a box under his parent's bed. In it was the same snake who'd bitten him. Machado knew this because he asked his father, a man who valued honesty above all else, and he had answered honestly. He could still remember the way his father would lean close when he had something important to say.

Machado's father told him he wanted to remember the day he almost lost his son. Machado had been upset by this. His father went on to explain he kept it to remember the fear he felt that day, to keep close the terrible image of his son writhing on the ground after being injected by the snake's venom. He wanted to always know that he could go to the shoebox in those times when he needed perspective.

Machado then asked his father if it could be made into a belt. His father didn't see why not, but before agreeing, asked why. Machado told of his bond with the snake. And how, even though he may look different, it's those differences who made him who he was.

He remembered his father's kind eyes in that moment. They always held a gentleness, but on that day, they seemed overly so. The warm orange glow of the setting sun sent a stray beam past the lip of his father's wide-brimmed hat stinging Machado's right eye and causing it to water. The falling teardrop trickled its way past the two scarred holes, marking the wounds that created this tear, before or after that day on the rocks, when the viper's poisoned teeth nearly blinded him.

While exploring the small farm where his parents worked, Machado came across a large rattlesnake sunning itself on the warm surface of a nearby rock. Being a boy of such a young age and curious about such things, Machado took to poking at it with a stick the length of his arm.

He could never recall the sensation of the bite itself. The snake's long, curved fangs penetrated Machado's face with such speed and force that he was knocked to his back with the snake still locked to his fleshy cheek. He woke in the local hospital two days later.

His father wiped the tear away with his thumb that smelled of the dried tobacco he'd harvested that day. He then removed the hat and placed it on the young Machado's head. Its shadow doused the light. His father pressed the hat down, firmly securing it as best he could to the top of his son's head. He spoke the words, forever etched in his mind.

What's mine is yours. Take the hat. Let it watch over you in the times I am not there. But keep it tight, because I'll be there in its shadow keeping that light out of your eye. I'll be watching on from above and when your mother and I feel it is time, we will call you forth on the voice of an angel. It will sound of your mother's dovelike voice and you will hear it rush your ear riding in on the gust of wind I send. It will swoop off your hat, no matter how tight you pull it that day. Its removal will strip away the dark shadow cloaking your every step since your fourth birthday. The light you are bathed in will call you home to your mother and me, who'll be waiting with open arms to give you the peace in death that I could not give you in life.

After Maria came into his life, Machado often thought about saying similar things to her but had not found the words. Machado's father had been a boisterous man who never seemed to be at a loss for words. Not a speaking man, Machado set out to write his feelings down. He'd secretly taught himself to write, practicing each night after Maria went to sleep.

Machado was a perfectionist in all matters of his life. The letter he challenged himself to write was no different. It was also the only letter Machado had written or ever planned to write. He had finished before his last trip and it rested atop the pile of cash lining the wall of his pantry. The letter waited patiently, for Maria knew she was not to go into the pantry unless he was dead. She asked him how she would know whether he was dead. He answered with a number. "Two." If Machado had not returned home within two days of his expected arrival, she was to immediately go to the wall behind the pantry.

She never looked to see what was behind the false wall. Machado had a thin piece of fishing wire hooked to the inside and in all the years she'd lived with him, Maria never looked inside.

Machado had grown weary of it all in recent years, but in his profession, retirement came in only one of two ways. Instant death, or a long, painful one. Machado had delivered both in equal measure over his years of service.

Machado knew well enough that he would probably never be able to enjoy a proper retirement but the money, nonetheless, accumulated to a sizeable rainy-day fund. And for Maria, his little flower, the three-hundred-thousand dollars resting underneath the letter would surely be sufficient to give her a bright future, should his life abruptly end.

She, of course, did not know any of that. She only knew that there was money if she needed it when he didn't return. He always wondered what her face would look like when she opened that pantry, knowing he would never get to see it.

Machado sat across from Maria as she delicately picked at her food. She looked at him and did not see what everybody else saw. To Maria, her father's tattered and sun-beaten suit, worn by Machado every time he stepped out to do his employer's business, didn't signify the coming of the Reaper's scythe. To the teenager across from him, Machado wore the wide-brimmed hat and suit of matching color to honor the man he loved most, in the hopes his father was indeed looking down on him from above and would one day keep his word, calling Machado home when his path had run its course.

And the item he revered above all others was the same one that had caused men to defecate themselves upon seeing it. Men died before intended, their hearts seizing at hearing its rattle. The snakeskin belt strapped to his wrist was the ungiven gift his father had planned to surprise him with on his ninth birthday.

Machado had never told his father he knew the secret, having caught sight of him working on it in the shed behind their home one night, the same night a murderous thief killed his parents in front of him. The masked killer took the turquoise bolo tie before the sound of a neighbor dragging a metal trash bin spooked him. The thief grabbed a shoebox set aside on the nightstand before disappearing into the night through the window he'd first entered. Machado's snake belt was in that box.

Machado spent three more hours inside that closet staring unmoved at the horror, unable to do more than breathe and blink. His eyes went back and forth from his dead parents to the open window. He imagined the slow breeze fluttering was the souls of his parents looking out the window and ensuring the bad man would not return. When the wind subsided altogether, Machado imagined their souls had deemed it safe, and he exited.

Machado spent his ninth birthday making his wish come true. He'd paid a man money he found in the back of a false door in the back of his father's dresser. It's where Machado got the idea for the one in his pantry now. The amount of money in the Machados' dresser enabled the young Machado to hire a man to do what he was too small and weak to do himself.

He sought the help of the local cobbler, who also doubled as a hitman hired to do the cartel's dirty work. Machado paid the assassin half up front with the demand that, upon finding the thief who'd murdered his parents, he'd wait to kill him until he could be there to watch.

On Machado's ninth birthday, he held a private party. Only three people were in attendance. The boy, the cobbler, and the thief. Machado stood over the man bound to a table and gagged with the same red bandana he'd worn the night he'd killed Machado's parents. He continued to look, refusing to let his eyes blink just like that night in the pantry, and watched as the beady eyes of the person responsible for robbing him emptied of life. Machado took back what was his, both the turquoise bolo tie and the snakeskin belt.

The cobbler and his wife were unable to bear a child, so he offered the boy an opportunity to live with them. Machado accepted and, as time went by, Machado took an apprenticeship at his adoptive father's shoe repair shop. Machado proved himself a capable cobbler but found his true calling in the second profession to which he also apprenticed. His first contract came at the age of twelve. The list had grown through the years and he had long since stopped counting. In the criminal underworld he was revered as the Boogeyman.

Maria saw through all of that, because she was the only person Machado had shared that with. And so she was the only person who saw him for the boy he used to be and not the killer he had become.

Machado's chance encounter of meeting Maria had been a unique twist of fate, a crossroads of sorts. He'd been assigned to kill the girl's parents. They were low-level drug dealers who worked for Mr. Fuentes, but they had shorted him five-thousand-dollars on a transaction. Machado's expertise was sought to ensure the message would be clearly received by anybody else. Machado had a particular gift in sending those type of messages.

On the day he'd planned to handle the task, Machado had arrived early to do his reconnaissance, but was dismayed to learn he arrived too late. A team of *Fuerzas Especiales*, or FES, were Special Forces like that of the United States Navy's elite SEALs, were already walking out. Maria's parents had been killed during the raid.

The girl was never part of the contract, and so was not a target. He was preparing to leave when he saw her drift away from one of the military men absently guarding her. Maria's face was dotted with her parent's blood. She looked--as Machado had when first walking out of the pantry--shell-shocked and lost. She wandered away from the military man and he did not even notice. Machado did as was done for him when the cobbler opened his door to him.

In the five years of living, Machado prayed each night that Maria had accumulated enough positive to erase the horror of that day. In exchange, she had done the same for him.

He pushed his plate aside and took a sip of dark roast coffee. Dealing in death meant that Jose Machado was aware of his own mortality and thought of it often. It never bothered him before. He had always assumed that the bullet of another would find him someday. He'd killed too many people to think otherwise. He hoped it would be a quick death. Machado had been at the hand of too many long ones to wish the same end for himself.

"Maria, you know where I keep it and you know what to do if I don't come back."

His phone vibrated before she could offer a roll of her eyes which usually accompanied this conversation. She disliked talking about death and avoided it at all costs. Jose found that to be one of the things he loved about her.

The call came from the only number who knew it.

Hector Fuentes' right-hand-man, Juan Carlos Moreno was on the other end of the phone. In the brevity that only he could offer, he had explained that Rafael Fuentes had attempted to kill his father. And then Moreno had killed Rafael. Moreno went on to explain the bulletproof vest Hector Fuentes wore deflected but did not completely stop the blade. Then the call quickly switched to the business at hand.

"I am indisposed outside of Rancho San Rafael cleaning up a bit of unpleasantness. Mr. Fuentes would like you to handle him? I'll send you their location. You might want to get moving. They're only thirty miles from your location but moving quickly and looks like they're heading for the river as we speak."

"And how would you like this handled?"

"Dead. All of them."

"Consider it done."

The phone clicked off. Machado took one last look at himself through the brown of Maria's eyes, seeing himself once more as the boy he was and not the killer he'd become. "I must go."

"But papa, you just got here."

"I know." He looked at the pantry with the money and back at the girl. "Two days."

"Two days." She repeated through a forced smile.

He stood up from the table and walked back to the coatrack, grabbing his wide-brimmed black hat and walking out into the sunlight to march, once more, to the orders of the devil.

THIRTY-SEVEN

The clotted blood clung to the gauze and angrily protested as Hatch adjusted the dressing on her left hand. Angela had Ayala's first aid kit ready to go the minute Hatch dove inside Ayala's beloved clunker.

The teen, relying on a health class from high school, had done a great job patching her up with the limited supplies on hand. Angela cleaned the headwound from the pistol whipping and, using some medical glue, she sealed it enough so the blood no longer rolled down Hatch's face. Her left hand was in bad shape.

Hatch knew why Moreno had chosen the left, instead of her right, to dig around inside the web of her hand with the long black fire poker. It was her shooting hand. Few knew it had not always been that way. The blast that ripped Hatch to shreds and gifted her right arm the wicked branching of scar tissue served as reminder. She made the compensation in a failed effort to remain in service to her team after tragedy struck.

In effect, Moreno's fire poker had only rendered one of her *two* dominant hands lame. She shifted the butt of the pistol to the right side.

Wind, following the contours of the bullet-riddled Nissan, whistled loudly in the hole where Ayala's rear windshield used to be while he muscled the accelerator pedal with the bottom of his boot as they raced to the location on his phone's GPS. He was using the address provided by his contact, the man who'd be meeting them and ferrying them the rest of the way to the crossing.

Ernesto Cruz was Ayala's most trusted friend and confidant. When it came to keeping alive, Ayala trusted one man above all others. Hatch had already heard the story of how Ayala had first come to know Arturo Sanchez, the former special forces operator who protected him during the fatal drug raid that left two parents dead and their flower-drawing daughter missing.

Hatch knew of the *Fuerzas Especiales*, Mexico's elite military unit with a specialty in maritime operations. She had had no direct experience with them during her time in the special operations community. Most of what she learned came by way of Alden Cruise, her former SEAL boyfriend, who spent several months in a water survival school with several of his Mexican counterparts.

Hatch remembered Cruise talking about his experience, but beside their involvement in Operation Black Swan, where they recaptured Joaquin "*El Chapo*" Guzman after his second escape from a Mexican federal prison, the only details she could recall now was how that unit got its nickname. The *Fuerzas Especiales* were more commonly known as the *FES*, coined after their unit's moto. *Fuerza, Espíritu, Sabiduría*. Strength, Spirit, Wisdom.

Those same three words described what was needed of all of them if they were to survive these dire circumstances. This was something Ayala said Arturo Sanchez had in droves. And this would be the man leading them down the snaking path of the river.

His combat skill was beyond reproach, but it was Sanchez's familiarity with Mexico's waterways, and his proficiency in navigating twists and turns of the Rio Grande, snaking its way across northern Mexico that would make all the difference in their escape attempt.

Sanchez took to the water shortly after the shooting of Maria's drug dealing father and the unfortunate death of her mother. He found peace in the ranging rapids of the river and became a whitewater rafting guide. It wasn't long before Sanchez heeded the call to serve again, this time taking a different approach to it however.

Ayala explained to Hatch that Sanchez hung his gun up after killing Maria's mother, vowing to never kill again. When Ayala reconnected with Sanchez years after the shooting, he told the military man about the work he was doing in freeing those enslaved and trafficked by the cartel. Sanchez used the snaked path of the river to transport victims to safety. And in cases such as Hatch and Angela's, finding a way across the border.

Ayala pulled off the road and made his own path through the dirt and weeds until the Nissan could go no further. Thirty feet from the riverbank, Ayala parked and shut the motor off. He looked at the red pushpin on his cellphone's mapping system. He was in the right spot. But there was no Sanchez. And no boat.

The trio left the car and Hatch scanned the perimeter. The only sound was that of the river. A white Lincoln town car skittered past too quickly for Hatch to get a view of the man driving, but took comfort in the fact she could see, in the passing blur, that he was alone.

EXPERIENCE TAUGHT HATCH THE REWARD OF PATIENCE. SHE applied it in the silent vigilance as she watched the Lincoln whiz by and continued watching the direction it travelled for several minutes after it disappeared around a bend in the road, shrouded by a cluster of rocks and trees.

Hatch didn't look away until the car vanished from sight. The reward of her diligence came in the red glow of the Lincoln brake lights illuminating. The car didn't stop, only tapping its brakes one time. Her hand instinctively hovering by the Glock tucked at the small of her back, Hatch waited until she felt the threat pass.

Ayala sighed and uneasily rubbed at the moist air accumulating on his brown arms. Hatch could see the strain on the reporter's face. "It's a river, not a road. I'm sure your guy will be here. If not, we drive."

"Driving would be more treacherous. Every passing car or truck has the potential to be loaded with the cartel's killers. Too dangerous. It's for this reason, we use the waterways whenever possible."

"Okay, then we wait until we can't." Hatch saw that Ayala was still coiled tight as a barrack mattress. "If it's not that, what's eating at you?"

"Goodbyes."

"We're a long way off from goodbyes. We still have to get down the river to the crossing."

"You. Not *we*." Ayala turned and, even against the obnoxious yellow of his Hawaiian pineapples peeking their way out from behind his fishing vest, looked blue. His sad aura was conveyed in the deep brown of his eyes. "I will not be making the rest of the journey with you."

"I don't understand."

Angela offered no response, verbal or otherwise, at Ayala's declaration. Hatch saw the lack of surprise in the teen. She assessed that Ayala must've already explained this to her in the interim while Hatch was having her less-than-pleasurable chat with Moreno.

"I should have told you my story when you so bravely shared yours. It's something I regret and something I hope to reconcile someday. Now, however, is not that day. All I'll say for brevity's sake, is that my mother died in that water many years ago. I've never set foot in it since. Look at me." Ayala held his hands out in front him. "Look at how I'm shaking just being around it."

Hatch did look and could see the tremors shaking his body as if a giant plow pushed along his entire body, spreading seeds which bore the fruit of its labor in the goosebumps popping up along his outstretched arms.

"I understand."

Ayala stopped shaking almost immediately. "I thought you were going to give me another pep talk. Like the one you gave me on the rooftop."

"The time for pep talks has long passed. Aside from that, I understand because I know the debilitating effects of fear."

"I don't see it. That's because the worst scars, the ones that never truly heal, are always the invisible ones." Ayala's eyes drifted to Hatch's right arm and the damage it spoke of, written in the pale twisted vine extending the entirety of it. "If what you say is true, I can't imagine the ones I can't see."

"You don't want to." Upstream, the red nose of a raft appeared.

In the rear of the sun-faded raft sat a ruggedly handsome man. His bronzed nut-brown skin shimmered in the late afternoon light. The setting sun's beams played with the water droplets in the air, casting him in a hazy glow, making Arturo Sanchez appear as though Hatch was looking at him through the smudged lens of an 80's Glamour Shot camera.

He navigated the raft to the rocky riverbank with a look of confidence matching the resume Ayala had heralded during their race to the river. The race now over, and Ayala's task of getting them there complete, it was time for Hatch to say goodbye.

"I'd like to see your smiling face walk through my doors at Cafe Rosa someday, and you and I can reminisce on the good we've done. And talk of the crack that we put in that boulder."

"Next time we talk again, I hope we don't just put a crack in it, I hope we've split the damn thing in half."

"I'd like that."

"Me too." Hatch hugged the man, favoring her damaged left hand while doing so.

Ayala faced his fear, or at least a portion of it, by walking between the two women he'd saved, as they made their way the last few feet.

The reporter turned human rights activist stopped dead in his tracks at the first wet rock, as if the water soaking its smooth surface was a forcefield barring further passage. And that is where he stood as Hatch looked upon the man who had risked everything to help a woman he didn't know find a girl he'd never met. A purity resonated in the kindness this man had shown.

In that moment, just as it did with Sanchez, the mist in the air combined with the sun to give him a glow. Hatch thought of Ayala's story, the one about seeing a glow around Maria that tragic day. Then she thought about the old woman who'd claimed to have seen a similar glow around Hatch before letting them into her home, knowingly sacrificing herself for people she did not know and had never met. She looked at the Peacock Man standing before her in the shimmering water's glow and wondered to herself, *was he glowing?*

The brightness surrounding Ayala, regardless of its significance, real or imagined, vanished into shadow as the man casting it fell into the water lapping at the rocky shore.

Miguel Ayala lay face down in the riverbank, exchanging a blood payment for crossing through its invisible forcefield. Hatch pulled Ayala from the water and into the raft as the second shot missed Angela, sailing by the teen's head with only a gnat's ass separating her from an instant death.

Without Angela's body to stop the shot, it continued its path to the rubber floorboard of the raft while nicking the thwart, a long inflatable cross tube used to keep the raft rigid.

That second shot did something else, maybe not for Ayala or Angela, but definitely for Hatch and most likely Sanchez. This bullet told of its origin. When the first shot rang out and Ayala dropped, Hatch had immediately scanned the jagged horizon for sign of the shooter. The second shot gave her that.

A black, wide-brimmed hat loomed above the scope of the rifle.

Sanchez shoved the raft from shore. Hatch didn't ask the why. When she had found the shooter, so had Sanchez. *A good operator is a good operator, regardless of the team they play on.*

And although Hatch and Sanchez had never before worked together, the training that molded them and the battlefields they were tested on *were* the same. And so, they too *were* the same. The bond of brotherhood, of sisterhood, occurring in those briefest of shared seconds, was established in a way few could achieve in a lifetime of friendship.

The battle cry of warfare instantaneously bridges years in minutes, forging while at the same time sealing a bond rarely broken. That happened in the millisecond both realized they were thinking the same thing at the exact same time.

The car can't be reached. The only way out is through.

Hatch was on point while Sanchez steered. Angela tended to Ayala's wound.

Hatch had her Glock out the second she safely placed Ayala in the raft. She tucked her knees between the lip of the man tub and the floorboard, stabilizing her shooting platform. The wet rubber was now more blood than water as Ayala's blood steadily drained from his shoulder. Hatch pushed the gun out and fired six steady, controlled shots in the direction of the hat.

The distance would've been tough for any shooter but the fast-moving river made it nearly impossible to hit the target she was aiming at. Hatch was not just any shooter, but even her skill was tested by this obstacle. So, she did the next best thing.

To keep the impending third shot from coming, Hatch used the rounds to keep the shooter's head down. That's not to say she didn't take aim. The shots weren't delivered in a burst. Rather, she paced her shots to conserve ammo while giving Sanchez enough time to steer in front of the rock the shooter hid behind.

It was Hatch's sixth and final shot that hit its intended mark, or at least close to it. In the moment before Sanchez brought the raft past the shooter's nest and blocking the aim of the man in it, Hatch saw the bullet hole.

Hatch found it strange the shot hadn't knocked the hat off. She reasoned it must've been glued to the man's head. The third shot never came. The only sound filling the aftermath came by way of Ayala's murmured groans and the sound of the rushing water, all of which were drowned out by the hiss of the leaking stabilizing tube as they raced down the river and away from the killer wearing a peculiar wide-brimmed black hat that now had a hole in it.

THIRTY-EIGHT

Blood leaked from Ayala's shoulder, soaking into his shirt, and transferring some of its spillage to Angela's clothes, whom Ayala had landed on top of when Hatch pulled him into the raft.

Everyone remained low, pressing themselves flat against the floor of the raft as best they could until they passed a thick cluster of trees and disappeared around the bend. With Sanchez handling the navigation of the river, Hatch requested Angela care for the wounded Ayala. When she turned, Hatch was happy to see the teen was already applying pressure. She'd undone his green fishing vest and used it to pack the holes on both sides with a relative degree of effectiveness. Hard to tell with the water mixing in, but the flow seemed to have slowed.

In the lull of the battle that followed the protection offered by rocks and trees, Sanchez offered his explanation as to why a third shot had never come after they passed by to the other side of the boulder.

He said, and Hatch agreed, it had been doubtful and highly unlikely the shooter, if still alive after Hatch's headshot, would have been capable of navigating the distance by foot. Sanchez had been correct in his assessment.

"Next place he or anybody else will be able to use will be a place called The Devil's Hand."

"What's with all the devil this and devil that?" Hatch asked, only half-joking. After having entered through The Devil's Pass, it seemed only fitting she'd pass by The Devil's Hand on the way out. She hoped, if the devil stopped by for a visit, Hatch would get to personally thank him for the hospitality.

The cross tube looked like a popped balloon. Deflated of its purpose, the raft became less manageable for the strong ex-special forces operator steering it. Sanchez' lean muscles worked the oar. The silver wings of the tattoo on his left forearm fluttered under the rippled tension of the constantly pulling water.

The tattooed emblem of Sanchez' former unit, the elite *Fuerzas Especiales* special forces unit he'd served with, depicted a green and black shield split by a yellow bolt of lightning and covered a silver anchor mounted on a silver pair of aviator wings. Under the anchor's pointed bottom were the words. *Fuerza, Espíritu, Sabiduría*. Strength, Spirit, Wisdom. And again, Sanchez exemplified them all. And after all they'd been through in their brief acquaintance, Hatch wholeheartedly agreed.

After navigating away from the kill zone, Sanchez explained the route used for the crossing and, more interestingly to Hatch, how he'd come upon it. After taking an early retirement from the service, Sanchez spent a month on the river in total isolation with nothing but his raft, camping essentials, and a gun in his search for understanding the post-military world. Hatch understood, because she too was on a similar path.

Sanchez told Hatch how he'd tried to wash free the invisible taint of blood covering his hands in the river's water. In that cleansing, he claimed to have found a new path by crossing paths with a very old one. During one of those honest conversations between two people after a moment when life bumps up against death and manages to stagger forward in fragile progression, Sanchez told of his crossroads.

Long ago before border walls and fences were put up, US citizens and Mexicans alike crossed the border without challenge and often with much regularity, depending on needs and resources, and their availability. One of the most important ways in which these border towns coexisted was in sharing medical supplies and facilities. These were, and still are, places where both come in short supply.

These informal and generally unregulated crossings were a normal part of rural life for generations. As years passed, border security tightened, and these communal partnerships died off, and were fast-approaching extinction.

While at a low point in his spiritual journey down the river, Sanchez hit bottom under the shade of a tree in eyesight of his father's grave. The house he'd buried his father in was gone, as was the marker he'd made those many years ago. Sanchez could still find his way to those bones layered not so deep beneath the surface, a depth only a small child of eleven could dig. On the day his father was shot dead by cartel bodyguards mistaking his van for a potential threat, he was delivering milk. No apologies were given when the mix-up had been realized. One of the men got out of the car and laughed at the sight of Sanchez' father gasping his last breath. Sanchez saw that man's face every time he pulled the trigger. A cartel hitman's mistake forged a burning fire inside a boy of eleven. That fire burned out of control and all the hate and anger he felt toward the cartel was fuel to launch a personal vendetta spanning ten years of service, until the day his gun had taken the life of an out-of-her-mind wife and mother. The fire was doused by her blood.

Sanchez had to bury his father without any help. A boy of eleven used nothing but a coffee can to claw through the dry dirt. His father's death left him an orphan. His mother having died of complications during Sanchez' birth.

He had always been able to tell when his father caught a glimpse of his wife in his son. Sometimes a tear of joy, sometimes one of sadness, but every time he reflected his mother's image, his father wept.

Sanchez never thought of his mother as dead though. The unbearable pain of knowing his entrance into life had taken the mother who'd given it to him nearly crippled him. To beat back his demons, Sanchez found a different perspective.

He envisioned that in a moment where the door between life and death were open, she slipped out as he entered. In that version of his life's beginning, Sanchez met his mother at the door. He still believed time stood still while he and his mother shared a moment. She laid a kiss upon his cheek and whispered in his ear all the loving comments a mother would say in a lifetime of loving their child. He claimed to have heard as he grew to be a man. In his mind, it had been her voice he heard in the wind the day he graduated from the grueling fifty-three-week course it took to become one of the world's elite.

His mother stepped up and offered one last smile followed by a playful wink before she vanished into a thousand stars, blinding him in her brilliant light. Rafting became his connection to her, seeing his mother's radiance reflected in the shimmering droplets caught by the sun's light.

Split between the shimmering river and his father's unmarked grave, Sanchez felt it a fitting place as any to put a pistol in his mouth. It's why he brought the gun with him in the first place. He was on a one-way trip to remove the pain he felt in taking his last shot. The bullet he'd sent ended the life of an unarmed mother of a child who wore her blood a second after it left the muzzle.

He vowed the next time his finger pulled the trigger, it would be done to end his own life. It was in that darkest of places, where he found the light.

Sitting under the shade of a tree with the cold steel of his gun clenched between his teeth, Sanchez received his new calling in the scream of a woman.

Nearby, but downstream from where Sanchez sat, a woman in a flowered sun dress clung to a thick rope crossing the river choke point where less than twenty feet of water separated the two countries. A young girl screamed for help when she slipped on a rock. The mother caught her daughter by the wrist while maintaining a hold on the rope, both of which were slipping. Her four-year-old-daughter was being pulled by the water.

A terrifying scene to behold, Sanchez couldn't help but notice the oddity in that the woman and child were not crossing out of Mexico, but into it. Odder, both were American. He was left with two distinctly different paths whose choices required a fraction of a second to make, both with life ending consequences.

Sanchez made his choice with time to spare and rushed to the aid of the mother and child.

The child's hand slipped free just as he met them at the halfway point where the water was deepest, coming waist high on the mother. Sanchez' arm shot out like a bullet and snatched the girl by the collar, pulling her to safety before the river had a chance to take her.

In that gift of life, on the dirt bank of the Rio Grande River, Arturo Sanchez had been given a second chance at life. He took the gun he'd been intending to use to kill himself and tossed it into the river.

Sanchez escorted the traumatized mother and daughter the rest of the way, which turned out wasn't far from where they'd crossed. The hospital in San Antonio del Bravo was only a ten-minute walk from the crossing. Sanchez learned from the mother that a US citizen can cross the border to receive medical treatment free of charge.

Sanchez hadn't known this. Even though he buried his father there, he had only been in town less than a week when his father was shot dead. Sanchez moved on, taking refuge with an uncle in Nogales. Learning a secret about the town his father was buried in greatly intrigued him.

San Antonio del Bravo, Mexico and Candelaria, Texas, total population combined to be less than two hundred. In Candelaria, Texas, sick people drove nearly three hours to get to the nearest hospital. That is, if they chose to remain within the boundaries of the US border. The choice became easier when the hospital was a roped crossing of a river, followed by a ten-minute walk. The woman had felt an unfamiliar pain in her side and was worried for the baby growing inside her.

He saw the mother and her two daughters every now and again.

They would always wave and Sanchez would send them a rare, dazzling smile. He'd been ferrying people ever since.

Born out of survival, two cultures merged to form one community, achieving a human connection unbound by any walls or boundaries.

Hatch continued to scan for a threat as the water raced them to the crossing near San Antonio del Bravo. Against the backdrop of a slowly setting sun, Hatch peered ahead at the river as it disappeared behind a large silhouette of a boulder. The water grew angry as The Devil's Hand grew larger.

THIRTY-NINE

The speed at which the raft moved down the river had increased exponentially over the last several minutes. Ayala was conscious, but weak. His wrist was adorned in his father's gaudy wristwatch which dangled loosely, its jingle heard over the sound of the water.

The naming convention for the boulder they were fast approaching was spot on. The Devil's Hand looked like a massive black fist of stone. The river caught the setting sun, bathing it in a reddish orange glow. To Hatch the devil's fist looked encased in hell's fire.

"Ready." Hatch lay flat across the right side of the raft. Her thighs pinched wet rubber. Her Glock contained eleven rounds of ammunition and sat at the small of her back. Angela had adjusted and tightened the bandage around Hatch's left hand. The fire poker had done some damage, and would require medical attention, but all five fingers still responded to her subconscious commands, although their response came slowly and with an incredible amount of pain. Hatch didn't like losing her gun hand, temporarily or otherwise, to Moreno's sadistic activity but was grateful she had another. She found the simplest plans to be the best. The one concocted by Hatch and Sanchez during the final stretch of water before reaching the boulder was as simple as they got. Sanchez was going to drop Hatch off before getting to the rock. Sanchez, knowing the area the way he did, assessed his memory of its layout and selected the best possible location for an ambush. When asked why, he said it's where he would take the shot.

Sanchez said The Devil's Hand was not one giant rock, but two. The largest boulder, the fist, rises thirty feet above the water it rests beside. Its misshapen body stretched along the bank for a hundred feet or so. The smaller boulder, the thumb knuckle where the rock formation's namesake originated, nestled itself ten feet down river from its bigger companion. The gap between the two rocks was where their shooter would most likely be. And that's where Hatch was heading.

The timing had to be perfect. Sanchez calculated an approximate window of time Hatch would have once released on the shore based the river's current. He factored it all in a matter of seconds and determined Hatch would have approximately one minute to get from the designated release point to the objective. Hatch suggested Sanchez park the boat while she swept the shooter's nest. His logic came from the sight of the black hat he'd seen, the same one that now bore the well-aimed result of Hatch's sixth shot.

Sanchez had a hushed reverence when he spoke of its wearer. And when he spoke the name aloud, Ayala, who was barely maintaining consciousness, widened his eyes and stared at the river guide. They called him *El Vibora*. The Viper.

Hatch listened to the tale of El Vibora told by Sanchez. The cartel hitman's story read more like that of a villain in a children's book. Hatch thought he would have fit perfectly in Ayala's story about the seed and boulder.

In Sanchez' retelling, one thing was abundantly clear, whether or not the tale of the killer bore embellishment. The Viper was not a threat to be taken lightly. And in honoring that wisdom, they decided pulling the raft ashore left them more vulnerable and less mobile should they encounter El Vibora or another of the cartel's hunter kill teams.

Hatch had one minute to get out of the water, cross the rocky terrain of the devil's fist, find the shooter and a vantage point to neutralize him, and all before the raft entered the crosshairs of The Viper's scoped rifle.

Sanchez promised to slow the raft as best he could. The bullet hole in the floorboard had been effectively patched but without the inflated bladder of the thwart to provide rigidity. The ability to stabilize the rubber vessel became harder the closer they got to The Devil's Hand.

Angela said it was as if the boulder was pulling them with an invisible lasso.

Sanchez offered the less fantastic and more scientifically acceptable reason for the tractor beam-like pull of the water. Currents strengthen on sharp turns, like the ninety-degree bend around the boulder. The churn is created in the dynamic shift in direction as water level changes. The Devil's Hand was a Class III Rapid, which meant they faced four- and five-foot waves crashing against the rocks lining the river beyond the turn.

Hatch was thrown overboard, and her one minute began.

FORTY

An unseen rock slapped the bottom and, with the stabilizing tube deflated, Sanchez had been unable to counter its effects before Hatch went over the side deeper than intended.

Hatch swam hard, taking the river current at an angle and bringing herself to shore one hundred feet further upriver than their plan dictated. A football field of mud and rock had been added to the timed obstacle course.

The cold water responsible for rinsing much of the blood caked to her skin and clothes was now responsible for the slipping and sliding she experienced while sprinting along her route. Her lungs burned. She barely kept ahead of the red rubber rocket in her left periphery. She could hear the tick of the countdown clock in each wet step she took.

Hatch scaled the jagged edges of the biggest boulder. The red of the raft disappeared into white froth and out of sight as Hatch followed the boulder's cool stony contours around and to the right. The sands of time fell more rapidly, matching the speed of Hatch's feet. The burning exhaustion stinging her muscles earned her the high ground. And as Sanchez had predicted, the sniper nested below.

The killer's wide-brimmed black hat cloaked the man in shadow. He knelt in the gap between the devil's fist and thumb knuckle. If these two boulders were truly The Devil's Hand, then Hatch stood thirty feet above the webbed gap between them, like the gauze-wrapped hole in her left hand.

The red appeared in her vision while she drew her Glock from the small of her back while navigating the uneven terrain on her path to high ground. But just as time ticked away and Hatch brought her gun up on the cartel boogeyman, she slipped.

Hatch's wet boot lost traction. Instinctually she reached out with her non-gun hand to catch herself. Hatch's left hand found no purchase with the sun-warmed stone; the wet, blood-soaked a gauze mitten had seen to that. Hatch fell down the side of the boulder. A loud cracking sound rose above the churning whitewater.

The loud crack was not that of a rifle, but instead came from Hatch's pistol. It smacked the rock which knocked it out of her hand. As the last grains of sand in the hourglass finished their descent, Hatch landed flat on her back. Her gun was out of her hand and rested on the wet water-smoothed pebbles within arm's reach. It didn't matter. It wouldn't have mattered if it *was* in her hand.

Action always beats reaction. Hatch survived un-survivable encounters by the grace of that principle instilled by her father and refined in the fifteen years of battle she tested it against. In those trials, in the world of combat, no truer fact existed. Action beat reaction and the hand of the devil literally held Hatch.

FORTY-ONE

Hatch lay flat on her back. Her stone mattress wet with the angry water's spray reminded her, painfully so, of the journey it had taken her to get from the ridge thirty feet above to where she now lay, looking up into the end of the killer's rifle. The legendary El Vibora. The Viper, serving his dark master's command, had turned his aim from the raft to her. One slip had shifted favor to the hand of the devil.

On the wet, rocky shore of the Rio Grande River, Hatch heard the words whispered to her on the wind brought to her from the churn of whitewater. As with all words of wisdom, they are only considered wise at the point in time where wisdom is needed. Hatch had used her father's wisdom to find strength in dark times and resolve when her measure was tested.

Many times, her father's lessons, living long beyond the twelve years they had shared together, had enabled Hatch to cheat death. *This* did not appear to be one of those times.

Laying on the rocky riverbank with the setting sun slowing descent and setting the sky ablaze, Hatch found that for the first time in her life, she had no way to capitalize on the words her father said in the woods behind their mountain home.

The first punch often ends the fight.

He'd been going on that day about action versus reaction and the importance of always striving to be on the offensive. It didn't make much sense to the young Hatch, at least not then and not as it did now. But on this day, it seemed the message he'd sent had been received by the man in the wide-brimmed black hat, standing above her.

His ghostly, nearly translucent skin peeked out from under his hat. Two distinctively lighter marks paired underneath his right eye. Dark storm clouds brewed in the eyes sighting down the long barrel of the rifle now pointed in the direction of her forehead.

The first punch often ends the fight.

El Vibora won the draw. The advantage was clearly in his favor, and the first punch was about to hit Hatch's forehead in the form of a bullet-shaped fist, traveling two-thousand-seven-hundred and ten feet-per-second from the end of the rifle.

Hatch met the eyes of her killer. In the brief unspoken exchange, two killers, regardless of their cause, locked eyes. Like rams locking horns, their souls were momentarily locked in the age-old battle of good and evil. Hatch stood face to face with The Viper in the open door separating life from death. It appeared to Hatch that Murphy's law had reared its head once again, this time tipping his hat in favor of the devil.

She tried to retrieve the image of Dalton Savage's face to replace the ghostly one hovering above. His face flickered but wouldn't hold. Her mind, in battle with itself, refused to drift.

El Vibora stood silhouetted by the warm oranges and deep reds of the setting sun. But that's not what caught her attention. It was the hole she'd placed with her sixth shot during their first encounter.

The sun sent its final goodbye to the day in the form of a cord of gold beaming like Zeus's lightning bolt through the small opening she'd created with her Glock. The goldenrod sailed a short journey until it found its end in the reflective surface of Ayala's father's watch from the raft. The reflection of light was intensified by the frothy mist created by the whitewater.

The beam bounced back toward the hole it had come from but at an angle, putting it in line with the devil's hitman's right eye. Then Murphy's Law changed hands with the devil and passed favor to the supine Hatch. And in the light reflecting off the Peacock Man's watch, El Vibora, The Viper, blinked.

A flood of tears marched down the killer's face, stretching a river across his cheek.

The first punch often ends the fight.

In the frozen speck of time Hatch realized something. It was the nagging part that wouldn't let her give way to her end. It was why she couldn't hold the image of Savage's face in her mind's eye. She couldn't do those things, because there was a second part to the message her father sent, a message the devil's right hand never got.

If you happen to take the first punch, you better make sure you damn well finish the fight.

And in that moment, Rachel Hatch did what she did best.

Hatch had been in a knock-down, drag-out fight with the devil and his henchmen. A fight that began over twenty years ago on a cold morning near the lowland brook behind her family's house in the small town of Hawk's Landing, where she found her father dead. But death had not ended the conversation between father and daughter that day. Nor any other to follow. Her father's words continued to find meaning in her life long after their first utterance. And the words fueled the stoked the fire inside her.

Finish the fight.

The age-old war between good and evil chose its battlefield to be the bank of a river, dividing two communities who used the rope between them to overcome their differences, outweighing those of politics and geography.

Then the devil's hound did as he was commanded. He stood with his back to the sun which, as any shooter will advise, is the best way to use the light to blind a target. And he did as training and experience taught him to do, as it had taught Hatch to do. But in the devil's haste, the killer he sent lacked the benefit of her father's wisdom.

If you happen to strike first, do not hesitate. With hesitation comes opportunity. And if it presents, you better take it.

The Viper's right eye leaked water like a broken spigot. The cartel gunman rapidly blinked his eyes, only strengthening the tear-made river rolling down his face. Hatch seized the opportunity of El Vibora's distraction.

The Glock within reach, Hatch grabbed it and got off one single shot before the man's eye had a chance to clear.

The blood flowing from the small hole in the center of The Viper's forehead at the T-intersection, where the bridge of the nose met his brow made its way down the right side of the legendary killer's face, joining the river of tears.

The rifle dropped from his hand. The Viper stood motionless, as if his body were in argument with death and not yet willing to concede his hold on life. The blood mixed with the saline of his tears and spread out like the twisted thorns of Hatch's scar. The blood running down made his face look as though the old scars of the rattlesnake's bite were opened and bleeding once again.

Just before The Viper fell, Hatch saw confidence in the man's eyes as he faced death, and she hoped to have the same when her time came. The fearlessness with which the killer walked away from the world was not all he demonstrated at his end.

In the last blink of his right eye, Hatch saw peace in its final closing. A peace that could be only achieved in death, but only truly appreciated by those who spent the better part of their lives walking hand in hand with death.

The darkness of his eyes fell with the gust of wind that knocked off his hat, a feat even her sixth shot had not been able to achieve.

Hatch watched the dead man's wide-brimmed black hat float down the river until it was swallowed by the raging whitewater.

FORTY-TWO

The raft served as a makeshift bed for Ayala. Sanchez rummaged the Lincoln for any medical supplies, and before finding a combat medic's first aid kit, the former FES operator came across a brown leather ventilated case with a large rattlesnake coiled inside. Hatch watched Sanchez release the snake away from the group into a cluster of rocks. The snake tasted the air with its tongue before disappearing down a dark hole. The noise of its rattle rang out one last time and then faded away.

Sanchez returned with the kit and he, with the assistance of Angela, went about tending to the wounded Ayala. The hole punched through the floorboard of the raft had torn wide open when they'd struck a rock. If Hatch hadn't fallen when she did, they would've been sitting ducks.

Ayala had the weak smile of a dying man on his face and limited words to accompany it. Time was of the essence and he needed to get to the hospital, the same one Sanchez had walked the pregnant mother and her young daughter to. The pale horse of the devil's servant would be used to ferry them the rest of the way. The white Lincoln Town Car had been parked behind the shade provided by a cluster of trees.

Before sending the dead man downriver, Hatch searched him to find in his pockets only one thing of interest. It was folded into fourths and nestled above *El Vibora*'s no longer beating heart.

The rattle on his wrist jingled one last time as she lifted his arm to retrieve a folded piece of paper found in his pocket. Finding the paper's content curious, she gave it to somebody who might be capable of translating it.

Hatch handed the folded paper to Ayala, ready to be shifted to the awaiting chariot. Tears mixed with river water on his face as he looked down at the image.

Ayala's face screwed up into a question he sought the words to ask.

"I don't know what it means. But it was in his breast pocket. Above his heart."

Ayala's eyes traced the contours of the lines in front of him before giving his opinion. "She's alive."

The piece of paper blew life into the fading light in Ayala's eyes. It was as if he was never shot, as if the bullet had never passed from the back end of his shoulder to his chest. It was as if the holes, both in his shoulder and in his heart, were miraculously healed by the picture and the image held in his hand.

The folded piece of paper held a colorful image of a lily blooming in springtime with the last droplet of morning's dew dangling at the edge of its light purple petals.

Ayala took a picture from his own pocket. He held it in his other hand. Ayala brought the photograph to his lips. He kissed it and then cast it into the water, before it was swallowed, just as the dead man and his hat had been.

He took and re-folded the girl's drawing and put it in his pocket, replacing the photograph that had just occupied that space. Before Hatch could ask, Ayala offered, "I'm trading an old memory for a new one. I'm trading dark for light."

A team effort took Ayala to the Lincoln. Goodbyes were exchanged, in that very particular way when friends know they will likely never see each other again.

Just before Sanchez sped away with the wounded Peacock Man, Ayala passed along his final words to Hatch.

"Try it sometime." He tapped a shaky hand on the breast pocket containing Maria's drawing. "Trading light memories for dark ones. If nothing else, take a moment each day to appreciate its end in those last threads of light. Take stock in the completion of the day's end in knowing that tomorrow's is yours to make."

And with that, Arturo Sanchez, a warrior born of the most horrific beginnings who eventually found peace, carted off Miguel Ayala, the Peacock Man of Nogales, who proved he could fly, if only for a few feet, to save two girls from a fate worse than death.

It had been a good day. Hatch had one more stop until she saw its end and the promise kept in doing so. With the teen close behind, she stood on the bank of the river.

Hatch's gripped the frayed knots of the rope and began to cross.

FORTY-THREE

Hatch sat on the other side of the Rio Grande, the warmth of the sun in her face. The sun's grip loosened its hold on the day as the last fingers of magenta touched the coming night sky.

Hatch enjoyed the shade of a tree as fire flicked her face, formed in flickering wisps of red and orange from the sleeping teen's hair being blown wild by the wind. The dry heat of the fading day stole the remaining moisture from Hatch's mouth as she gently caressed the teen while they waited not-so-patiently for the arrival of Sanchez' contact on the other side. He said his name was Ben, and that he could be trusted. Hatch had seen the demonstration of Arturo Sanchez' code tattooed under the anchor of his former team.

Fuerza, Espíritu, Sabiduría. Strength, Spirit, Wisdom.

The man had demonstrated to Hatch all those qualities and more in their brief but intense time together. She took his word as his bond and waited.

As the teen slept the sleep of a thousand lifetimes, Hatch took a moment to reflect. She shifted positions as subtly as possible, so as not to wake Angela. Hatch looked up the river to the bend where the rocky whitewater shredded the raft. She looked out on the rock named The

Devil's Hand. From her position across the river, it no longer looked like one giant rock. Instead, the gap where Hatch had made her final stand against the devil, divided the two boulders. A tall cypress rose from behind. Beyond its treetop and barely visible amidst the dying embers of sunlight, the orange-colored sun-glass-wearing walrus, mascot of the cartel-run Solarus Juice Company could be seen.

Looking at it another way, maybe in the way somebody like Miguel Ayala or his companion Ernesto Cruz would, Hatch adjusted her lens. And this is what she saw when she blinked them open.

A massive cypress split a massive boulder in two, sending the troll high into the air where his tormented cries could no longer be heard.

In that rare moment of peace, Hatch understood the story Ayala had told her. Hatch was ready to tell her version. There was a little girl and boy in Colorado who desperately needed to hear it. Hatch pictured her niece, Daphne, and her nephew, Jake.

Tornadoes of dust chased a dark colored SUV as it pulled to a stop. Hatch's hand was on the Glock under her thigh.

A tall muscular man wearing dark jeans and a denim shirt of lighter blue stepped from the driver's door. "Daphne?"

"See any other half-dead people under a tree matching our description?"

"Not today." He laughed.

Angela hardly woke during her transport from Hatch's lap to the backseat of the Tahoe. Hatch climbed into the passenger seat. Nothing was said as they drove off. The details had already been arranged through Miguel and Sanchez' contact. Ben was to take Angela to a specified location outside of Austin, where her parents were already traveling to after receiving word their daughter had been found.

Hatch would not be there for any of that. She would part ways in Austin and set off to close a door that had been open for way too long. Its salty California breeze held answers to a question only one person could answer.

"Got a paper and pencil?" Hatch asked.

"Check the glove box. Should be a couple napkins and a pen if that works?"

Hatch spread the napkin on her thigh and uncapped the pen. Her letter began like this:

Have I ever told you the one about the seed and the boulder?

FORTY-FOUR

The Very Thought of You by Nat King Cole played on the radio, just above the rattle of Ayala's yellow Nissan, as they watched the cafe from a block away. Ayala wore his favorite Hawaiian shirt for today's occasion. He'd retired it four months ago when a bullet tore through it. The yellow of the pineapples were a little darker on that side, but he figured, you can't appreciate the light without a little bit of the dark.

Other than the music and the air conditioning at full blast, neither men spoke as they watched the front of the cafe where Hector Fuentes was finishing up a midday meal.

In the months since Ernesto Cruz's death, Sanchez searched for a pattern in the cartel leader's itinerary that could be exploited as weakness. Everybody had them. And with the right set of eyes, anybody could find them. And he found it in the tip from a reliable informant who worked at the restaurant where Mr. Fuentes was now dining.

He told Sanchez that the restaurant was rented out whenever he came to eat there. No other customers were allowed in or out. He posted one guard by the door at all exits, and kept his personal bodyguard, Juan Carlos Moreno, with him at all times. He tightened his security ever since his son had tried to kill him, and public appearances had become almost non-existent. It was rumored that the psychological impact of his firstborn's attack and then subsequent death had unhinged the man. And with that, his power was starting to wane.

Sweat formed on Ayala's brow, coating him in a light sheen, as he waited patiently for Sanchez' thumb to move. It was resting just to the side of the red detonator switch in his hand. Sanchez had used his primary skillset from his time with the special forces. Demolition.

The long bike chain securing the rusted bike to the base of the tree trunk was actually a thick strand of det cord, shrouded in a plastic coating and shaped to look like a bike chain. It was connected to the bike, but only so the signal receiver, underneath the bike seat, could run the thin, black wire along the frame of the bike.

The luncheon lasted nearly an hour and a half. And even with the air conditioning running, both men were now soaked through with sweat, further darkening the stain on Ayala's Hawaiian shirt.

"I think I can see them moving around in there. Looks like the party's breaking up."

Ayala gnawed on the end of the unlit cigar in his mouth. The man at the door stepped forward, his head swiveling from left to right. He kept his gun hand close to the pistol underneath his sports coat. He looked back into the cafe and nodded. The doors opened a moment later.

Hector Fuentes exited with Juan Carlos Moreno close to his side, moving him towards the limousine that pulled up, like he was a dignitary under protection. Moreno shut the door on his boss and began to make his way around the back end of the vehicle to speak with the security man who had been posted at the door.

Sanchez moved his finger over the red plastic button. With no hesitation, he pressed it. Silence followed the click until a moment later, it was broken by the detonation.

White light exploded out in a concentric circle from the tree.

The driver and doorman were killed instantly. It took a second to find Moreno because the cartel head of security's body was scattered in several different places. It wasn't until Ayala saw Moreno's head impaled on a stop sign that he let out a breath.

A loud crack followed the initial explosion.

The blast had badly damaged the limo. But somehow, Hector Fuentes had survived.

Ayala watched him crawl away, badly injured, but alive. The cracking sounded again. It rumbled the ground and felt and sounded like an earthquake.

The explosion severed the massive tree. The cracking was the release of the thick trunk's resistance to the blast. It fell forward onto the fleeing Fuentes, who was incapable of escaping its path, and crushed him under its branches.

The cigar fell from his mouth as Ayala's jaw dropped wide. He thought of his good friend, Ernesto, and left the cigar where it lay. He looked on at the sight before him one more time before driving away in his patched-up Nissan.

He thought, how wonderful it would've been for Ernesto to see him prove to the devil himself, *the seed is mightier than the boulder.*

FORTY-FIVE

On that day I was to kill your parents, fate put me in line with you. As you have rightly guessed at but never asked, I am not a tobacco farmer. I am a killer of men, women, and children. I know where my journey ends. I will be in good company as the fires of hell lick at my flesh. But rest assured, I do not fear this end or its consequence for the life I have led. I say this not out of a bout of boastful machismo, but for the simple reason that the path I walked led me to you. And for that, I would roast in a thousand hells if it meant I could do it again.

If you are reading this, then you know I am gone. Hopefully in the five years of life we have shared together you have felt in some small measure a fraction of the love and adoration I had for you.

I will not feel the lash of the devil's whip, for my spirit will wander above it all. I will be with you in the wind that passes through your hair. I look on as you live the rest of your existence in peace and tranquility. In those moments of doubt, when you need a father's hand, you will hear my wisdom in the rustle of leaves.

For you were more than a servant girl who became my daughter. You were the girl who planted the seed of love that blossomed into a flower, replacing darkness for light.

In you, I see a different path than I have traveled. And on it, I hope you continue to spread your seed wherever the wind takes you.

Maria stepped out of the busy café onto the street and walked over to the man in the blue ambulance carrying her heavy satchel. He turned to face her. "Are you the one they call Azul?"

"I am."

Maria then fished out a metal box the size and shape of a brick. A turquoise bracelet dangled loosely at her wrist with beads that rattled noisily. Azul accepted the box containing twenty-five thousand dollars. Maria hoped it would do well for the man she'd read about in the newspaper.

The article had struck a chord with Maria when she'd first read it. The three hundred thousand dollars Machado had left her was more than she'd ever know what to do with in two lifetimes.

She set aside enough to carry her through the rest of her life. And then looking at the pile left over, Maria contemplated how to best use her newfound wealth. The answer came with a breeze pushing its way through the clustered branches of a nearby tree. Maria was instantly found by a hissed whisper and set forth to do its biding.

Standing beside Azul and looking upon his blue ambulance, Maria was suddenly inspired to do something else.

Maria pulled a paintbrush and palate from her oversized satchel. She then took a step back. Holding the bristled end of the paintbrush in front of her, she angled it and turned it and angled it, squinting her eye while taking in the blurred image of the blue backdrop. And thought of the flower she planned to paint.

The whisper she'd heard had told her what to do with the money. In the leaves jostling, she heard Machado's slithered tongue tell her what to do. She heard it as plain as if the man, who she had loved as a father, said four words to her.

Make light the dark.

And Maria planned to, using the money gifted her to help those in need. Maria looked at her canvas and it came to her. The flower would be a rose. It seemed a fitting flower for the van, since Maria planned on meeting with the reporter who'd written the article at a restaurant called Rosa's Café.

Maria squirted a deep red into the recessed bowl and, looking at her canvas, she wondered if the reporter, Miguel Ayala, would like to see one of her flower drawings.

READ on for a sneak peak at AFTERSHOCK (*Rachel Hatch Book 7*), or order your copy now:
https://www.amazon.com/dp/B08X93GBZ9

Join the LT Ryan reader family & receive a free copy of the Rachel Hatch story, Fractured. Click the link below to get started:

https://ltryan.com/rachel-hatch-newsletter-signup-1

L.T. RYAN & BRIAN SHEA

THE RACHEL HATCH SERIES

Drift

Downburst

Fever Burn

Smoke Signal

Firewalk

Whitewater

Aftershock

Whirlwind

Tsunami

Fastrope (Coming Soon)

RACHEL HATCH SHORT STORIES

Fractured

Proving Ground

The Gauntlet

AFTERSHOCK
RACHEL HATCH BOOK SEVEN

by L.T. Ryan & Brian Shea

Copyright © 2021 by L.T. Ryan, Liquid Mind Media, LLC, & Brian Christopher Shea. All rights reserved. No part of this publication may be copied, reproduced in any format, by any means, electronic or otherwise, without prior consent from the copyright owner and publisher of this book. This is a work of fiction. All characters, names, places and events are the product of the author's imagination or used fictitiously.

AFTERSHOCK CHAPTER 1

The moon hid under a thin veil of wispy gray clouds but still managed to cast its glow over the freshly fallen snow.

Chris Macintosh's hot breath melted the flakes falling in front of him and covering his face in a glimmering sheen. He snapped an icicle from his nose with the rough edge of his sleeve. The leaking pipes that were his nostrils worked to replace the stalactite of snot. The cold air pinched his throat and stung his lungs. He'd forgotten how much he hated the cold. Breakneck, Alaska, was a lifetime away from his Austin, Texas, childhood. The company he currently kept worsened his tolerance for the cold, wet embrace of Mother Nature.

Lank cursed under his breath as he turned his face from the wind. The man assisting Lank's right side complained in hushed curses, most of which were washed out by the high winds that blew in their faces every few minutes or so. "How much did you say this guy weighs?"

Lank's pitchy voice irritated Macintosh to no end. He'd been listening to Lank moan for the past ten minutes since they'd pulled the body out of the trunk of the Bronco a half mile back. Todd Lankowski, better known as Lank, was by all accounts an idiot. And his question about the weight was the third time he'd asked, thus making this Macintosh's third attempt to explain. "Because he's dead weight."

Lank spit. The wind blew it back into his face, instigating another round of expletives. His use of the f-bomb would give a sailor pause. Lankowksi peppered that word into just about every sentence the wire-thin man uttered. Macintosh tolerated Lank out of necessity. In other circumstances, Macintosh would've probably already punched him in the face.

Macintosh had spent the last two weeks kissing ass with the scrawny lackey in the hopes of getting an audience with the king. He'd spent the last seven years at Spring Creek Maximum Security networking himself into this position. And the last two weeks had led to this moment.

"Are you sure he's gonna be here?" Icy wind stung the back of his throat.

"He said he was." Lank stopped walking. The dead weight of the man between them anchored Macintosh. He turned in annoyance to see Lank eyeing him.

"You seem real eager to see Grizz."

"I am. Been waiting a while."

"Doesn't mean the feds couldn't have gotten to you."

Macintosh balled a fist. "Accuse me of it again and you'll be the second asshole I drag up this hill tonight."

"I'm just sayin' is all."

"You think I did ten years in Spring Creek just to cop a deal? And you remember, it was Ray Winslow who tapped me and brought me in. I didn't go looking for any brotherhood. It found me." Macintosh tapped at the swastika tattooed in dark black against the side of his neck.

"It's just—ya know—been crazy ever since Grizz whacked those three Marshals."

"Then we best not be wasting any more time out here."

Lank began moving again, although the lion's share of the load was still being shouldered by Macintosh.

AFTERSHOCK CHAPTER 1

A few feet from the door, Lank's feet shot out from under him like a poorly placed Charlie Brown kick after Lucy had just yanked the football away. The unconscious man between them broke his fall.

A long slow grunt rumbled from their prisoner.

The prisoner muttered something unintelligible. The wind obscured any sound not absorbed by the rag taped to his mouth. Macintosh pressed on the man's shoulder, keeping him pinned to the ground while Lank scrambled to get his feet under him.

Macintosh knew the unconscious man's name was Dawes. He also knew Dawes was a member of the United States Marshal Services Special Operations Group, as indicated by the OD green patch sewn into the shoulder of his black tactical uniform. Dawes had been unconscious for the better part of the past twenty-four hours since they'd captured him after a failed breach of their compound.

"Grab his damn arm," Macintosh barked. Lank pulled Dawes' other shoulder. "We have two feet to go to the door. Do you think you can do it without falling on your ass?" Macintosh was cold, he was tired, and he was terrified of what lay on the other side of that door, and what he might be asked to do.

They made the last few steps across the glass surface. The light above the door bathed Lank in a pale glow, making his bony form look more skeletal in the light.

Macintosh adjusted Dawes' weight and gripped the doorknob. As he turned the knob to open it, Macintosh knew one thing for certain. Today would be somebody's last.

AFTERSHOCK CHAPTER 2

Hatch sat in the same restaurant booth they'd shared years ago. Being back here felt odd. She'd always wondered what it would be like to see Cruise again after all these years. Ten years with the SEAL Teams before opting for the private sector. Their six-month love affair following the amphibious assault course where they'd met had proved they were just as intense in the bedroom as they were on the battlefield. But the brightest flames burn out fastest, and it wasn't long before life and circumstance interfered.

Sitting at the café where they'd said their last goodbye seemed like as fitting a place as any to pick up again where they'd left off. If Cruise hadn't alerted Hatch to the Talon Executive Services hunter-killer squad sent to kill her, it was unlikely she would've been able to get ahead of the power curve. She owed him a debt of thanks but couldn't ignore the question burning a hole in the back of her mind. *How did Alden Cruise know?*

The person capable of answering that question walked in. It'd been five years since Hatch last saw him. She felt the tingle in her scar return. Hatch rubbed her fingers along the raised puffiness of twisted thorny branches wrapping her right arm from wrist to shoulder. The wise café owner in Africa had taught her she had nothing to hide, nothing to be ashamed of. And she'd accepted his wisdom. She embraced her ravaged flesh as a reminder of times long past.

Hatch no longer hid her damaged arm from view. But seeing Cruise approach, she felt ashamed. She felt an irrational urge to cover it. Cruise hadn't been touched by the ravages of time since they had last been together. In fact, he somehow looked even better. The years between them had had markedly different impacts, at least outwardly. Hatch looked at the chiseled former SEAL as he made his way toward her.

"Rachel Hatch in the flesh."

In the flesh. Even his words had an unintended effect. His eyes immediately shot to her damaged arm. Cruise tried to casually retract his glance, but Hatch could see the shock resonate on his face. She met his gaze and he offered an apologetic look. *Great.* The last thing she wanted was a pity party.

Hatch stood. The two embraced. Cruise leaned in for a kiss. Hatch redirected its intended destination of lips for the side of her cheek.

"I should've been there for you." Cruise slid into the opposite side of the booth.

"You were deployed. It didn't matter anyway. Whatever we had ended long before this." Hatch slapped the scar.

"I heard you died."

"I heard that too."

"Well for a dead person, you look great."

Hatch felt her cheeks warm with a redness blocking her pale complexion. She knew Cruise well enough that, beyond his charm and golden boy looks, he was more than a cookie-cutter superhero.

She remembered it being one of his most endearing qualities. Beneath his tough exterior was a kind soul. Cruise had laid it bare to her while on a midnight picnic overlooking the San Diego Bay. Cruise had taken her to Turner Field, a grassy sports field located on the Naval Amphibious Base in Coronado. The Silver Strand Boulevard separated the main base from the SEAL candidates being run through the grinder of the Basic Underwater Demolition/SEAL, or BUD/s. Cruise had been named Honor Man for his class, a distinction earned by outperforming all other trainees. He hadn't stopped at surpassing his peers but went on to dethrone the obstacle course longtime record holder.

As they'd shared a glass of wine and looked out on the lights of the bridge connecting Coronado to the San Diego mainland, Hatch remarked at the stillness of the bay water compared to the ocean feeding it. She had said the moon looked as though it were kissing the water. Then he proposed to her using a piece of foil he'd shaped into a ring. He deployed for eighteen months the next morning. Hatch had just been selected for Task Force Banshee. Even if the foil ring had been real, it would've ended the same. Married to the military left them lonely in life. Or at least for her it did. Cruise now wore a black plated tungsten wedding band.

"They still make those coffee cakes?" Hatch asked.

"Best in the world. My humble opinion, of course." Cruise leaned back in his seat and called over in the direction of the kitchen, "Sherry, two of the usual."

Sherry, a cute waitress in her late twenties, approached with the two plates balanced in one hand and a coffee pot in the other. Cinnamon sugar filled the air. The waitress topped off both mugs before returning to the kitchen.

"How did you know about that Talon team coming for me?"

"Same old Hatch. You don't beat around the bush."

"Never really been my way." The warmth of Hatch's coffee warded off the coolness still clinging to the air of the spring morning.

"There's a long and short answer to that question."

"That's not an answer."

"I'm with Talon."

Hatch nearly spat her coffee. Her mind reeled. She quickly scanned the interior of the café. No threat.

"Relax. It's me. Just me."

"I don't understand."

"You've got Talon all wrong. It's not what you think. They are on the cutting edge of defense contracting, handling some of the most dangerous missions in the world."

"Like hunting a woman and her family? Are my niece and nephew these dangerous threats you speak of?" Hatch felt a surge of rage rise up inside her.

"What happened to you was an anomaly. It's a private security company, plain and simple. Government contract work, foreign and domestic. What happened to you was done by a rogue element, a couple old war horses with skeletons in their closet."

"My dad was one of those old war horses."

"I know."

"That's all you got?" Hatch suddenly wasn't as hungry.

"I only came upon it by accident. I was putting together a proposal to bring you in and make you an offer. I was using our internal system to draft the request when I found your name had been flagged. When I tried to access it, it was beyond my clearance. At the time I thought there was nobody beyond my level.

"I eventually gained access. I thought somebody had already begun the recruitment process. Having a female with your skillset is rare. And we are always looking to add the right people to our ranks. But that wasn't the case. You weren't being recruited. You were being targeted. Being targeted by Talon is never a good thing." He broke into a smile. "Unless your name is Rachel Hatch."

"This is your recruitment pitch? I killed a group of your hired guns and now you want to offer me a job?"

"Not exactly. But sort of. The upper echelon wants to call a truce. And their peace offering is in the form of a job opportunity."

"Why would they want me to work for them?"

"Something about keeping friends close and enemies closer."

"I'm an enemy?"

"Not to me. Their words. Not mine."

"Why not kill me?"

"They tried killing you. It didn't take."

"Why not kill you for interfering?"

"They don't know. All they know is that you survived an encounter that should never have left an entire team dead. But somehow you single-handedly stopped them all."

Hatch thought of Nighthawk's well-timed shot that had saved her life and knew the fallacy in Cruise's assessment.

"If you accept this offer, you'll be safe."

"Handling the world's most dangerous missions doesn't sound like a safe offer."

"It would mean your family would be safe. You'd never have to worry about them again. Nobody's coming for you ever again if you accept."

Hatch felt a lightness she hadn't experienced in a very long time. She was grateful for the momentary interruption when Sherry returned to warm their coffee.

"I know this sounds crazy. It was the best plan I could come up with to save your life."

"I'm not sure what kind of life that leaves me with."

"I know you. I know the type of person you are. I know your code. In my division at Talon, we help people, good people in bad situations."

"What division would that be?"

"Kidnapping and ransom risk management. All ex-military and police special operators like yourself. We handle private high-dollar contracts, both domestic and abroad. Our team cuts through bureaucratic red tape like a warm knife through butter. We save lives. And get to put down some bad guys in the process.

"What is that thing you always used to say? Something your father told you about helping good people? That's what we're doing. I mean we're dealing with life and death situations. Doesn't get more real than that. Plus, we've got a damn good track record of bringing those victims back."

Hatch pondered the opportunity while sitting in the shadow of the Hotel Del Ray, which was blocking the view of the sand berms where future SEALs battled shore breaking waves in hopes of serving in a Tier One capacity. Hatch was being given an opportunity to rejoin the life she'd left behind. Since leaving Mexico, Hatch had been giving thought on how to best honor her code as she moved forward.

"How do we do this? Set up some type of job interview? Do I have to give you a résumé?"

"You just did." His smile broadened, stretching across his golden skin. "Does that mean you're in?"

"I'm in."

"Let me be the first to welcome you to Talon Executive Services."

"I do this on one condition. I can walk away at any time. No questions asked. Nobody comes looking for me or my family. Once I do this, they are off the radar forever. Understood?"

"They were never on any radar of mine. I hope you know that."

"I wouldn't have accepted this offer if I thought otherwise."

"I think I can work all that out. Your family is safe. You have my word."

"What's next?"

"Funny you should ask, on my way to meet you I got a message. I've got to go in for a briefing. Wheels up in two hours."

"Will you call me when you get back?"

"No. You're coming with me. We've got a rapidly evolving hostage situation."

"Nothing like hitting the ground running."

"We'll have to get you a change of clothes."

"Why's that?"

"We're going to Alaska."

AFTERSHOCK CHAPTER 3

Macintosh stood facing Walter Grizzly, Grizz, as he was known to most, a six foot-nine, three-hundred-eighty-pound behemoth. His muscle was only matched by his will. A thin layer of fat insulated his bulging muscles. It was bitter cold outside and not much better in the concrete shed they were standing in. Yet Grizz wore nothing but a sleeveless hooded black sweatshirt in lieu of a coat. He looked like a cross between Bill Belichick and Rumblebuffin, the fabled giant from CS Lewis's Chronicles of Narnia.

His body was covered in tattoos. The overlapping images coated his flesh and disappeared under the thick red of his beard. Grizz's head was shaved smooth. A solitary red triangle with a thick black W was tattooed on the back of his enormous head.

Grizz was the founding member of their Aryan brotherhood. Full membership could only be attained through the rite of passage. Full initiation meant the prospect had to commit murder. The red triangle pointing up was symbolic of The Way's belief structure. "Blood is the only path to purity. Blood is The Way." Macintosh's tattoo was etched into the side of his neck using a prison made tattoo needle. A skin infection, a byproduct of the unsanitary process, left a section of the W blotched with scar tissue.

Macintosh earned his ink while at Stone Creek Correctional. He'd saved Ray Winslow, one of The Way's founding members, during a prison yard fight. Macintosh had seen the other inmate, a wild-eyed man by the name of Paul Banyan, make a move on Winslow with a shiv made out of a toothbrush handle. Macintosh had knocked the weapon out of Banyan's hand just before he would've struck paydirt in Winslow's jugular. Banyan died in the yard that day.

Although Banyan's death could not officially be laid at the feet of Macintosh, the State did find cause to extend his seven-year sentence for a failed armed robbery by three years. It'd also earned him a place among The Way.

The ankle holster concealed along the inside of Macintosh's left leg just above the ankle seemed heavier now, as if the gun itself was somehow rooted to the poured concrete floor Macintosh stood on. Deputy US Marshal Dawes was duct taped to a metal folding chair in the center of the room. Underneath was an eight-by-eight drop cloth.

Grizz towered over all the men in the room. But with Dawes seated before him, he looked even more menacing.

He said nothing, standing with arms folded behind the chair. He stared at the man between them who was groaning. His head was bobbing more steadily as he tried to bring it up. Macintosh looked at the man's eyes as they flooded open, and then saw the shock and horror of them when they recognized the man standing behind the chair. He twisted against the restraints, and only worked to kink up the tape, further cutting off his circulation. Dawes' hands were a shade of dark purple, matching the bruising along the side of his beaten face. His eyes shot wildly around the room and locked with Macintosh's. He was begging. No discernable words penetrated the gag in his mouth. Tears started to stream down the man's blood-crusted face.

"US Marshal Dawes, do you know what this day is for you?" Grizz growled. "It's a reckoning. You think you can come to my home and take from me? Your laws don't apply to me. We are sovereign. You cannot impose your will on me."

Dawes whimpered.

"I am the only law that matters. The other three I killed should have served as a warning. But just like Waco, you government types can't seem to help yourselves."

"Lank, it's your time to earn your mark." Grizz continued.

The scrawny Lankowski straightened. He pulled out a small black revolver from his waistband and pointed it at the federal agent's head. "Just give me the word, Grizz. I'll put a bullet through his thick skull."

"Wait." Macintosh nearly choked on the word.

Grizz turned his emerald stare to Macintosh. His voice boomed like someone beating an empty barrel with a wooden mallet. "Did you just speak out of turn?"

"Killing him is a bad move."

Lank turned the gun toward Macintosh. "I told you there's somethin' off 'bout this one. He ain't right."

"You best be pointing that gun elsewhere." Macintosh squared himself to Lank. He thought of the ankle holster. No way he could get to his piece before Lank got a shot off.

"Let's see what he has to say." Grizz stepped forward and rested his beefy hands on the shoulders of Dawes. "Tell me why this man here deserves to live."

"They already tried to breach once. If you kill him, nothing will stop them from rolling a tank through the front gate. Keep him alive and you have leverage."

The big man stirred. He adjusted his forearms and returned them to their folded position across his barrel chest.

"It's how we survived the prison riot. We took a guard hostage. It became our saving grace. Plus, we got a lot of intel about how the other guards planned to stop us. It gave us the tactical advantage and enabled us to hold the prison for over ten days. Might be worth a shot to do the same thing here. But this isn't my show."

"You're damn right it isn't!" Grizz's cheeks reddened to the color of his beard. Then he let out a huge sigh. "But right is right. You may be onto something."

Lank still held the gun out and pointed in the direction of Macintosh.

"Put that thing away before you shoot yourself." Macintosh sneered.

Lank holstered his pistol. "So we just gonna take the newbie's word as gospel?"

"He's a marked member. You remember that next time you point that thing in his direction. I'll cut your throat myself."

Lank resumed his slouch.

"Since you're full of ideas, what is it you suggest we do next?" Grizz redirected his attention to Macintosh.

"We need to establish communication with the feds, so we can keep them from assaulting the compound. At least buy us enough time to slip away."

A loud rumble rolled through from a distance. It shook the small building and nearly threw Macintosh on top of Dawes. The lights went out.

"What in the hell was that? The feds? It felt like an explosion." Lank shot a panicked look at the door.

Grizz's voice roared above the noise. "That's no explosion. That's a quake."

Order your copy now:
https://www.amazon.com/dp/B08X93GBZ9

AFTERSHOCK CHAPTER 3

Join the LT Ryan reader family & receive a free copy of the Rachel Hatch story, Fractured. Click the link below to get started:

https://ltryan.com/rachel-hatch-newsletter-signup-1

ALSO BY L.T. RYAN

Find All of L.T. Ryan's Books on Amazon Today!

The Jack Noble Series

The Recruit (free)

The First Deception (Prequel 1)

Noble Beginnings

A Deadly Distance

Ripple Effect (Bear Logan)

Thin Line

Noble Intentions

When Dead in Greece

Noble Retribution

Noble Betrayal

Never Go Home

Beyond Betrayal (Clarissa Abbot)

Noble Judgment

Never Cry Mercy

Deadline

End Game

Noble Ultimatum

Noble Legend (2022)

Bear Logan Series

Ripple Effect

Blowback

Take Down

Deep State

Bear & Mandy Logan Series

Close to Home

Under the Surface

The Last Stop

Over the Edge (Coming Soon)

Rachel Hatch Series

Drift

Downburst

Fever Burn

Smoke Signal

Firewalk

Whitewater

Aftershock

Whirlwind

Tsunami

Fastrope (Coming Soon)

Mitch Tanner Series

The Depth of Darkness

Into The Darkness

Deliver Us From Darkness

Cassie Quinn Series

Path of Bones

Whisper of Bones

Symphony of Bones

Etched in Shadow

Concealed in Shadow (2022)

Blake Brier Series

Unmasked

Unleashed

Uncharted

Drawpoint

Contrail

Detachment

Clear (Coming Soon)

Dalton Savage Series

Savage Grounds
Scorched Earth
Cold Sky (Coming Soon)

Maddie Castle Series

The Handler
Tracking Justice (Coming Soon)

Affliction Z Series

Affliction Z: Patient Zero
Affliction Z: Abandoned Hope
Affliction Z: Descended in Blood
Affliction Z : Fractured Part 1
Affliction Z: Fractured Part 2 (Fall 2021)

ABOUT THE AUTHOR

L.T. Ryan is a *USA Today* and international bestselling author. The new age of publishing offered L.T. the opportunity to blend his passions for creating, marketing, and technology to reach audiences with his popular Jack Noble series.

Living in central Virginia with his wife, the youngest of his three daughters, and their three dogs, L.T. enjoys staring out his window at the trees and mountains while he should be writing, as well as reading, hiking, running, and playing with gadgets. See what he's up to at http://ltryan.com.

Social Medial Links:

- Facebook (L.T. Ryan): https://www.facebook.com/LTRyanAuthor
- Facebook (Jack Noble Page): https://www.facebook.com/JackNobleBooks/
- Twitter: https://twitter.com/LTRyanWrites
- Goodreads: http://www.goodreads.com/author/show/6151659.L_T_Ryan

Printed in Poland
by Amazon Fulfillment
Poland Sp. z o.o., Wrocław
10 October 2023